# Praise for *A Stranger Here Below*

"Deeply imagined and intricately plotted, *A Stranger Here Below* marries richly textured historical fiction with the urgency of a mystery novel. Fergus knows certain things deep in the bone: horses, hunting, the folkways of rural places, and he weaves this wisdom into a stirring tale." —Geraldine Brooks, author of *March* and *People of the Book*

"The kind of mystery Lee Child would have Jack Reacher tackle if he placed a story in the 1830s." —Michael McMenamin, author of *The Liebold Protocol*

"With luminous and deftly sketched prose, Charles Fergus takes us into an American past that is both deeply familiar and utterly strange. Sheriff Gideon Stoltz patiently unravels a series of crimes and secrets, while also examining his own life, his past, and the beauties and tragedies of life itself." —Jeffrey Lent, author of *Before We Sleep* and *In the Fall*

"Some writers are natural storytellers and have an instinct for the reader's interest. Others can invoke mood or a sense of place, handle landscape, or create precise imagery. Every now and then you find a writer who has all of these skills, and because of that they invoke the magic of fiction. They make the chair you are sitting on disappear. Charles Fergus is one of those writers, and *A Stranger Here Below* is one of those books." —Craig Nova, author of *All the Good Yale Men* and *The Good Son*

"Imbued with Michael Connelly's gumshoe skills and the vivid historical descriptions of Charles Frazier, *A Stranger Here Below* is a stark procedural set in the backwoods of Pennsylvania circa 1830." —Brad Smith, author of the Virgil Cain mysteries

"A dark, engrossing tale that introduces a decent, sympathetic hero in the young sheriff Gideon Stoltz. The novel's special strength is its imaginative saturation in the community of Adamant, a violent, haunted place of dreams and visions, a place as hard and unforgiving as its name." —Castle Freeman, Jr., author of *The Devil in the Valley*

"In Gideon Stoltz, Charles Fergus has created a unique 19th-century Eastern lawman who struggles not only with wrongdoers but with his own griefs and travails. *A Stranger Here Below* kept me reading late into the night." —Dan O'Brien, author of *The Indian Agent* and *Stolen Horses*

"Fergus puts you firmly in Gideon Stoltz's rough-hewn world where a 'foreigner' with the wrong accent has to watch his back even if he wears a sheriff's badge. A cracking good mystery." —Scott Weidensaul, author of *The First Frontier*

"A rich novel of a distant time and a man who is 'Othered' in most aspects of his life ... Although clearly crime fiction, the book is equally an exploration of the soul." —*The New York Journal of Books*

"A writer of nonfiction about the natural world, Fergus brings his appreciation for nature to this well-paced blend of mystery and western. An appealing debut that deserves a boost from enthusiastic hand-sellers." —*Booklist*

"This novel works as a compelling and complex historical mystery, but it's more ... The details, whether of a grouse's feathers or a horse's gait or burning charcoal for an iron furnace, are flawless. This is a gem." —Matthew Miller, Nature.com, The Nature Conservancy blog

"If you've grown tired of formulaic mysteries and thrillers, then you're in for a treat with *A Stranger Here Below*. The characters are built not from clichés, but through Fergus's deft descriptions of their thoughts, desires, and secrets, all while creating a tone that keeps the reader entranced . . . A pleasure to read." —Elaine Meder-Wilgus, *WPSU's BookMark*

"Fergus has created a strong character in Gideon Stoltz . . . Some themes are universal, and the jealousy, cruelty, and greed that Stoltz uncovers are as prevalent today as they were in 1835." —*Historical Novels Review*

# A STRANGER HERE BELOW

**Books by Charles Fergus**

**Fiction:**

*Shadow Catcher*

*Nighthawk's Wing*

**Nature and Nonfiction:**

*Swamp Screamer*

*Summer at Little Lava*

*The Wingless Crow (nature essays)*

*Thornapples (nature essays)*

*Trees of New England*

*Trees of Pennsylvania*

*Wildlife of Pennsylvania*

*Natural Pennsylvania*

*Bears Wild Guide*

*Turtles Wild Guide*

*Common Edible and Poisonous Mushrooms*

*Make a Home for Wildlife*

**Hunting:**

*A Rough-Shooting Dog*

*A Hunter's Book of Days*

*Gun Dog Breeds*

*The Upland Equation*

# A STRANGER HERE BELOW

## A GIDEON STOLTZ MYSTERY

**CHARLES FERGUS**

An Arcade / CrimeWise Book

Visit our website at www.arcadepub.com.

10 9 8 7 6 5 4 3 2 1

Library of Congress Cataloging-in-Publication Data is available on file.

Cover design by Erin Seaward-Hiatt
Cover artwork © Slava Gerj/Shutterstock

Print ISBN: 978-1-951627-44-7
Ebook ISBN: 978-1-5107-3851-5

Printed in the United States of America

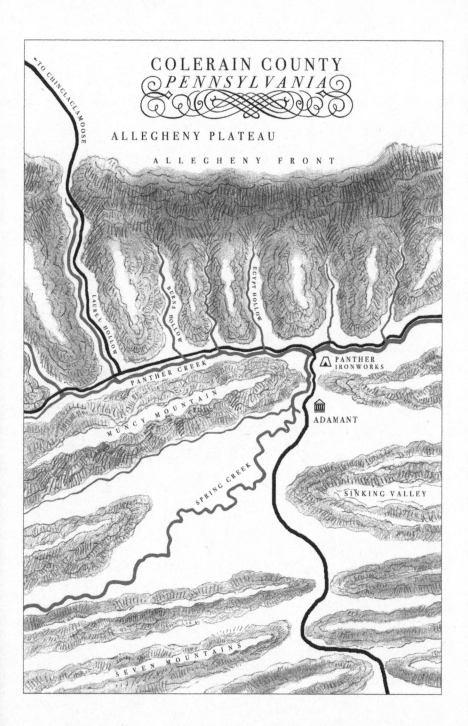

*I am a stranger here below,*
*And what I am is hard to know.*

From the shape-note hymn "Jackson," 1810

*And if on earth we meet no more,*
*O may we meet on Canaan's shore*

# One

——⊗⊗⊗——

GIDEON STOLTZ STOOD IN THE DARKNESS, SHOTGUN IN HIS HANDS. His breath clouded in the chill air. He didn't see light in any of the windows in Judge Biddle's house. Had the judge overslept?

Yesterday, on the way home from hunting grouse, they'd passed a pond where ducks were coming in. The judge had stopped the wagon and, in the evening light, they had sat side by side on the hard bench seat and watched the ducks fly over, heard the rapid *whick-whick-whick* of their wings, then splashes as one, and another, and another lit on the water and began quacking.

Gideon had suggested they come back first thing the next morning. He was the county sheriff; young for that job. He respectfully pointed out to his friend and mentor, Judge Hiram Biddle, that the pond was no more than a quarter hour's walk from town. They wouldn't need the wagon. Tramp there, get in a quick hunt, and be back in time for the day to begin.

Finally, the judge had nodded.

Now Gideon stood fidgeting in the dark outside the judge's house. In his mind's eye he could already see the ducks floating on the water, bright as jewels. He and Judge Biddle would creep up on the pond. At first light they would rise up together on the brushy bank. Startled, the ducks would lift off. He imagined the brilliant streams of water trailing from their bellies as their wings grabbed the air, mallards with emerald heads and sprigs with long pointed tails and wood ducks with ruby eyes and speckled breasts. How many would they get? He could practically taste roast duck already.

He waited for what he figured was another five minutes. Clearly the judge wasn't out of bed, and his housekeeper, Mrs. Leathers, hadn't arrived yet.

Five more minutes passed. Still no sign of activity from within: no sudden glow as a lamp was lit, no muffled footfalls, no creaking of stairs.

He walked around back to where the judge kept Old Nick. The red setter danced at the end of his chain and whimpered and licked Gideon's hand. When Gideon returned to the front of the house, the dog started barking. Surely that would rouse the judge.

Nothing.

He tried the door. Unlocked. He knew it was a presumptuous thing to do, but he let himself in anyway. He closed the door behind him and stood in the entry. All he could hear was the ticking of the big walnut-cased clock in the judge's study. Gideon knew how the house was laid out: the judge had invited him there for drinks and conversation. They were friends, improbable as that sometimes seemed, the young sheriff from away and the senior jurist who'd had a long and distinguished career in Colerain County. Friends united by their love of sport, the admirable hunt, the gentlemanly art the judge called "shooting-flying."

He called out: "Judge Biddle?"

Nothing.

He leaned his shotgun in a corner, felt his way down the hall, and turned left into the kitchen. Well, they'd be late, but maybe the ducks would still be on the pond. He put his hand on the stove, felt a remnant warmth. A lamp sat on the table. He opened the stove's door. He picked up the poker and prodded around inside the firebox until he saw an orange glow. He got a splint from the tin box on the mantel, held it to the ember, and blew on it gently. He smelled brimstone as the splint flared. He carried it to the lamp, lifted the globe, and held the flame to the wick.

"Judge Biddle?" he called again.

Dead silence. And now he began to worry.

He told himself that Hiram Biddle must still be asleep in bed. The fact that his calling had gotten no response didn't necessarily mean there was a problem. The judge was old. A bit hard of hearing. And no doubt worn out from slogging through the brush all yesterday. Or maybe he was ill—maybe he'd been stricken with an attack of some sort, maybe even expired in his bed. Gideon shook his head and tried to banish that thought.

Holding the lamp in front of him, he went down the hall. He looked into the dining room. Chairs were neatly positioned on both sides of the drop leaf table. He checked the parlor. No one there. The door to the judge's study was half-open. He pushed it the rest of the way.

His nostrils flared at the acrid smell of combusted gunpowder. The tang of blood, like wet hay gone sour, hung in the air. Cutting through those scents, the stench of *dreck*.

Judge Biddle sat sprawled in a chair. He didn't move. In the center of the judge's chest a fist-sized hole punched through his vest. At the edges of the hole the green woolen cloth was charred black.

Gideon groaned. He almost dropped the lamp but managed to set it on the table with a clatter, the flame leaping wildly. He felt a weird prickling sensation gather in the center of his back, then spread out across his shoulders. It almost took his breath away. He knew the feeling, remembered it from the past.

Judge Biddle's eyes were half-open. His head lolled back. His cheeks and forehead were chalk white, his nose pinched and greenish. Blood had pooled in his mouth, run down the side of his neck, and dried there. The chair in which he sat faced the table. The judge's shotgun lay on the table, its buttstock braced against the wall, its twin muzzles aimed at the judge in his chair.

*Lieber Gott.*

Gideon felt his spine stiffen. Looking at the judge, he no longer saw the body of his friend. Instead he saw something that had dwelt in the back of his mind for years, crouching there like some fearsome ungovernable beast, always ready to spring forth.

"*Memmi*," he whispered.

He saw her plain as day. Lying on the floor, her skirt rucked up around her waist. Her one leg, bruised, wedged against the *brodehonk*. Right there in the *kich* where she always was, where she cooked their meals, where she baked those pies—he liked shoo-fly the best, the gooey kind with plenty of *molosich*—all the goodies she knew he loved, cookies and cobblers, cakes and pies. They smelled like she did, warm and good. Now what he smelled was blood and *dreck*. The air in the kitchen had seemed to be blinking. It pulsed with yellow and purple light. The world had held still for a moment; then it had shuddered into motion again, a new and terrifying place.

He shook his head, forced a deep breath, and made himself return to the here and now. *This is not my mother. But it is bad.* Yesus Chrishtus, *it's bad. Judge Biddle. Dead! Killed by his own hand.*

He heard a rustling and jerked his head around. He came back solidly to the present when he found himself staring into the face of Alma Leathers, Judge Biddle's housekeeper. She stood in the doorway of the judge's study, in the elegant house on Franklin Street, in the town of Adamant, Pennsylvania, in the year 1835. And Gideon was not a ten-year-old boy any longer, but a man of twenty-two.

Mrs. Leathers had hold of the doorjamb. Slowly she slid down it until she was kneeling on the floor, her legs hidden beneath voluminous skirts. She pulled her eyes away from the judge and fixed them on Gideon's. Their gray irises were ringed with white.

"No," she said. She looked at him, seeming to beseech him—as if he could somehow turn the clock back and make things right again.

So many times he had wished he could do that for his *memmi*.

"I waited around for a while and then let myself in," he stammered. "We were going out hunting. Ducks. A big flock of them on a pond. We saw them last night."

"No!" she said again.

He helped her to her feet. The room was growing light from the day coming on. The tall clock in the corner ticked loudly, implacably, ticking away the seconds, ticking away life.

"Go out to the kitchen," he told Mrs. Leathers. "Start the fire. Make some coffee. I will take care of things here."

She turned and walked woodenly down the hallway.

He looked back at the judge, his friend and hunting partner, the man he most admired in the town, slumped in the chair, dead.

He tried to unkink his shoulders and draw air into his lungs. He looked around the room. A poker lay on the floor beside the judge's chair. No overturned furniture, no belongings strewn about, nothing suggesting that an assault or a robbery—or a murder—had taken place.

Next to the judge's shotgun lay a paper with writing on it, held down by a book. He set the book aside, picked up the sheet, and read: a date, some legal verbiage about this being the last will and testament of Hiram Biddle, and superseding all others, and being of sound mind—*How could anyone of* sound mind *have done this?* His brain barely registered the words until he saw his own name.

I leave my setter, Old Nick, to Gideon Stoltz, Sheriff of the County of Colerain, Commonwealth of Pennsylvania. I leave my Manton shotgun, including gun slip, case, and contents thereof, to Gideon Stoltz the same. I leave the spring wagon, my shooting brake, to Gideon Stoltz, also the bay horse Jack, along with harness and tack. The remainder of my estate, house and grounds, carriage, furniture, household goods, and personal belongings, shall be sold at auction and the proceeds used for the upkeep and betterment of the County Home for the Poor and Indigent.

Instructions for a coffin, funeral, headstone. The judge's signature at the bottom of the page. Nothing else. No reason given why Judge Biddle had killed himself.

Gideon read through the will again. It seemed carefully written and logically ordered—although it must have issued from a deeply troubled mind.

A mind he thought he knew. A keen mind that dispensed a balanced justice in court. A mind that planned their hunts with an almost military precision. He remembered the judge just yesterday saying in his even, matter-of-fact tone: "The wind has now turned into the north. Let us hunt up the steep gully and give Old Nick the advantage of having the scent in his nose." Gideon wished they were there now, on the piece of ground the judge called Seek No Further on account of an apple tree of that variety growing near the cellar hole of a failed homestead, beneath which there always seemed to be a grouse. He wished they could wade into the brush following the setter. A breeze combing the maples, their leaves fluttering red-white-red-white, the tang of fallen apples, the toasted-bread scent of frost.

Instead he smelled blood and *dreck* and the musty air of a cold room.

He said to himself: *You have tasks. Now do them.*

But what could he do beyond saying a prayer, informing the state's attorney of this dreadful event, and seeing to it that Hiram Biddle's body went gentle into the ground?

*Soon as from earth I go,*
*What will become of me?*

# Two

⸻⸙⸻

S UICIDES BURNED IN HELL.
Gideon stumbled along the muddy street past brick and stone and log and clapboard houses, past stores and shops. Smoke from wood and coal fires hung low. Rain began to fall, a few drops, then dozens drumming down on roofs and plinking in puddles.

Well-nigh impossible to absorb what he had just seen. Hiram Biddle had shown him kindness and respect. He had been for Gideon an example of how one ought to comport oneself, how one should behave and live. And now this.

He passed the gray limestone bulk of the courthouse. The rain and the wind picked up. He came to Lawyers Row. A sign dangling from an iron bracket creaked in a gust: A. FISH ESQ. He stood for a moment, then shook off his reluctance, mounted the steps, and cleaned his boots on the scraper anchored in the stoop. He knocked three times and opened the door.

He edged his way into the office. Alvin Fish already sat working at his desk. The Cold Fish, as Gideon's deputy, Alonzo Bell, called the state's attorney behind his back.

Fish wrote by the clean white light of a whale oil lamp. He held up his left hand, palm outward, while continuing to scratch with his pen. Finally he set down his pen and raised his head. Fish was a gaunt man with a heavy beard that, freshly razored, made his hollow cheeks look gray. He took off the spectacles that pinched the bridge of his nose. He looked at Gideon for a long moment.

"Speak," he said.

"It's Judge Biddle." Gideon heard himself say *Chutch*, his *Pennsylfawnisch Deitsch* accent betraying him yet again. He suddenly remembered to doff his hat. "He killed himself."

Fish slowly half-rose from behind his desk. "What? Judge Biddle? Killed himself, you say?"

Gideon nodded.

"You are telling me that Hiram Biddle is dead?"

"He shot himself. Last night. I just came from his house."

Fish searched Gideon's face with his dark inquisitorial eyes. He was an aggressive prosecutor; Gideon had watched him tearing into witnesses in Judge Biddle's courtroom. Wrinkles deepened at the corners of Fish's eyes. Then the corners of his mouth tugged fractionally upward.

"How shocking," Fish said. "How tragic, utterly tragic. I take it you've done nothing with the body yet?"

Gideon shook his head.

Fish straightened all the way up. He tapped his spectacles against his palm. "Go fetch the coroner. Inform him that I want an autopsy done. Right away. Tell him I will assist. And I want your report on my desk by the day's end."

The state's attorney made a flicking motion with the fingers of one hand. "Get to it."

Gideon went back outside. Raindrops smacked against his hat brim. Water gurgled into rain barrels beside buildings. The hills hemming in the town peeked through the lower edges of gray clouds, their steep brushy slopes dressed with autumnal yellows and reds. He scarcely noticed the colors as he trudged to Dexter Beecham's house.

He knocked and waited for what seemed like hours, until the doctor's wife opened the door. She had a doughy, sleepy face. Her husband came down the hall behind her, yawning, slipping galluses up over his shoulders. "Well, well," he said. "Sheriff Stoltz. Good morning."

Gideon didn't think it was a good morning at all.

"Judge Biddle is dead," he said. "He shot himself in the chest with his shotgun."

Beecham blinked. "You don't say." His face was red—it was always red, as if he were perpetually embarrassed or had just run a mile.

"Mr. Fish wants an autopsy."

Beecham rubbed his red face.

"He wants it right away."

"As in, before breakfast?" Beecham gave a little laugh.

"He says he will assist."

"All right, then," Beecham said. "Let's get a wheelbarrow."

They found the wheelbarrow in the doctor's barn. They set off, Gideon holding the handles and pushing, Beecham grabbing the barrow's front end and helping to pull it through muddy places. People were now opening up shops and passing by in the street. *They don't know yet*, Gideon thought. *Will they even care?* Some of the more curious paused and watched the two mismatched men with the wheelbarrow: Beecham short and rotund, Gideon tall, with broad shoulders and big hands.

Judge Biddle's house was a particularly fine one, built of limestone and set back from the street. Green-painted shutters framed the windows. Twin fountain-shaped elms arched over the yard, beginning to turn yellow. The wind shook the trees, and a flurry of wet leaves came tumbling down.

In the house, Beecham spoke condolences to Mrs. Leathers. Gideon led the way down the hall, the doctor waddling along behind.

The judge remained slumped in the chair in the study. The shotgun lay on the table with its buttstock against the wall. It went through Gideon's mind that the gun ought to be cleaned: black powder residue ate away at Damascus steel at a fierce rate.

The judge's will lay on the table, although the book that had held it down was gone. Put away by Mrs. Leathers? Again Gideon looked about for a suicide note. Again he failed to find one.

Beecham stood in front of Judge Biddle with his arms crossed. He reached out a hand and slowly moved the judge's jaw from side to side. Then, using both hands, he moved the judge's head. He pushed down the eyelids with his fingertips. He stood back, cupping his chin in his hand. He bent forward again and touched the edge of the gaping wound in the judge's chest. He clucked and wagged his head.

"Yep, suicide. Has to be. Last evening, I would guess." He shook his head. "Well, I'll be damned."

*No*, Gideon thought. *It is Judge Biddle who is damned.*

He grimaced as he helped the doctor wrap the body in a blanket that Mrs. Leathers brought. He smelled again the *dreck* that had leaked out after Judge Biddle died and lost control of his bowels. The corpse was rigid and unwieldy and felt surprisingly light, like a husk instead of the dead weight that Gideon had expected. He took hold of the shoulders while the doctor lifted the feet, and together they carried the bundled body down the hallway, angled it through the front door, and placed it on the barrow. The barrow lacked sides but had a front piece. The doctor tucked in the blanket's ends and used a rope to tie the bundle in place.

People had begun to gather in the street. Eight, ten of them, standing there gawking in the rain. Gideon saw them looking at the blanketed corpse, and looking at him as well. He couldn't read their faces. How had they learned of the judge's death? Mrs. Leathers must have told someone. Or maybe the doctor's wife. And that person told someone else. Soon the news would be all over town.

"Who will lay this body out?" he asked Beecham. He envisioned someone, maybe Mrs. Leathers, maybe himself, washing the judge and clothing him in his best suit for burial. Would there be a wake? The judge hadn't put it in his will. Did you even do that when someone killed himself?

"My wife will take care of those things." Beecham jammed his hat down on his head and turned his collar up against the rain. "She'll make a shroud for the judge here. You know, Sheriff, an autopsy don't leave a real pretty corpse." He gave Gideon an inquiring look. "Want to be there when I open him up?"

Gideon shook his head. He lifted the barrow's handles and pushed it down the walk. The barrow's wheel, a sycamore round, wobbled and squeaked across the stones.

\*\*\*

In the lot behind the judge's house, Gideon fed the horse and dog. Both were ravenous. The gelding pitched into his hay; the setter wolfed down his tripe. Old Nick pushed his bowl around, licking up every scrap. The judge had been proud of the dog; he said he had a "long nose," which meant he could pick up bird scent at a considerable range, then go charging or pussyfooting in, depending on what was needed to pin the bird. Gideon thought about all the times he had watched the red setter weaving through the brush, homing in on a hidden grouse or woodcock: the bell going silent as Old Nick came to a halt, his head low like a snake's, his eyes bulging, his feathery tail sticking out behind. Such a sense of anticipation, as they crept up on the point. The sudden whirring of wings as the bird flushed; the abrupt thunderous shot. When the judge called "Fetch!" Old Nick would run on ahead and find the bird brought down by Gideon or the judge (usually the judge), bring the game back, and lay it in his master's hand.

Gideon went back inside the house. He disassembled the judge's shotgun and took the barrels into the back yard. He got some soap and a pot of hot water from Mrs. Leathers and scrubbed clean the barrel that had fired the fatal shot. He dried the barrels with a rag and greased them. In the study he put the gun away in its leather case.

A third time he searched for a suicide note and failed to find one.

He walked back to the jail through the rain and hung up his coat and hat. He wondered where his own gun was, then recalled that he'd left it at the judge's house. The judge had given Gideon his old shotgun last year after Gideon had accepted, with great enthusiasm, the judge's offer to take him hunting. And now Judge Biddle had willed him his graceful Manton 16. Such a beautiful firearm it was! He felt a moment of greedy delight that quickly dwindled to despond.

His deputy, Alonzo Bell, handed him an old sack. Gideon used it to dry himself off.

"Why in Pete's sake did he do it?" Alonzo said.

Gideon shook his head.

Alonzo was in his early forties, twenty years older than Gideon. His big jaw and protruding lower lip always put Gideon in mind of a contented horse. But now Alonzo looked as agitated and confused as Gideon himself felt. "Well, for crying in a bucket," Alonzo said, then went stumping off to attend to chores in the cell block.

Gideon sat down at his desk. He got out a quill and ink bottle and paper to prepare a report. He stared at the sheet and wondered how to begin.

***

It was dusk when he got home.

"True," he said to his wife, "something terrible has happened."

She hugged him hard and kissed him on the lips. "Mrs. Sayers told me over the fence."

Their baby, David, seven months old, lay on a blanket on the floor. The child crawled jerkily toward his father, craning his neck upward, smiling and burbling and reaching out a tiny hand. Gideon picked David up and held him to his chest.

True laid her hand on her husband's shoulder. "Was it you who found him?"

Gideon nodded.

"Oh, Gid." She raised her hand and cupped his cheek. Her eyes searched his. "I heard he killed himself."

"He left his will sitting out on a table."

"Did it say why?"

"No. Just a will. Nothing else, no explanation."

"You must be heartsick."

He let out a sigh. "Why would he do such a thing?"

"Maybe you will find out by and by." True took the baby from him and gently laid him on the blanket. "Supper's ready. We need to eat right away so we can get to the singing."

He had forgotten. "I don't want to go."

"You need to go. It will make you feel better."

★★★

The rain had subsided to a drizzle. True had swaddled David against the miasmas that rose from the earth at night, carrying disease. They hurried along through the muddy streets.

The Methodist church was a low log building. Inside, tallow candles gave off a pungent smell and a wavering light. No organ, such as the one in the brick Episcopal church on Spring Street where the town's better citizens worshipped; not even a piano. Here were only the voices folks had been born with.

Forty people filled the church. They picked up the oblong tune-books and sat down on benches made from split logs. Gideon sat with the tenors. True, holding David, sat to his right with the trebles. On the tenors' left were the basses, and on the opposite side of the hollow square sat the counters.

Before they began, an elder stood up and announced that Judge Biddle had killed himself: "Blew himself 'most in half with a shotgun." Gideon saw people looking at him. Of course they knew he was Judge Biddle's friend. Of course they'd heard it was he, Gideon

Stoltz, the Dutch Sheriff, who had found the body. Two of the basses leaned their heads together and traded whispers. One was a laborer named Bevins, the other a fellow named Raines who worked at the hotel. They straightened and stared at him, their faces hard and their eyes narrowed.

What was that about?

The lead tenor announced the first song: "Idumea," on page twenty-five. He pitched the starting notes up and down the scale and the singers tuned in, the sound swelling as the parts found their places: the high trebles, the lower tones of the counters, the grave voices of the basses, and above them the higher tones of the tenors, all blending into one sonorous trembling chord.

The harmony was raw, in the minor mode, utterly different from the predictable, mellifluous *Hoch Deutsch* hymns of Gideon's childhood. The congregation had been singing this new music for over a year, ever since a singing master had come down from New York and taught them to read the music. They'd dug deep into their pockets to buy the tunebooks—True made him contribute five whole dollars! At each singing they might do twenty, thirty hymns, with names like "Northfield" and "Delight" and "Cowper" and "Schenectady" and "Primrose" and "New Jerusalem." The minister was glad, since the vigorous new hymns were building zeal and bringing more people to church. Gideon enjoyed the strange and unexpected harmonies; he often found himself humming or singing the songs later, when splitting firewood or working at his desk or riding somewhere on his horse. The hymns' poetry, their lyrics, never failed to move him. Each song, it seemed, had the power to inspire him, or terrify him, or uplift him—or wound him. Some of them made him recall things he didn't want to remember. Like his *memmi's* death.

He hadn't mentioned this to True, who loved the singing. She said it strengthened her faith and brought her closer to God. She made sure they never missed a single Wednesday night.

With his hand the leader beat out the tempo. The people sang out *faw* and *sol* and *law* and *me*, voicing the syllables of the differently shaped notes—triangles, ovals, squares, and diamonds—printed in the books. The second time through, they launched into the words. They sang loud and strong. Gideon let his voice soar. He knew "Idumea" by heart; the congregation sang it every Wednesday night and sometimes during Sunday service as well.

> *And am I born to die?*
> *To lay this body down!*
> *And must my trembling spirit fly*
> *Into a world unknown?*

Others in the chorus kept time, arms rising and falling, hands clapping down on thighs, feet tramping the floor.

> *A land of deepest shade,*
> *Unpierced by human thought;*
> *The dreary regions of the dead,*
> *Where all things are forgot!*

The words pierced Gideon's own heart. He thought of Hiram Biddle's soul wandering restlessly in the dreary regions of the dead, with no hope of entering into the light of God's saving grace.

> *Soon as from earth I go,*
> *What will become of me?*
> *Eternal happiness or woe*
> *Must then my portion be!*

The judge had committed suicide. His portion must be eternal woe. Yet Gideon prayed that Hiram Biddle's soul might somehow find salvation.

*Waked by the trumpet's sound,*
*I from my grave shall rise;*
*And see the Judge with glory crowned,*
*And see the flaming skies!*

This Judge was God in all His power. On the day of redemption, those who had kept the faith would rise from their graves and join Him. The voices filled the church as the people sang the repeat, belting out again those final, awful words: *And see the Judge with glory crowned, and see the flaming skies!*

Gideon could almost see the heavens red with fire, hear them crackling from one horizon to the other. But his mind stayed stubbornly earthbound.

By killing himself, Judge Biddle had spurned the gift that God had given. There had to be some reason for him to have taken an action so dire. Was it something from the past? Something that he'd buried and tried to forget, only to have it emerge anew? Something evil, or scandalous, or grievously sad?

Gideon felt resentment well up. The judge should have realized that it would be he who would find his body. He would have to forgive Judge Biddle for that.

And he wanted to understand.

He made up his mind to learn the reason *why.* Yes, he would do it. He would look, and ask, and listen, and figure out what had caused Hiram Biddle to throw away his life, on earth and in heaven everlasting.

*Give joy or grief, give ease or pain,*
*Take life or friends away*

# Three

⸙

T HE RAIN HAD LET UP. WALKING HOME THROUGH THE DARK AND quiet town, Gideon carried David, fast asleep. During the singing Gideon had looked across at his son, held in True's arms, and seen him smiling and waving his little hands and making hooting sounds as if trying to join in singing the hymns.

True linked her arm in his, and he told her about the things that Judge Biddle had willed to him. She looked up at him, clasping his arm tight. "The dog and gun would have been more than enough for you to remember him by. But a horse and wagon! What a generous gift! And him in such turmoil and pain."

At home, Gideon banked the fire while True nursed David and put him in his cradle. She snuffed the candle, took Gideon by the hand, and led him to their bed. They undressed and lay down together. It seemed they always made passionate love after singings—and tonight especially Gideon wanted to lose himself in her. True ran her hand through his sandy hair. She kissed him gently on the mouth, then slowly moved her lips down his neck and chest. His stomach fluttered as her lips went farther down. She brought him nearly to a climax, then stopped. She lay down on her back, and he covered her with his body. She wrapped her arms and legs around him. He felt himself go deep inside her, even as he went deep inside himself, and as they moved together and approached the sudden cleansing release, he heard their cries as if from far away.

Later, coming back to awareness, he heard her whisper in his ear.

"You should see your legs," she said. "I peeked when you dropped your drawers. Scratched and scraped all over."

He cracked one eye open. "From hunting in the briars, I guess."

She nibbled his earlobe, chuckling. "I like it when you talk Dutch."

"Hmm?"

"'Haunting.' What you just said."

"I meant . . ." His voice trailed off.

"I know what you meant. If my brothers heard you say 'haunting' instead of 'hunting,' they would ride you hard." She chuckled again. "Though not the way you ride me hard." She kissed his ear. "Foreigners, that's what we call you Dutch."

Dutch. It meant German. *Pennsylfawnisch Deitsch* was the dialect Gideon had grown up speaking.

His people had lived in Pennsylvania as long as True's Scotch-Irish clan, but that didn't stop the *Deitsch* from being treated as foreigners, along with the French, the Catholics, and the Jews.

He disliked it when others made fun of his accent or scorned him for being of German descent. But True could tease him all she wanted. He knew what she was trying to do: take his mind off the day's events. Well, he'd play along. "We Dutch are the worst of the lot," he said. "We love to hold a grudge. *Schtubbich*, set in our ways. Some of us even refuse to learn English."

"It didn't trouble me any, you being Dutch. I wouldn't have cared if you were a Frenchman or a Jew or even an African. Though if you'd've been black, I expect the jaybirds would've killed you."

"Jaybirds" was what True called her brothers: James, Jackson, Jared, and Jesse Burns. All of them worked at the iron plantation at Panther, east of Adamant, where True had grown up. Gideon had a hard time pronouncing his J's. To him, those rugged men were Chames, Chackson, Chared, and Chesse.

True kissed him on the lips. And again. "Dutchman or not," she said, kissing him one more time, "I do love you."

"I love you, too."

He lay upon her, resting his weight on his forearms, breathing in her scent. He felt safe in the warmth of her embrace. He dozed off.

Suddenly she was pushing at his chest, grunting, "Get off!"

He rolled onto his side.

She sat up, her head lowered and held between her hands, her hair draped over her arms.

"True, honey, what is it?" He reached out, placed his hand on her back.

"I saw something." Her voice was small and quavering. She took rapid breaths. She raised her face and looked at him, her eyes wide. "It just . . . came into my head. I saw it like it was right in front of me. Two people, a woman and a man. They were arguing. Screaming at each other! I couldn't hear what they were saying, but I could tell they were angry, angry and in pain."

She shuddered beneath his hand.

"Then they were gone, and I saw two candles flickering on a table, side by each. All of a sudden, they both guttered and went out."

Gently Gideon rubbed her back. True had told him that sometimes she had visions, saw things that had happened in the past—or would take place in the future. She called this troubling ability "the second sight," or just "the sight."

But who could believe in such things? Gideon considered himself a rational man, a man who saw only those objects that were in front of him, in the here and now. He had no time for visions and superstitions. Then he thought with a start of how, when confronted with the judge's body this very morning, he had suddenly seen his *memmi*. He had seen her vividly, as if she lay on the floor in front of him, bloody and ravaged and dead. But that wasn't a vision—it was just a horrible memory, one that had been burned into his brain, a memory he'd never been able to get rid of.

True lay back down. He settled the quilt over them both. He turned his body toward hers, rested his hand on her hip, and pressed his lips against the soft skin at her temple.

"It's the sight," she said. She stared up at the ceiling. "I wish I didn't have it. Seems like nothing good can ever come of it." She shivered and pulled the quilt tight around her. She claimed to have gotten this unwanted gift from her gram, who believed it hit every other generation.

He had met True's grandmother once, at her parents' cabin at the ironworks. Arabella Burns was the mother of True's father. Gideon had been introduced to her quite casually, which seemed to be typical of the way True's people behaved, even at times when you'd think they'd be formal and polite. The old woman was small and thin, yet she seemed large and powerful in some strange way. She had said little, sitting perched on a stool in the corner of the room, erect and proud, watching over things with a sharp eye.

"When I was little, Gram had this raven's foot," True said. "It was big, black as tar, with scales all over it and sharp claws. The toes were clenched most of the way shut, except for this little hole between them. She could look through that hole and see things that would come to pass."

True turned her face toward his. He could barely see her features in the dim light. Her hair was dark and thick, her eyebrows arching. Gideon thought of the trim strong body beneath the quilt and felt himself wanting her again.

"Gid, do you believe in the sight?"

He paused before answering. "No. I can't say that I do."

She looked away. "Well, at least you're honest."

He knew she wasn't stupid or silly. But he didn't share her belief in visions or spirits or the supernatural—or being able to read the future or perceive the past.

"Maybe you just had a dream," he said.

"No. I wasn't asleep." She turned back toward him. "I *did* see something. A man and a woman, arguing. And two candles that went out. I don't know who those people were, or when it was, or where. But I tell you, I saw it."

He didn't respond right away.

"You don't believe me."

"True," he said, "I don't have to think the same way you do. I don't have to believe everything you believe or see everything that you see. I love being with you, talking with you, loving you. I will never get tired of that." He was quiet for a moment. "I'm sure you did see something. I just wish I knew what it meant."

Before she could reply, he kissed her on the lips. Her mouth opened to his. He circled his hand over her belly, then moved it downward. She caught her breath and pressed against him.

*My silent dust beneath the ground,*
*There's no disturbance there*

# Four

⁘

"**G**O AHEAD AND SHOOT!"
Alonzo Bell, deputy sheriff, lay on his back at the far end of
the ore pit. He had taken off his hat. Against the orangish dirt, his
bald head appeared pale as a dab of early snow. Jutting up between his
bent knees was a weathered board four feet tall. On the board Alonzo
had used a piece of charcoal to make a target, a black circle three
inches across.

*Ganz narrisch* it was: completely crazy. "Alonzo!" Gideon yelled
to his deputy. "This is not safe!"

Yesterday Gideon had found Judge Biddle's body. This morning
the coroner had delivered the autopsy report. There were no surprises:
death from massive wounding to the heart and lungs caused by a self-
inflicted shotgun blast. Now Hiram Biddle's enshrouded remains lay
in the walnut coffin that the town's best carpenter had built and
taken to Dr. Beecham's house. Tomorrow, the coffin would go into
the ground.

After getting the coroner's report, Gideon had gone to the judge's
house, put a bridle on the gelding Jack, and walked him to the livery
barn where he kept his mare Maude. He dreamed of someday owning
a place with a barn and a fenced lot and maybe even enough pasture
to keep horses. But for now he would have to pay board for both
Maude and the gelding.

After arranging for the livery to take Jack, Gideon had gone back
to the judge's house. He wheelbarrowed Old Nick's wooden box to
his own house, the dog following along obediently. He set the box in

the back yard. True had come out and given Old Nick some meat scraps. The setter had wagged his tail and licked her hand.

At the jail, Gideon let Alonzo talk him into riding out to shoot mark, even though they had a prisoner. Henry Peebles was sitting in a cell awaiting trial for gouging out one man's eye and biting off another's thumb during a brawl in Hammertown, as the seamy side of Adamant was known. Gaither Brown, a part-time deputy with a leatherworking shop down the street, agreed to bring his work—he was tooling some leather for a saddle—and sit in the jail's front office, keeping an eye on things while Gideon and Alonzo went out and practiced shooting.

"Your gun's loaded!" Alonzo yelled. "Go ahead and empty it!"

Gideon had already shot at stumps and old bottles, sending shards of green and brown glass whizzing across the ore pit. After each shot, he swabbed the rifle's bore, then poured powder down the barrel, used the hickory rod to ram home a lead ball wrapped in a linen patch, and primed the pan.

His ears rang. When he swallowed, he tasted burnt gunpowder. In the matter of shooting the charge now loaded in the rifle, Alonzo was correct: For safety's sake, before being placed in its scabbard for the ride back to town, the weapon should be discharged. Though not necessarily in the direction of a man with a target clamped between his knees.

Gideon winced as he settled the butt plate against his shoulder. Tomorrow that shoulder would be purple as a bunch of grapes.

He thumbed the hammer back and peered down the barrel. Earlier he had aimed at a bottle, squeezed the trigger, watched the hammer fall—and the gun had failed to shoot. One second had passed. Then another. When he lifted his head, the *verfluchta* thing chose just that moment to go off, the wooden stock slugging him in the jaw so that his teeth clashed and he saw stars. No idea where the ball had flown.

The rifle's sights wavered past the black bull's-eye, danced across gray-clad knees. Gideon lowered the gun. "I can't do this!"

"Yes! You! Can!"

He sighed and raised the weapon again. One didn't shoot a rifle the same way that one fired a shotgun. The rifle was concentration and precision; the shotgun was fluidity and grace. Judge Biddle always said that the two skills didn't mix—you couldn't be a good shotgun shot and a good rifle shot both. Gideon figured he wasn't any great shakes at either.

He remembered something else the judge had told him. He had quoted some learned man, a lawyer or maybe another judge, saying: "The law is a gun, which if it misses a pigeon kills a crow; if it does not strike the guilty, it hits someone else. As every crime creates a law, so in turn does every law create a crime."

The idea of a law creating a crime didn't sit well with Gideon, who believed that laws were drafted by wise and sober men to prevent crimes by spelling out what people shouldn't do. Such as shooting a .50 caliber ball at a target held by some *dummkopp* a good sixty yards off.

Was Alonzo a pigeon or a crow?

And who was the real *dummkopp*? If he jerked the trigger instead of squeezing it, if there was another hangfire and the ball somehow went astray and hit Alonzo, killed him—*manslaughter*. Gideon imagined the state's attorney Alvin Fish—the Cold Fish—prosecuting him with vigor for such an offense.

"Go ahead and shoot!" Alonzo yelled.

Gideon took a deep breath. He let out half of it. He steadied the rifle so that the bull's-eye nestled on top of the gun's sights. He tightened his finger, felt the trigger's slight creep. Then the hammer fell, flint struck frizzen, smoke gouted from the barrel and spurted from the touch hole as the gun went *CRACK* and bucked back into his shoulder.

He lowered the rifle. Peered through thinning smoke. Up came Alonzo in his labored trot, grinning like the butcher's dog. He held up the board. "Right on the mark! By gee, you could win a turkey shoot!"

★★★

The road led through brush growing thick above blackened ground. A stand of forest had been logged off here within the last few years to make charcoal for the ironworks; once the colliers had moved on, someone had set the patch on fire so the huckleberries would grow.

"When we get back, you can clean these rifles," Gideon said. Alonzo loved fiddling with guns, scrubbing out their bores after shooting, dressing their moving parts with whale oil, coating their barrels with rendered sheep fat or wax.

"Been holding my water all morning," Alonzo announced from atop his tall gelding. "I'll mix some hot piss in with the water, so I will. You can't beat it for cleaning burnt powder out of a gun barrel."

They passed a shallow pit where men chinked with picks at an ore bank. Other men shoveled the broken rock into baskets, then carried them to a wagon and dumped them in the bed. Gideon and Alonzo overtook a laden wagon on the road. The teamster sat astride the left-side mule closest to the wagon. He called out "Whoa," pulled back on the reins, and the six-mule team walked to a halt.

The teamster's head was level with Alonzo's. Seated on his little mare, Gideon had to look up.

"Heard you'uns banging away," the teamster said. His cheek bulged with a quid. "One of your balls flew over my head."

The hangfire. "I hope no harm was done," Gideon said quickly.

The teamster squirted tobacco juice onto the road. "No harm, Dutchman. Woke these mules up, so it did."

"This here is Sheriff Stoltz," Alonzo said. "And you are likely aware that I am his deputy."

"I am aware, 'Lonzo Bell, that you are a windbag who couldn't find his own ass with both hands and a coon dog."

"The sheriff is perfecting his marksmanship," Alonzo said, ignoring the teamster's gibe. "At first he couldn't hit a target even if it was as broad across as your wife's bee-hind. Now I believe he could take the head offen a squirrel at fifty paces."

"That'd be good shooting," the teamster said. "But it would ruin the best part."

Gideon's stomach gave a jump. More than once Alonzo had tried to talk him into eating what he called "a mess of brains": fried squirrel brains, considered a delicacy in these parts. Cook the heads in lard, crack them open with a knife, and feast on what was inside. The thought nearly made him gag. It must have shown on his face, because the teamster barked a laugh.

"So you figure on making a frontiersman out of this tadpole?" the man said.

Gideon flushed. Even though he held a position of authority, he was not much respected in Colerain County. Too young, for one thing. And people called him the Dutch Sheriff. They sniggered at the way he got his V's and W's mixed up, and his sentences all backward. Like the time he was digging in the garden and shucked off his muddy breeches before coming in the house, and called out to True, "Honey, throw me down the stairs my other pants." She laughed so hard she almost wept.

Two years ago he had gotten on his mare, Maude, and ridden her west to this remote backwoods place. He had left his childhood home in Lancaster County to get away from his grim, narrow-minded *dawdy*, who drove him like another beast of burden. And, if he was honest with himself, to get away from what had happened to his *memmi*. Though maybe that hadn't worked so well. Maybe you could never get away from something like that.

In Adamant, he got hired as a deputy. He did well at it, even solved a crime on his own by arresting a ne'er-do-well who was stealing items out of barns and sheds and reselling them to a peddler who took them elsewhere and sold them again. Then, just last year, Sheriff Payton had fallen dead with a stroke of apoplexy while walking in the jailhouse door, and the county commissioners appointed Gideon Stoltz, only twenty-one years old at the time, a stranger and a Dutchman to boot, as the new sheriff.

"... devil of a thing," the teamster was saying, "I mean, him bein' a judge and all, and what does he do? Goes and shoots himself with that fancy shotgun."

Devil of a thing indeed, Gideon thought. And now that shotgun is mine.

They bade the teamster goodbye and rode on. The valley lay before them. On the long, parallel mountains hemming in the vale, and between the farms scattered through it, stood the forest. The trees were straight and tall, green pines and darker green hemlocks, towering chestnuts and oaks and maples and beeches whose leaves showed tints of yellow and red and bronze. A flock of pigeons crossed the bright blue sky, black specks flowing southward in an undulating stream of life, a flock for which no beginning could be glimpsed, nor an end.

They came back to Adamant. "Let's go up on Burying Hill," Alonzo said.

The horses huffed as they climbed the steep track. On top, the riders walked their mounts past slate and sandstone markers. Past a newly dug hole where Hiram Biddle's corpse would soon go to rest.

Gideon looked out over the town. The courthouse's copper roof dazzled. On a hill opposite it stood the academy, a three-story building whose peaked roof bristled with chimneys. On the Diamond, where Franklin and High Streets met, white sheep and red cows grazed. Along Franklin stood a dozen fine houses, brick and stone, Judge Biddle's among them. Smaller log and frame houses, including Gideon's, dotted the lesser streets of the town. He found his cottage, a speck of brown—it looked tiny, insignificant, yet he knew it to be full of peace and love; he thought of True, and of little David.

His gaze shifted to the big spring around which the town had grown. From the spring issued a stream of water that ran off toward the east. Farther along, Spring Creek had been dammed in several places, its flow harnessed for a gristmill, a sawmill, a slitting mill for making nail rods. On the far side of the creek lay Hammertown—another of those tough English words, which Gideon invariably pronounced *Hemmertawn*. And a tough place it could be. In Adamant proper, you bought your meat and tinware and flannels and flour and got your boots cobbled and your chin shaved, and when you worked up a thirst or had a base urge you went downhill, crossed the covered bridge (a sign said WALK YOUR HORSE OR GET A 2 DOLLAR FINE), and sought out the saloons in Hammertown. Loose women there. Bad whiskey. Fights, like the one that had landed Henry Peebles, eye-gouger and thumb-biter, in jail.

Spring Creek cut through a gap in the hills to join larger Panther Creek. There in the far offing Gideon could just see the ironworks with its furnace and forge, its mills and barns and pale dots of workers' cabins, a thin veil of smoke hanging over it all.

"Let me show you something," Alonzo said.

Gideon expected his deputy to dig a pamphlet out of his pocket condemning the Whigs, or extolling the Old Hero and current president, Andrew Jackson—or an advertisement for a new firearm manufactured on the percussion-cap system, which should be purchased for the armory; it seemed Alonzo agitated in favor of this modernization at least twice a day. Now, however, Alonzo did not appear intent on discussing firearms or politics. He drew a thick leg over his gelding's back and came off like a slide of ore, the horse bracing patiently as his rider clumped to the ground.

Alonzo rubbed his chin and looked around. "There's a grave somewhere around here."

Gideon dismounted and put the reins over Maude's head so she could graze among the tombstones.

Alonzo's chin needed a shave. He had a paunch and an ample rear end that he referred to as his "back porch." His big jaw and heavy brow made him look dull. But he was smart and resourceful, and Gideon often thought that Alonzo Bell would make the better sheriff, though it didn't seem his deputy had ambitions in that direction.

Alonzo set off toward the far end of the graveyard, Gideon following. Grass gave way to goldenrod and hawkweed.

Alonzo tramped down some weeds, exposing a small gray marker dappled with lichens and standing slightly off plumb: REV THOS McEWAN 1752–1805.

Alonzo squatted and looked at the stone. "McEwan preached over to Panther," he said. "Ought five. I was pretty young, and Ma wouldn't let me watch them hang him. So I run off into the forest and didn't come back till after dark, which that put her in quite a tizzy, figuring I had run away or met with some evil end."

"This man was hanged?" Gideon said.

Alonzo nodded. "The reverend here killed a man. The first murder in the county, if you don't count rubbing out a few score of Indians."

"Who did the preacher kill?"

"Fellow name of Nat Thompson. The ironmaster's brother."

"Why?"

"They got in a fight. After the preacher brained Nat, he tried to hide the corpus by burying it in his own garden, imagine that. Why do murderers always want to bury a corpus? There are better ways of disposing of someone you have killed. Cut the body up, leave the parts in the woods, and let the wolves and bears eat up the evidence. But no, they always want to bury it, usually near where the deed was done."

"Someone found the victim's body?"

"The sheriff did. When it went to trial, the preacher confessed. They took him to the gallows tree and put a noose around his neck."

Gideon's gaze shifted downhill to the white oak spreading its brawny limbs beside the courthouse. In autumn, pigeons sometimes roosted in the great tree; people went there at night with catchpoles and killed bushels of them. The old oak would no longer be used for hangings, however: the state legislature had just passed a law specifying that all executions would take place in the walled yard behind each county's jail.

Alonzo straightened with a grunt, his knees popping like gunshots. "Folks say Judge Biddle was never the same after he sentenced the reverend to hang."

*Your joys on earth will soon be gone,*
*Your flesh in dust be laid*

# Five

DIG IT DEEPER.

He listened to the uncanny words: like an urgent whisper by a voice old and hoarse.

*Dig it deeper.*

Trying to locate the source of the sound, Gideon looked up. Against the gray sky, the bare black branches of two trees scraped together.

Yesterday he had stood in the sunshine here on Burying Hill while Alonzo showed him the grave of the preacher that Judge Biddle had sentenced to hang thirty years ago. Now the judge would go into the same ground as the man he had condemned.

Crows flapping overhead cast wary glances at the figures below, then let out scathing caws. The wind picked up, and the trees' limbs began chattering in a tongue Gideon didn't understand.

The mayor, Osgood Jolly, read from the *Book of Common Prayer*—something he had been loath to do, telling Gideon, "I don't care if he *was* a judge, the service is not to be used for any 'who have laid violent hands upon themselves.' Says so right here." Jolly had pecked his fat finger against the book's page. Gideon had replied, "It was the judge's wish that the service be read. He wrote it in his will." The mayor frowned and shook his head. Gideon had declared, "I will read it then," not wanting the task, what with his accent thick as *nudelsupp*, but figuring, correctly as it turned out, that Jolly would not wish to give up his authority.

The mayoral voice intoned: "Man, that is born of woman, hath but a short time to live, and is full of misery."

Surely so, thought Gideon, though to temper that misery might come great joy: the love of a woman, the miracle of a child.

"In the midst of life we are in death . . ."

Last night, as he had sat by the coffin in the doctor's parlor, Gideon had prayed for Hiram Biddle, asking God to take the judge's soul into heaven. He had also spent time thinking back over the last day of Hiram Biddle's life, a day when he and the judge had gone hunting for grouse in the brushlands outside of town.

One thing he'd remembered clearly from the hunt was an excellent and artful shot the judge had made. A cock grouse had come clattering out of the brush in front of Old Nick, flying low and fast, and Judge Biddle swept up his gun and snapped off a shot: a cloud of russet feathers, and the bird cartwheeled and thumped the ground. Old Nick found it and brought it back. Then, instead of pouching the bird, the judge had stood with his gun resting on his left arm, holding the grouse in his left hand, while with the fingers of his right hand he had spread the grouse's tail like a fan so that the reddish-brown feathers showed all pretty. The judge had stood there looking at the fanned tail, his head bowed, for a long time. Like he was praying. Or considering. Coming to some decision, maybe. When finally he pouched the bird, Hiram Biddle's face had looked old and weary and . . . hopeless, that's how it had seemed, thought Gideon. Hopeless, and terribly sad.

And when they'd returned to town, having made plans to go duck hunting before dawn the next morning, Judge Biddle had addressed him as "Gideon." He couldn't remember the judge ever using his Christian name before. At first it was the formal, polite "Deputy Stoltz," and then, after his promotion, "Sheriff Stoltz." Another odd thing: The judge had given him his take of game, three plump grouse and two woodcock, a nice addition to Gideon's brace of grouse and a single woodcock. Judge Biddle had never given away his game before.

"Thou knowest, Lord, the secrets of our hearts . . ."

Gideon decided that only God knew the secrets of Hiram Biddle's heart.

". . . grace of our Lord Jesus Christ, and the love of God, and the fellowship of the Holy Ghost, be with us all evermore. Amen."

A thin chorus of amens echoed from the gathering. Only a handful of people had come to the burying. The judge's housekeeper, Mrs. Leathers. Some folks from the courthouse. The editor of the town's weekly newspaper. And the headmaster of the academy, a white-haired gent dressed in old-fashioned blue pantaloons, a dark blue coat trimmed in red, silver-buckled shoes on his feet, and a tricorn hat on his head.

The custodian and his helpers took hold of the ropes and lowered the coffin into the ground. Two other men stood waiting. They wore black frock coats with silk facings on the lapels; their hands, gloved in black leather, held stovepipe hats. Fish and Blake. Fish, the state's attorney, the county prosecutor; Blake was a lawyer, too. The two men set their hats down carefully on nearby slabs, took up shovels, and snicked them into the pile of fresh earth. They cast the dirt into the grave.

Gideon heard the clods thump hollowly against the judge's coffin. And all at once the prickling pins-and-needles sensation blossomed across his shoulders and back. The debilitating feeling that had overcome him when he found the judge's body. The same feeling that had stricken him when he'd been confronted by his *memmi,* lying dead in the kitchen twelve years ago. His vision swam, and now he heard the dirt drumming down on his mother's coffin, sealing her away in the earth—forever. She was gone for all time, he would never see her again, never kiss her or feel her hand caressing his cheek or ruffling his hair. He looked across at his sister Joanna holding little

Friedrich by the shoulders, Friedrich's hair all *stroobly*, their *memmi* would never have let him go out like that. Friedrich was *rutsching* around, trying to get loose. Their other sisters, Hannah and Sarah, held onto each other, tears running down their faces. But no one held onto Gideon. Their *dawdy* stood there like an ox about to have a hammer brought down on his head. Gideon's uncle, for whom he'd been named, wept and wrung his hands. Many others had come to the burying. Of course, it was something out of the ordinary, something to break the monotony, the routine of farming. He had stared at the men, unable to stop wondering: Did you kill *mei memmi*? Jacob Reifsnyder, from the next farm over, short and wiry, with a beard almost as red as his neck—was it you? Or maybe you, Sam Wechsler, big *doplich* Wechsler, you were always laughing and gay when you talked to her, standing there now beside your dried-up skinny *frau*, leaning your head toward hers and saying something, a half smile on your lips, as if nothing so very dreadful has taken place. His eyes had passed slowly over the other men, one by one. *Was it you? Or you? Or you?*

The thudding of dirt ceased. The two lawyers, Fish and Blake, put their shovels aside and brushed off their hands.

Gideon straightened and tried to relax his shoulders and breathe air into his lungs.

A movement drew his eye toward the end of the cemetery. There, beyond the last scattered markers and the sere grass and weeds, stood a horse. A horse like a vision. A beautiful horse, tall and black. Even on this dull day, its coat glistened. The horse had a deep chest and sloping muscular shoulders and an arched neck; it stood perfectly balanced on its long legs. *Ein hengshd*: a stallion. It had to be. He drank in the horse's beauty, used it to anchor his mind in the present.

A man stood by the stallion, holding the reins. The man wore a brown workaday coat and had kept his hat on his head. Beneath the broad brim, Gideon recognized the face of Adonijah Thompson, owner of the Panther Ironworks. Gideon had never met the ironmaster, although he had seen him from time to time in town. The black stallion must be the one called Vagabond. Everyone in the county was talking about the horse, how fast and fiery and potent he was, and many had put their mares to him.

The ironmaster placed a black-booted foot in the near stirrup and swung up into the saddle. He sat there, tall and erect, staring at the people gathered around Hiram Biddle's grave. Then he turned the stallion aside. A lane intersected with the burying ground and the stallion strode onto it, taking long fluid steps, heading off beneath the trees. The ironmaster didn't look back.

★★★

Walking down Burying Hill, Gideon fell in with Fish and Blake. Fish was gaunt and somewhat stooped. Blake had a big bearish head and tended to mumble through a ginger-colored beard.

"A sad day," Gideon offered.

The Cold Fish looked resolutely ahead. "Felo-de-se is always hard to accept."

Gideon didn't know the Latin words but assumed they referred to suicide.

"This is not a backwoods settlement any longer," Blake said. "Adamant is an up-and-coming town. For such a prominent figure to take his own life . . ." He shook his head.

"It will be in newspapers all over the state," Fish muttered. "It's unseemly, that's what it is."

"It wonders me," Gideon said—he winced at the Dutch usage and started over again. "I am . . . astonished that Judge Biddle would do this. The day he killed himself, he and I went . . ."—he caught himself before the pronunciation *haunting* slipped out—". . . hunting for grouse."

Fish gave a dismissive shrug. He lengthened his stride, and Blake followed suit.

Gideon walked faster to stay with them. "It seemed to me that Judge Biddle was not on that day his usual self. He seemed, I suppose you would say, troubled."

Fish shook his head. "What's done is done."

"The other day in court he was quite himself," Blake mumbled.

"A keen sense of justice," Fish said. "Knew the law inside out, and never applied it out of rancor or for personal gain."

"Vigilant," Blake added. "Could never sneak anything past him."

"And now the black ox has trampled him," Fish said.

The lawyers increased the pace of their downhill march again.

Staring at the lawyers' backs, Gideon felt like a child tagging along behind his elders. He had worked with Fish to investigate several crimes, including the theft of those small items from barns and sheds, and, more recently, a case in which a husband used a rod to beat his wife bloody, and the affray down in Hammertown during which Henry Peebles injured those two men. Fish had treated Gideon like some tool to be used and then set aside. Now people were saying that Fish would be the new judge.

They reached the streets of Adamant. People went in and out of stores. A boy wearing a leather apron dashed past. A man pushed a handcart filled with packages.

*They go on with life as if nothing has happened*, Gideon thought. It had been the same when his mother was killed.

He took several long strides, stepped in front of the lawyers, and turned to face them. They had to stop or run into him.

"Mr. Fish, Mr. Blake. Both of you have known Judge Biddle for years. Is there anything in his past that could have made him decide to kill himself?"

Blake looked off to the side and murmured, "In this world ye shall have tribulations."

Fish stepped around Gideon as if the sheriff were a pile of horse manure that a man wouldn't wish to dirty his boots in.

Blake touched his hat brim while brushing past on the other side.

Black hats bobbing, Fish and Blake continued down Lawyers Row. They climbed identical sets of limestone steps and let themselves into their offices.

\*\*\*

The hotel worker, Raines, was out behind the big brick lodging house scrubbing out a spittoon. A wooden bucket filled with soapy water sat next to another half-dozen of the ornate brass vessels yet to be cleaned. Raines went to the same church that Gideon and True attended.

"Hello, Mr. Raines," Gideon said.

Raines looked up. When he saw who it was, his stare became as hard and unfriendly as the ones he and his friend Bevins had directed at Gideon after the judge's suicide was announced during Wednesday evening's hymn singing at church. Those stares had aroused Gideon's suspicion at the time. "I wonder if you would mind answering a question or two," he said.

Raines's unfriendly stare became downright hostile.

"The other night in church. When they said that the judge had killed himself, you and Mr. Bevins put your heads together and whispered to each other. Then you both turned and looked at me."

"Well, what of it?"

"Do you know something about the judge's death? About why he killed himself?"

Raines squinted. "Why in the blazes would I know anything about that?"

"I don't know, I just wondered."

"Course not. Me and the judge, we weren't exactly bosom friends."

"You disliked the judge for some reason?"

"What?" Raines looked baffled. "I ain't saying that at all. I am just telling you I wouldn't have nothin' to do with no judge. Not like him and me drank whiskey together, or went out traipsing around the countryside hunting little birdies."

Gideon felt his face redden. "Then why did you and Bevins look like you knew something? Why did you stare at me like that?"

Raines sniffed. "The reason we looked at you? Because we wonder why you are the sheriff." He lifted his chin. "You are barely breeched. You're a stranger. You don't come from around here. And every time you open your mouth, you advertise yourself as a dumb Dutchman." His voice was full of scorn. "Sheriff Payton, he was all right, too bad he had to die. But why should they go and make you the sheriff over us all?"

Gideon was nonplussed. And embarrassed for being dense enough to think that this man and his friend might have any particular knowledge that could shed light on Hiram Biddle's death.

"Mark my words, come the next election, you'll get voted out," Raines said. "You think we want a Dutchman wearing a badge, struttin' around with his thumbs tucked in his vest, lording it over us? I think not. No, sir. This ain't your county. Adamant ain't your town."

"Sorry to have bothered you," Gideon said.

*Broad is the road that leads to death*
*And thousands walk together there*

# Six

A FTER CHURCH ON SUNDAY, GIDEON HITCHED THE BAY GELDING
Jack to the wagon that Judge Biddle had willed to him. He
helped True up onto the seat, then handed little David up to her.
They drove out of Adamant on the road to Panther. Gideon let Jack
walk; the three-mile trip would take slightly under an hour. True sat
next to Gideon, holding David in her lap. She smiled at her husband.
"Remember the day we went and found that preacher?"

"How could I forget?" Gideon grinned. "You rode my mare, and
I walked along beside, and I was the happiest man in the world." He
added, "Now I'm even happier."

"I'm happy, too, Gid." She looked down at the sleeping baby.
"God has truly blessed us."

It still wondered him, how he'd met this wonderful woman at a
frolic in Panther, where they would soon be visiting True's kin—
which, if he admitted it to himself, was not exactly something he
looked forward to. At the frolic, True had caught his eye from across
the hall. They seemed to swim toward one another through the
crowd of bodies, the young people all chattering and smoking and
drinking and laughing and dancing, and came together. They couldn't
hear one another very well over the blaring voices and the cater-
wauling fiddle, so they put their heads close together. He felt her
breath on his ear when she said her name and asked his. Then she
smiled and put her arm through his and they went outside. They
strolled in the semi-darkness, in the orange and faintly pulsating glow
cast by the iron furnace. True told him she worked in the mansion

just across the way, helping to take care of the ironmaster's house. Gideon said he had just gotten a job as a deputy sheriff in Adamant. "So you are a lawman," the girl said in a teasing tone. In the company of this lively young woman—*wunnershee,* such a beautiful girl!—he felt like he was soaring. His hip grazed hers, and he felt a fire run up his side and spread throughout his body. When they parted, she gave him a kiss on the cheek, pulled back a little, and smiled as her eyes lingered on his. They agreed to meet again, at a revival meeting on the following Friday night.

At the revival they paid no attention to the preacher on the stage shouting and gesticulating and writhing as he proclaimed the imminent second coming of Christ, nor the people weeping and prostrating themselves and crying out "Amen!" in the flickering light of torches. Instead, they went off into the woods together. The next morning they found the preacher again. He was just finishing shaving over a basin outside the open flaps of a tent. He looked tired and rumpled, and his eyes were bleary. Before he would marry them he made Gideon cough up a half-dollar and told them to lay their hands on his Bible and promise to go to church regularly and worship the Lord and turn aside from Satan and his conjurings and temptations, and then he tied the knot. Afterward, Gideon had boosted True up onto Maude and led her back to the house he was renting. They loved each other heedlessly for two days.

The following Sunday, when finally they had gone to her family's cabin at the ironworks, they found her brothers seated at a table with their father at the head; Gideon figured they were plotting what they'd do when they got hold of him. True stalked into the room with him in tow, shy and fearful. Her father banged his hands on the table, jumped up, and lunged at him, bellowing, "You god-damned bastard!" Gideon was taller than Davey Burns; at a shade over six feet, he was taller than most men, and years of farm work had made him strong. Still, he ducked back from the barrel-chested man pushing toward him. It turned out he didn't have to fight. True jumped in between them, stuck her face up into her father's and said in a tone no less belligerent than his: "We are lawfully married! I picked him out. I will bear his children. *Your grandchildren.*"

Gideon thought about that—being picked out. When all along he thought he'd done the picking.

Now he drove the wagon carrying himself, his wife, and their child, on the way to that cabin in Panther where he knew he was still resented. As he drove the bay gelding, he looked off to the side of the road where Spring Creek went gliding along in its bed. Tan leaves spun down from dapple-trunked sycamores and lit on the water and went floating along in the current like a fleet of tiny boats. Uphill from the road, the trees had all been logged off for charcoal to power the blast that melted the ore, the crucial step in making iron. The trees' stumps and root systems had sent up thousands of new shoots, a jungle of brush that was lush green in summer, flecked now with autumn's colors. Brambles curved up among rotting limbs that the coalers had left behind. Rain had cut into the ground, rivulets carried the soil away. To Gideon, the hills looked deeply wounded; to True, he figured, it was the way they had always been.

"This Jack is a good wagon horse," Gideon said. "He's calm and strong. Now that we have a wagon, all of us can ride in style whenever we visit your kin."

"A plain old wagon," True teased. "What kind of style is that? If only Judge Biddle had willed you his phaeton." She laughed. "It was kind of him to give you his horse and rig. And the dog and gun. Imagine, him thinking of you in the midst of whatever it was that tormented him so."

"There's a Dutch word, *faschtwarre,*" Gideon said. "Puzzled, it means. That's how I feel about the judge shooting himself. It doesn't make any sense."

"It's hard, losing a friend. I think about my cousin all the time."

The previous autumn, that unfortunate young woman had been stirring apple butter in a kettle over an open fire when her skirts caught flame; burned severely, she died the next day.

"Death is all around us," True murmured. "We'd best be ready— ready to go home to the Lord."

Gideon thought of a line from one of the shape-note hymns they sang in church: *My soul should stretch her wings in haste, Fly fearless through death's iron gate.* He wasn't sure about that, longing for death, with the ascension to heaven the reward at the end of what might have been a bitter, painful life—or one cut cruelly short. Having that thought made him wonder if his faith was sound. Because he was plagued with doubts. It had been that way ever since he'd found his *memmi* . . . True was right, one had to be ready. Death might steal in with the diphtheria or the yellow jack, or come crashing down on a lightning bolt, or arrive pell-mell in a cutter pulled by a runaway horse. It might take you in its embrace when you opened the door to someone with rape on his mind and murder in his heart.

David remained asleep in True's arms, a bonnet shading his face. If only he could have shown this little one to his *memmi*. But if she hadn't been killed, would he ever have left his home? Would he have journeyed west, and met True, and had this child with her?

"Honey, your whole life you have lived here," he said. "What can you tell me about Judge Biddle?"

"Nary a thing." She gave him a mischievous smile. "I'm sure you realize that my kin are all law-abiding citizens who would never have dealings with a judge."

Gideon smiled back. According to True, her people held no great regard for the law. The Burns family was linked by marriage to clans called Price, Ross, and Bainey—farmers and laborers who, True told him, might proudly proclaim: "Every man is sheriff of his own hearth." Were that so, thought Gideon, there would be precious little work for a real sheriff to do, save patrolling the roads and traces that lay between.

They cleared the gap in the hills and entered Panther Valley.

"I've always liked this prospect," True said. She turned her face to the east, toward a long, wooded ridge. "They call that the Muncy Mountain, for a town north of here along the Susquehanna where the ridge first rises. I've never been there, but my pa floated past Muncy on an ark, taking iron down to Port Deposit in Maryland."

Across the valley from the mountain, and running perpendicular to it, lay a series of parallel hollows. From the floor of Panther Valley, each of those narrow vales rose toward the Allegheny Front, tall and haze blue, the long-reaching rim of a high plateau. The land on the plateau was rolling, mostly forested, and very wild. Gideon had been there twice, accompanying Sheriff Payton—once to hold a sheriff's sale for a failed gristmill, once to arrest a man who had beaten his own brother half to death for making a lewd comment about the man's wife.

Presently the road they followed changed from dirt to pale blue slag, refuse from the ironmaking process. The road lay before them like a pretty ribbon unspooled on the land.

At a small fenced-in graveyard, True handed David down to Gideon and, in her light and agile way, dropped down from the wagon. She went into the yard. The small stone marker read EMMA ROSS 1816–1834. True had brought a bouquet of fall asters bound together with yarn. She knelt and placed the purple flowers in the dirt, where the ground had already begun to settle.

★★★

The blue road took them past fields where corn stood in shocks, then past a big barn and a gristmill. They came to the furnace with its pyramidal stone base and tall brick stack. From the ironworks came a muffled roar accompanied by the creaking of a water wheel and the *thump-thump-thump* of the leather blowing tubs as they forced air through the tuyere into the hearth. The furnace stayed in blast around the clock, save during a mechanical breakdown or to repair a cracked hearth. It was allowed to go out only in the dead of winter when the stream froze, stilling the water that powered the blast.

The road skirted a grassy common with a roofed well at each end. Cabins built of squared logs clustered around the common. Ash from the furnace had grimed the cabins' whitewashed walls. "Black snow," True had called it, saying that the women of Panther forever complained about how hard it was to dry clothes on the line without them turning black.

"True Burns!" A heavyset woman set down a bucket whose contents she had just slung into her weedy yard. She came lumbering out through a creaking gate in a picket fence. "Ain't seen you in a month of Sundays."

"Hello, Mrs. Craigie," True said.

"Call me Bet, you're a growed woman now. I want to see that baby of yourn. Named after your pa, I heard."

True handed David to the woman, and the child came awake, yawning and waving his arms, then smiling and cooing. Gideon grinned. David was such a pleasant, easy baby.

A small bowlegged man got up from a bench and hitched himself over to the fence. Leather braces held up the man's broadfall trousers. The man's face was a sun-baked brown crazed with painful-looking pink fissures.

He looked at Gideon. "Got us another Dutch gov'nor down in Harrisburg," the man announced in a challenging tone. "Fifth in a row. It's plain to see they are taking over the whole damned state." He clasped a fence paling in each hand, lowered his head between his arms, and spat. He jerked his head up and looked hard at Gideon. "Now we even got us a Dutch sheriff upholding the law."

"Don't pay that cockerel any mind," Bet Craigie said. "Sheriff Stoltz, being married to our True, you are as welcome here as anyone."

Gideon smiled at Mrs. Craigie even though he doubted her.

***

"Iron," Jim Burns said. He put his work-hardened fists on the table's planks. The light from the window fell upon the table, around which sat the jaybirds, their father Davey Burns, and Gideon. "In the cities they take our bars and blooms and turn 'em into bolts and locks and horseshoes. Mr. Thompson says the nation is starved for iron."

"We need the canal to come here," Davey Burns said. "If we could get our iron to market cheaper, we'd make more money."

"You mean Mr. Thompson would make more money," Jesse Burns said. The rest of the jaybirds laughed, and Davey Burns cracked a rueful smile.

"The canal gets here, we'll have all kinds of foreign trash showing up wanting our jobs," Jackson Burns said.

"The Irish will come in, damn their papist eyes." Jim Burns folded his arms. "The Dutch are here already, and more every year. They smell limestone soil, they're on it like flies on shit."

"They band together and pay top dollar for a farm," Jackson Burns chimed in.

"No one's got a nigger's chance against 'em," Jim said.

"Look what's going on over in Sinking Valley," Davey Burns blurted. "The Dutch swarming in, buying up all the best land. Bunch of dirt-grubbing krautheads . . ." He reached his big hand across the table and gave Gideon's chest a push, causing his son-in-law to rock back on the bench.

Davey Burns winked and grinned. The jaybirds roared with laughter.

Gideon wasn't sure whether this goading reflected real animosity or if it was just meant to rile him.

His father-in-law lifted his chin. "Vell, boys, I guess vee had better vatch vut vee say, in front of the Dutch Sheriff of Colerain Cawnty."

Raucous laughter all around.

Not a bad imitation of a Dutch accent, Gideon had to admit:

about like himself when he wasn't working to tone it down. Without looking at her, he knew True had stopped whatever she was doing in the kitchen with her mother and sisters-in-law and was standing there listening. No doubt this ribbing was intended as much for her as it was for him.

"Brother Gideon," Jesse Burns said. He was the youngest of True's brothers and the sassiest. Unmarried, he was something of a rounder, according to True, who was not even sure where he lived these days. Like his father and his brothers, Jesse was employed by the ironworks, although Gideon had never learned what his job was. Now Jesse smiled maliciously at Gideon. His eyes were dark, almost black, and his forehead and cheeks had little divots left by the smallpox. He poked his chin at Gideon. "Say somethin' for us in Dutch."

Gideon thought for a moment. "All right. Here is a proverb, in pure, one hundred percent *Pennsylfawnisch Deitsch.*" He cleared his throat. "*War fel shwetst, legt fel.*"

"What's it mean?" Jesse demanded.

"'Whoever speaks much, lies much.'"

Silence. One of the jaybirds belched.

"Do you suppose Brother Gideon is saying we're a bunch of liars?" Jesse said.

"Here's another one," Gideon said. "*War 'm onara ein grub grawbt, flot selwar nei.*" He paused. "'Whoever digs a grave for others, falls in himself.'" That earned a few nods and chuckles. "Ah," Gideon said. "The most important one: *War de duchter heira wil, holt sich mit der mudder.* 'Whoever wishes to marry the daughter must keep on the good side of the mother.'"

"Well, that might make some sense," Jesse said, "if you hadn't already stole our sis. Because I don't recall you courting her proper, or even meeting my ma and pa before you run off with her."

"That's enough." True's mother spoke from across the kitchen. "Gideon had durn well better stay on my good side if he wants anything to eat. You, too, Jesse Burns."

"I know why she fell for him," Jesse said. He looked at his brothers, then grinned at True and winked. "Lookit the size of his thumbs. Brother Gideon is *all* thumbs. You can tell a lot about the size of another part of a man's body just by looking at his thumbs."

"Must be why your thumbs are the size of thimbles," True said, clapping down a platter of cornbread in front of Jesse.

In the uproarious laughter that followed, Gideon felt the tension leave his shoulders.

A special dinner had been prepared for the visitors from town: beans, carrots, potatoes, and chunks of ham cooked in broth. The women crowded into one end of the kitchen near the hearth, chattering gaily. True went back to work at a small table, while one of her sisters-in-law bounced David on her knee, playing a peekaboo game with him. The other children, nieces and nephews too many for Gideon to remember their names, had been shooed outside.

"Mr. Burns," he said to his father-in-law, "can you tell me anything about Judge Biddle?"

"What about him?"

"I knew him from court," Gideon said, "and he and I went haunting sometimes." He purposely let slip the Dutch pronunciation, making the jaybirds snicker. Well, why act like someone you are not? Gideon decided he didn't care what these *narre* thought of him. "I'm trying to figure out why the judge killed himself. I wonder if it was something from his past, something that finally became too much for him to bear."

"Well, God rest his soul," Davey Burns said. "I got hauled in front of old Hiram oncet. Back when I was young and tough, or at least I fancied I was tough. That time I went on quite a spree. Which it ended in a fight with somebody, can't recall who it was, but I believe I broke his head." He grinned and rubbed the knuckles of his big right hand. "The judge give me two weeks' labor on the county roads. A fair enough punishment, I reckon.

"I can tell you one thing," he continued. "The ironmaster has always hated the judge. The two of 'em got crosswise a long time ago when the judge ruled against Mr. Thompson in a lawsuit."

"The lawsuit was one thing," said True's mother, stirring the contents of the big kettle suspended over the fire. "But it was a woman really set them at odds."

"That's so," her husband said. "The judge and Mr. Thompson were both sweet on the same girl. Way I heard it, Mr. Thompson asked for her hand, but she turned him down and picked the judge instead—though they never did marry. She was the daughter of . . ." He arched an eyebrow. "Now there's a story for you. She was daughter to a preacher name of McEwan, who got himself hanged for killing the ironmaster's brother."

"My deputy showed me the preacher's grave," Gideon said. "He didn't say anything about the preacher having a daughter, or the judge being engaged to marry her."

"I can't remember all the particulars," Davey Burns said. "Those days I was always off with a pack train or an ark, carrying iron to wherever the market was best. Now my ma, she knew all of them people. She worked for the ironmaster in the big house. She even watched the preacher hang. Judge Biddle, he had to watch, too. Imagine that, sending the father of the woman you love to stretch a rope." He grunted. "Maybe that *could* finally persuade you to shoot yourself."

"Let's not talk any more about hangings," True's mother said, "or folks shooting themselves. It's the Lord's day. Davey, you offer the blessing. We will all thank the Lord for watching over us. And remember," she said, ladling out a bowl of stew, "never trouble trouble till trouble troubles you."

True took the steaming bowl and set it in front of Gideon. She ruffled his hair. "My husband is the sheriff, as you well know," she said. "Sheriffs are attracted to trouble."

As usual, Jesse had to have the last word: "Tell him to keep his Dutch nose out of other people's business."

*So death will soon disrobe us all*
*Of what we here possess*

# Seven

⟨∞⟩

Frist thing Monday, Gideon went to the courthouse down-hill from the jail.

The court clerk was one of those people who, when talking with another person, close their eyes. He heard Gideon's request. When Gideon offered nothing further and just stood there waiting, the clerk finally replied: "The Reverend Thomas McEwan. I know of the case, though it was tried before I came to this place." His eyes still kept shut, he held up his palm. "Don't ask. No records for cases before 1810. A fire that year gutted the old courthouse. All of those old transcripts and documents went up in flames. We pretty much ignore anything before that date. Call it ancient history.

"On the subject of hangings," the clerk continued, his eyes stay-ing hidden behind their lids, "there was this fellow eight, ten years ago, name of Hicks. Gerald R. Hicks. Strangled his wife, on account of he suspected she was laying with another man, then burned the house down to make it look like an accident. But he couldn't keep his mouth shut and bragged on what he'd done, which got him arrested and convicted. The sheriff threw a rope over a limb on the old oak, and Hicks danced the floorless jig." The clerk snort-laughed, then fluttered his eyes open. They looked pensive. "You want my opinion, there's plenty of other folks around here could benefit from hanging."

Outside, Gideon strolled along the street. A hammer pinged in a wheelwright's shop. People walked past, rode horses, parked wagons. He had lived in this town long enough that he recognized many of the faces, even if he didn't know the names. Most of the residents were white, although a few Negroes called Adamant home. Strangers appeared with fair frequency: on foot, or riding horseback as he himself had done, or disembarking from the coach that jolted over the rough road through the Seven Mountains twice a week, except in winter. Singing masters and revival preachers included Adamant on their circuits. Phrenologists and homeopaths stayed in the hotel and put up handbills advertising their services. Temperance lecturers gave long-winded speeches. A religious pilgrim clad in motley robes once walked down High Street with seven grimy female disciples following behind him, one after another. You might meet a traveling abolitionist in Adamant—or slave catchers hunting runaways. Peddlers aplenty, carrying trunks on their backs or driving carts or wagons, hawking pots and pans and spices and fabrics, and bringing news from afar. But most of the newcomers were young men looking for work, finding it often enough at the mills, the brickyard, the tannery, the ironworks. Sheriff Payton had called them "wild cards" and didn't trust them. Yet, thought Gideon, he had trusted one Dutch stranger enough to hire him as his deputy.

He wondered what Sheriff Payton would have done had the judge killed himself a year ago. Would he have investigated the death? It was clearly not a murder. Under early common law, suicide was a crime, in fact a felony—was that where the term felo-de-se came from? That didn't make any sense, though, because you could hardly charge or punish someone who had already killed himself. To Gideon, *selbstmord* was more of an aberration, an event outside of predictable, understandable life. In this case, since it was his friend the judge who had taken his own life, it upset him deeply. But was it really his responsibility as sheriff to try to find out why Hiram Biddle had committed suicide?

He sat down on a bench and put his back against a store's sun-warmed wall. He closed his eyes and straightaway saw the judge in his study, sprawled dead in his chair. Then the judge's image faded, and he saw his mother lying on the kitchen floor. He forced his eyes open. Ever since that day, he had been unable to think of his mother without seeing her dead. Why couldn't he recall her alive and happy? Something would make him remember her, and he would see her face, and then it would go from light into shadow as if a fast-moving cloud had covered the sun—and he would be a ten-year-old *bub* again, frozen in place, trembling, scarcely able to think or even breathe, staring at her as she lay with her dress hiked up, her chest covered with wounds, drenched in her own blood. In his mind, even her memory had been murdered.

The night of the killing he had crawled into bed with Friedrich, in the same house where someone had come in to murder. Why hadn't their father sent them elsewhere? It was late summer, the room stifling, but he shivered under the blanket. Outside, a dry wind rose. The moon was full. Shadows of tree limbs swaying in the breeze made sharp, sudden movements across the bed. Katydids sounded their ratcheting calls, so persistent and loud that he could barely hear his sisters sobbing in the next room. Friedrich slept. Gideon didn't. He wrapped himself into a ball. He couldn't close his eyes. He couldn't cry. He lay there paralyzed, wondering if the killer would come back. In the morning, nothing had changed and everything had changed. His *memmi* was dead. He would never see her again. Or at least he would never see her alive again. Because he knew he would not stop seeing her broken, ravished body in his mind's eye.

\*\*\*

At home that evening Gideon lay on the floor and dandled David above him. He held the baby around his middle and boosted him up and down so that his little feet danced on his father's chest. Gideon sang a Dutch ditty that had to do with an *eil*, an owl, and every time he hooted like an owl he would boost David up high, the child bug-eyed and windmilling his arms, laughing and squealing with glee. "Careful he don't puke on you," True said.

For supper she served stew with grouse meat in it. "You should shoot a few more of these," she said.

Gideon laid his spoon down. "I don't have the heart for it. I don't have the judge to go hunting with anymore. I just have his dog and gun."

"Speaking of that dog, I can't get used to his name," True said. "Don't you know that Old Nick is another name for the Evil One? Why'd the judge ever give that nice dog such a vile name?"

"I never asked," Gideon said.

"If it's a joke, it's not a very good one."

"Well, it's his name now, we can't very well change it."

"Of course we can. A dog will answer to just about anything. How about Toby? Or Sam?"

Gideon looked at True. She appeared to be serious about this matter.

"You could call him Old Dick," she said. "Sounds about the same."

Gideon took a deep breath and let it out slowly. "We'll see."

She smiled then, and looked at him with sympathy. "I never got to know Judge Biddle like you did. I only saw him in his carriage or walking to the courthouse. What was he like?"

Gideon thought for a moment. "Dignified. Careful. In the court-room he was always in control. To me he was friendly and respectful. He always tried to make me feel welcome, in many different ways. I think he was happy to find someone else who liked shotguns and bird hunting." He shrugged. "He didn't really get to know me all that well. And I guess I didn't really know him all that well, either."

"Why would such a man kill himself?"

"I don't know. But I intend to find out. Because there has to be a reason. You don't just sit down in a chair and aim a shotgun at your breast and press the trigger for no reason."

True took David onto her lap. She tried to spoon some broth into his mouth. David made exaggerated smacking motions with his lips while most of the stew dribbled down his chin.

"Did the judge hold himself high and mighty?" she asked.

"I don't think Judge Biddle ever looked down on anyone." Gideon had noticed how sensitive people in Colerain County were to any perceived slight. Even True was that way. Almost resentful, they seemed to be. Many were laborers and servants, so maybe they were used to being looked down on. "I would call him generous," Gideon said. "In his will, Judge Biddle gave almost everything he owned to the poor people of the county. He gave a hundred dollars to his housekeeper, Mrs. Leathers. And he gave those things to me."

"How much do you think that gun is worth?"

He saw where this was going and kept his mouth shut.

True turned an amused smile on her husband. "It was the judge's gift to you. You don't want to sell that gun, it's up to you. Though we could use the extra money. That second horse is going to be expensive to keep. And I wouldn't mind having a nice table to eat on."

Gideon thought their current table was just fine. He decided to change the subject.

"I want to talk to your grandmother," he said. "Ask her what she remembers about the preacher, his trial and hanging. In fact, I plan to go see her tomorrow."

True quit trying to feed stew to David, who had begun to fret. She opened her blouse and gave the child her breast.

"My gram might tell you something," she said. "Get her talking, she'll go on half the night, fill you up with coffee—or rum—and tell you story after story. But you're a stranger, even though you're married to me. She might just run you off." She gave Gideon a sympathetic smile. "I'm sorry my kin don't treat you better."

"I'll win them over." Gideon grinned. "Maybe I just need to show them that Dutch folks can be more than"—he thought of what her father had said—"dirt-grubbing krautheads."

"Don't talk like that." She grew serious. "We're a clannish bunch. More than once I've heard my gram say, 'The bad and no good on the back of a stranger,' or 'Put the stranger near the danger.'" She touched her lips to David's downy head. "I have told you before, she's got the sight, same as I do." She looked critically at Gideon, as if challenging him to contradict her. "And she has an evil eye. My pa says it's so powerful and so little under her control that she daren't look at a creature belonging to herself and admire it too much, or it will lay down and die." She rested her cheek on David's head. "When I was little, she scared me. Truth be told, she still does."

*I'll go to Jesus,*
*Though my sin hath like a mountain rose*

# Eight

⊶⊷

H E WORE THE STAR, CARRIED A RIFLE IN THE SADDLE SCABBARD.
Dark clouds massed over the mountains to the west. They seemed to come from a single source beyond the horizon, as if a great fire raged there. The wind lifted Maude's forelock. It whistled among the branches and poked chill fingers down Gideon's collar. The sun rising behind him cast a lurid glow on brambles and popple stands—then was cut off by the thickening, spreading clouds.

Maude had a neat economical shuffle, a running walk that was comfortable to sit. She had a lot of spirit; she could run like crazy when he let her go—he'd won races on her back home. The mare had been a present for his fourteenth birthday.

Gideon felt a twinge. His father would have never given him the filly if he'd known his firstborn son would ride away on her six years later, leaving behind the carefully tended farm where four generations of Stoltzes had lived and worked and prayed, and where two generations—no, three generations now—lay buried.

Staring into the past, he no longer noticed the mudholes and shale ledges in the road past which Maude quickly and smoothly made her way.

★★★

After leaving the farm, he had ridden her west through the settled farming country to the gray-green Susquehanna. At Harrisburg, wagons by the score were lined up to cross the wooden camelback bridge spanning the mile-wide river. Not wanting to wait or pay the toll, he turned Maude north and rode out of the town. The next day they found a broad quiet stretch, shallow water partway across until it deepened and Maude had to swim. He gave her the reins. She held her head up and grunted and snorted, churning her legs as the current pressed against her right side, pushing them downstream. Finally she cleared the channel and regained the rubbly riverbed. She splashed through the shallows and clattered through the rocks on the far bank. She shook herself and, seeming to decide for them both, turned north again.

Later they left the river and continued west on a rough road hewn down a tight valley. The few farms they encountered had been freshly cut out of the forest, stumps still standing in the fields, cornstalks pushing up around them in erratic fashion. He bought lodging one night at a farm; the next night at an isolated cabin where dwelt a taciturn Negro man. When his money ran low he worked at a tannery for a few weeks. Then he rode on, following the barest trace of a road through a water gap in a ridge and into an adjacent valley. He continued down that valley. He met a lumber crew and stopped again and worked for another fortnight, bucking up big chestnut trees that the axmen had cut down.

From the day he left home, he spoke not a word of *Deitsch*—only the English that he knew he needed to make his way.

One day a man fell in with him at a crossroads. The Tattered Man—for that was how Gideon had thought of him ever since—rode a big black mule. He said he was a preacher and dug out of his saddlebag a Bible whose cover was as worn and shiny as his coat. He aimed the book at Gideon, sighting along the spine. "I will not sermonize at you," he said, "for I can see that you are a man who knows his Redeemer liveth." The Tattered Man grinned, revealing broken brown teeth. "You show the inner light," he said, "even if you are a blamed Dutchman."

The way climbed past walls of lichen-scabbed rock. It wound

among thick-trunked oaks and pines with huge spiky cones that looked like medieval weapons. At the top of the ridge, the Tattered Man halted his mule.

Before them the mountains lay jammed together, the rugged terrain covered with forest. Gideon could see the green rounded tops of the hardwood trees occupying the slopes, the darker green spires of hemlocks jutting up from the stream bottoms. Ridge followed ridge to the horizon. The view made him think of a great green blanket laid down on trash and rubble. A proverb came to him: *We's lond, so de leit.* As the land, so the people.

"The Seven Mountains," the Tattered Man said. "Paddy and Long and Thick and some others which I don't know their names, or if they even got names." The man intoned: "'The seven heads are seven mountains, upon which the woman sitteth.'" His face, grimy and unshaven, assumed a genial smile. "The woman being the Whore of Babylon. Revelations, chapter seventeen." He continued, his voice swelling until he roared like a revival preacher. "'And upon her forehead was a name written: Mystery! Babylon the Great! Mother of harlots and abominations of the earth!'" He fell silent, winked at Gideon. "Git ye up, mule," he said. He boot-heeled his mule once, twice, and on the third wallop the big twitch-eared beast commenced walking again.

The trail switchbacked down into the wooded valley. As they descended, the Tattered Man told story after story. He once shot a panther just as it sprang at him, the ball striking the cat in the open mouth, and the varmint fell dead at his feet with its whiskers touching his boot. He nearly smothered when the well he was digging caved in, and he lay there with the cold clay stopping up his mouth, listening to people screaming and hollering as they worked to dig him out, and a bright light shone before his eyes, the word of God entered into him, and his whole being was filled with peace. Right then, he knew he would follow the Lord. The Tattered Man explained how he and his brother had stood a donkey on planks and put him to a big plow mare to make this mule, his people had always rode mules instead of horses, on account of mules were smarter and stronger and had more staying power.

When he could get a word in, Gideon asked if the Tattered Man was going all the way to Adamant. He'd heard it was a go-ahead town, a place growing by leaps and bounds, a settlement where a man could find work, make a new start. And he was intrigued by the name: It meant unshakable, steadfast, determined. Just as he was determined to make of himself something more than a digger in the dirt, a tiller of the land.

"Adamant," the Tattered Man said, "Well, of course I am going there with you. Wouldn't be a Christian thing to do, now would it, to leave you here alone in this wilderness."

The sky had grown gray and dark, and Gideon smelled rain. He did not look forward to spending a wet night in the woods with no shelter. And something about the Tattered Man had begun to bother him. Maybe it was the way he *bobbl'd* on, as if his stories were the only thing of interest in the world. Or maybe it was something else, something more sinister. He had no idea who this ragged, grubby stranger might be. Gideon tried to think of a polite way to detach himself from the man. But he didn't want to get lost in these seemingly endless mountains, either.

As if divining his thoughts, the Tattered Man said, "You could turn tail right now, Dutch, and head back to wherever it is you are from. I won't tell you no lie, there's peril amongst these ridges. Wolves and panthers and bears as common as barnyard fowl. Rattlesnakes and copperheads ready to strike out and pizen your horse. Wildfires that can burn you up, floods that can sweep you away. And there's bad men, like William Jewell Jarrett. You heard of him?"

Gideon shook his head.

"Where do you come from, you have not heard tell of William Jewell Jarrett?"

Gideon thought about where he did come from. He pictured the fertile fields sectioned off by rail fences. Big red barns and white-washed slat-sided tobacco sheds and stone-built houses with holly-hocks next to the door, and peach and cherry and apple orchards and creaking mills along each stream and graded roads that went orderly from farm to farm, and all at once he was more homesick than he had ever imagined he could be.

The Tattered Man reined in his mule. He chuckled, looked side-long at Gideon.

"Speak of the de'il," he said, "and his horns appear."

From the brush next to the trail in front of them stepped a gray horse. Its rider wore a brimmed hat with a low crown, a butternut blouse, and a long unbuttoned duster. The man had a scraggly beard. Above a hooked nose the man's dark eyes showed as much emotion as a copperhead's. The Tattered Man walked his mule up to the gray. The mule touched noses with the horse, whimpered softly, and passed along to stand beside the horse, facing in the opposite direction.

Maude flicked her ears back, and Gideon glanced over his shoul-der. Another horse and rider had emerged from the brush behind them. The horse stood sideways across the trail. In his hand the rider held a sword with a long blade.

"*Oh, once I had a glor'ous view,*" sang the Tattered Man in an off-key baritone, "*of my redeeming Lord.*"

Beneath Gideon, Maude began to dance. *Yesus Chrishtus.* Money they would want, though he had precious little.

"*My God has me of late forsook, he's gone, I know not where.*" The Tattered Man whooped out a laugh.

They would take Maude. Yes, they would take her, and they would take his life. His heart hammered and he felt a liquid warmth fill his chest. He closed his hands on the reins and thought *Go!* and Maude shot forward, her iron-shod hooves clanging on rock. The highwayman's hand whipped across his body, grabbing for a pistol at his belt. As Maude spurted between the skittering gray horse and the stolid black mule, Gideon felt his knees slam into both men's legs.

Maude lunged, and they were through. She pounded down the trail. He dug his fingers into her mane and leaned forward on her fast-flexing back. He heard a deep *boom* and a *yowl* past his head like an angry hornet and another *boom*. The top of Maude's ear suddenly vanished. Onward she ran.

\*\*\*

His heart pounding, he surfaced from the memory of an event more than two years past that remained as fresh to him as if it had happened yesterday. He took a deep breath. He was in Colerain County, in Panther Valley, riding to the house of his wife's grandmother to ask her about any memories she might have concerning Judge Biddle. He looked at Maude's ear, saw the missing incurved top inch. Ever since that day in the Seven Mountains, her pretty head had been all *schepp*, lopsided.

If only that had been the worst of it.

He stretched upward in the saddle, sat down again, and worked a kink out of his back. He rubbed Maude up and down her neck, murmuring to her, and watched her ears swivel back toward him. They continued their way down the valley. Forest walled the road on both sides. A raven croaked from a snag, then shut up and watched them pass.

They forded a small stream that came murmuring out of a side hollow. Passed a log schoolhouse in a clearing, its single window covered with paper greased to a translucency with lard. No horses were hitched up outside, no smoke rising from the chimney. Lessons would not commence until the harvest was in.

They rode on. Out the corner of his eye he spied a strange object in a tree—as he stared, Maude came to a stop beneath him. *What is that thing?* His first impression was that it was a human heart plucked out of someone's breast, pierced and hung on a branch six feet above the ground. But no, it was only a *hannselnescht*, a hornets' nest, constructed around a branch in a small maple. A dead nest—the frosts had killed the hornets, and their nest hung there gray and heart-shaped and unraveling, paper tatters fluttering in the wind.

He clucked to Maude. He felt her sweet, easy gait beneath him. It took him back into the past again, back to the Seven Mountains.

***

Fleeing, he had pushed Maude on for most of a mile. Where the trail leveled out and the footing was good, he urged her to gallop. When he figured he had put some distance between himself and the bandits, he stopped and dismounted. Maude's sides heaved, and sweat foamed her chest. On her ear a maroon ooze of blood surrounded a white rim of cartilage. The wound had bled down into the fuzzy ear opening. Maude shook her head, pulled at the reins, sought to graze.

*Du bisht ein zwickel, ein fulshtennich zwickel.*

*You are a fool, a great fool.*

He'd stopped because he had spotted a spring in a glade that the trail cut through. He led Maude to the spring, and she drank from the spring's outflow. Finished, she took a few steps and began gathering in the green grass with her lips, clamping the blades between her teeth and tearing them off with little sideways swipes of her head.

What if they'd hit her in a hindquarter? What if he'd put his head on the other side of her neck? The ball that had clipped her ear would have drilled his skull.

With shaking hands, he scooped water and drank. The sweetest water he had ever tasted. In the bottom of the spring the water came bubbling up from a pea-sized opening in the sand. It looked like a mouth. The mouth opened and closed, opened and closed, saying: *Fool. Fool. Fool.*

He mounted again. The Tattered Man had praised the staying power of his mule. Gideon knew mules. From the age of eight he had plowed behind a three-mule hitch. Mules were patient. They didn't give up. He considered the broad muscled rump on the Tattered Man's mule as he urged Maude onward.

After an hour he stopped again and made his way off into the woods on one side of the trail. He draped his slicker over his shoulders, sat down heavily against a tree. Maude stood at the end of her reins. Clouds snagged on tall treetops, flowed around thick trunks.

He had no idea where he was. He had tried to keep to the better-traveled paths where twice the trail had forked. He had come upon no recent marks of wheels or hooves.

Rain rattled against the leaves high overhead. His stomach growled. That morning he had eaten the last corn dodger he'd bought from a farmwife two days past. He was bone tired. He leaned back against the tree and pulled the slicker around himself. Figured he'd rest for a minute.

When he opened his eyes, it was almost dark.

He lurched up in a panic. He had let go of the reins, but Maude hadn't gone far: he spotted her, a black shadow among the trees. He stood in the gentle rain and heard a far-off rumble of thunder.

The Tattered Man had played him for a fool. They had shot at him, tried to kill him. If he went home now, wouldn't he have a story to tell? But he hadn't struck out on his own just to go back and point at a mare's ear and say, "Let me tell you about the time when . . ." No, he was not going back. He was going on ahead, through the mountains to the town called Adamant. He would not give up. He would never give up.

Hastily he led Maude through the trees in the direction of the trail. He slowed as they drew near the place where he thought they'd left the path. He crept onward in the waning light, his eyes scanning the ground. Where was the trail? His stomach constricted—was he now utterly lost? No, there it was: a band of dirt slightly darker than the forest floor.

On the path were imprints of large rounded hooves. The mule. He crouched and studied the dirt. He didn't see any other tracks.

He swung up into the saddle as quietly as he could. He dared not go back the opposite way—the two other men might be following. He had no weapon. If he went forward, he might blunder into an ambush. Why had he let himself fall asleep? He startled momentarily, glanced this way and that—had he heard a voice calling?

*You're a fool, a fool, a fool.*

He rode Maude at a walk. It was almost dark. After a while he saw something out in front—he mightn't have noticed it if Maude hadn't lifted her head. He ran his hand along the side of her neck, claiming back her attention. He stopped her, stood in the stirrups. He let his vision shift from side to side. Now he could see it, a black form moving slowly, rhythmically, up and down. He heard the soft cuffing of hooves. He waited until he could no longer hear them.

He considered leaving the trail again and spending the night in the woods. It didn't seem as if the Tattered Man was following Maude's tracks—he'd ridden past the spot where Gideon had first left the trail. Overnight, the rain might wash his tracks away.

Or it might not. And in the morning he would have to ride this way again.

He let Maude stride out until he heard the mule's footfalls again and the dark form emerged from the blackness. Gradually it grew larger in his vision. It became a man seated on a beast. He kept expecting the Tattered Man to hear Maude, turn, and shoot—two shots had been fired earlier, so either the highwayman Jarrett had two pistols, or the Tattered Man also had one.

Closer. The mule kept plodding out in front. Closer. With a squeeze of his calves Gideon asked for speed. He stood on his left foot, freed his right boot from the stirrup. As Maude shot past, he reached out with his boot and shoved the Tattered Man off the mule. The mule sprang ahead, the rider hit the ground hard, something black and heavy went clunking off into the darkness. Maude skittered on a ways until Gideon turned her.

The Tattered Man lay motionless at the edge of the trail. The mule stood quietly. Gideon walked Maude back and dismounted. With the reins in one hand, he used his other hand to turn the Tattered Man over. The man was loose-limbed as a rag doll. Gideon smelled the cloying sweetness of whiskey. The clunking black object must have been a jug. He checked the man's waistband and found nothing. He ran his hand down one leg. In the boot, something round and hard: a knife handle. He drew the blade from its sheath and tossed it aside. In the other boot, a pistol. He sniffed the barrel, caught the peppery fresh-fired scent.

He put the pistol down. Why had the Tattered Man split off from the others? Maybe they'd given up on him, and the Tattered Man had set off in search of another victim. Or maybe the others were following and were not far off. As Gideon placed his fingers against the man's neck to search for a pulse, the Tattered Man shot up his hands and grabbed Gideon by the throat.

The Tattered Man yelled and wrenched him sideways. Gideon hit the ground hard and felt air *whoosh* out of his lungs. The man straddled him, pressing his thumbs into Gideon's neck. Gideon struck at the man's face. The man snarled and choked him harder. Gideon's other hand fell upon the pistol. Red and orange sparks flew at the edges of his vision. He swung the pistol as hard as he could and struck the Tattered Man on the side of the head. The man came down as if poleaxed. His forehead thumped the earth next to Gideon's head.

He fought his way out from under the Tattered Man. He knelt there panting.

Hoofbeats. Fifty yards away and coming fast.

He scrabbled to his feet and grabbed Maude's reins. He hauled himself into the saddle and turned her down the trail. She galloped.

★★★

Gideon came out of his reverie. He looked around at the bright autumn woods in Panther Valley. He was a lawman now, the sheriff of Colerain County. He hadn't planned it that way, but it was what he'd become. He was doing his job, he told himself, riding to True's grandmother's house, wanting to hear from her own lips the story of a preacher's hanging, a strange and disturbing happening from thirty years in the past. He stopped in the road and reviewed what True had told him: At the mouth of a hollow on the north side of the road, look for a cabin and a log barn with a bunch of deer antlers nailed to the gable end. Take the branch road between the house and barn, ride up the hollow, and you will come to the Burns place.

He figured he still had a ways to go.

He let Maude move out. Again he let his mind drift.

★★★

After a week had passed, after he'd arrived in Adamant and found work digging a house foundation, he went to the county jail. He had decided to explain to the sheriff what had happened, what had occurred in the Seven Mountains when he'd been set upon by the highwaymen. He stopped on the stoop, hesitated before opening the door. The jail was built from the same pale-gray limestone as the courthouse in town. He wondered, *Am I weak, to feel the need to explain what I have done, to justify my actions?* A stronger, harder man would feel no guilt at beating down a robber who'd tried to kill him, then riding off and leaving the man unconscious and perhaps badly hurt on the road. But he knew himself, and he figured he would not have peace of mind until he'd gotten it out in the open, told someone in authority what had taken place.

He knocked, went in the door, and introduced himself to the sheriff, a placid-looking, gray-haired man named Israel Payton. When the story was out, and Gideon stood there holding his hat in his hands, the sheriff came out from behind his desk. He shook his head and said No, he had heard nothing about such an incident. He had never even heard of a highwayman named William Jewell Jarrett. *However*, he assured Gideon, a bemused look on his face, *no jury in Colerain County, no prosecuting attorney or judge, would consider it anything other than justified to strike back at a man who was trying to throttle you to death*. The sheriff examined the yellowing bruises on Gideon's neck. He looked Gideon up and down. *You are a well-put-together young fellow*, he said, *with at least some sense of right and wrong. Can you read and write?* Gideon nodded. The sheriff smiled. *It so happens I need a deputy. You want the job?*

*Come, oh thou traveler unknown*
*Whom still I hold but cannot see*

# Nine

∞∞∞

A BRUPTLY MAUDE PLANTED HER FEET. AHEAD OF THEM THE ROAD curved through a stand of tall laurel. Gideon spied a horse and rider half-screened by the slick green leaves. The rider called out, "Good day to you, fellow traveler!"

The man walked his horse forward out of the long green tunnel. He stopped twenty feet away. The horse was a dun, maybe fifteen hands tall, lean and fit. The rider was about Gideon's age. He was clean-shaven, had dirt smudging his cheeks and chin, and wore a low-crowned carriage hat pitched back on his head.

The man rested his hands on his saddle's pommel and looked at the star on Gideon's coat. "Hullo there, sheriff." The man lifted his head, sniffed at the air. "I believe we're in for some weather."

Gideon studied the man's face. It appeared to be open and guileless. For some reason the man reminded him of himself two years back. He also made Gideon think of the Tattered Man. Maybe it was the way they'd met on the road. Or the fellow's tone of voice, forward and conspicuously friendly. *Well, this is all rather foolish,* Gideon thought. *It is only because I have been remembering that fight in the Seven Mountains that I feel suspicious toward this stranger.* Was that what being a sheriff did to you, made you look at people as if they were all potential outlaws?

"Good day to you as well," he said. "I am Gideon Stoltz, the county sheriff, as you noticed. Your name, please?"

"George England, sir." The man fingered his hat brim. "From a little burg called Chinclaclamoose, 'bout a day's ride west of here.

Tongue-twister of a name, ain't it?" His smile broadened. "I am headed to Adamant in search of employment. Can a man find a job there?"

"The ironworks hires a lot of men, and there are mills and some other businesses."

The young man nodded amiably. "So I'd heard. Pardon me for asking, but ain't you a bit young to be a sheriff?"

Gideon frowned; decided not to answer that question. "Where did you stay last night?"

The man shot a thumb back over his shoulder. "At a farm up one of these here side hollers, four, maybe five miles down the valley."

"What was the family's name?"

The man shrugged. "I never ast. Paid for my lodging by splitting half a cord of wood. They worked me hard, but they fed me good."

Gideon studied the man's eyes. Sheriff Payton had told him to look carefully into the eyes of any person he spoke with. Little shadows or tightenings, twitches, coldnesses, hard blinking, a sudden oblique glance—they told you things the owner of those eyes might not want you to know. But there seemed nothing evasive or suspect in George England's level, friendly gaze.

"Safe travels," Gideon said. "I hope you find Adamant to your liking."

The young man touched his hat brim again and passed by, still smiling.

★★★

The forest gave way to a hayfield on one side of the road, a picked cornfield on the other. At the edge of the cornfield three people gathered pumpkins. A woman in a gray cloak and bonnet waved to Gideon from the seat of a wagon. A young girl struggled at rolling a pumpkin half as big as she was. A boy took the pumpkin from the girl, hefted it to his shoulder, placed it on the wagon's bed, then stood and stared at the strange passerby.

Gideon arrived at what must be the mouth of Burns Hollow. As True had said, the offshoot road led between a farmhouse and a log barn whose end bristled with racks of deer antlers. He followed the road, and after another mile through the woods he came to a pasture. A cow stood rubbing her chin on the top rail of a fence. A horse kept in with the cow whickered.

The cabin sat in a flat where three small drainages met. "The old 'uns put the house there on account of the spring," True had told him. "I can taste that good freestone water yet."

In front of the cabin Maude shied and danced sideways. Something hung from the gate post, and the breeze had shifted it. It took Gideon a moment before he identified the object: an owl, hanging upside down, dead. The bird's broad brown wings dangled stiffly downward, and dried blood matted the pale speckled breast. The owl's meat-hook beak gaped open. Feathery tufts, like little horns, adorned the owl's head. The owl hung from a cord knotted to one feather-clad leg. The other leg was a bloody stump.

Smoke scudded sideways from the cabin's chimney. One end of the log structure attached to a smaller building, a dozen feet square, stone-built to the gables: a relic of the days when the first thing a pioneer family built was a stronghold against Indian attack. Vertical slits interrupted the stone walls. Gideon wondered if he was being watched through one of the slits, perhaps over the sights of a gun.

He sat patiently on Maude. Made sure his face and the star on his coat stayed visible. After a while he heard footfalls, then the sound of a bar being lifted and set aside. The cabin's door opened.

Gideon touched his hat. "Mrs. Burns, I am . . ."

"I know who you are."

Her hair was long and gray. She wore a linen dress cut short enough to reveal heavy brogans on her feet. A shawl covered her shoulders. She held her arms crossed at her breast. Lifted an eyebrow above a dark and guarded eye. "What's the sheriff want with me?"

"It has to do with Judge Biddle." He hadn't prepared a speech and wondered how to go on. "He killed himself last week."

She nodded toward the field. "Turn your mare in with my stock. Then come in the house."

*But when I hated all my sin,*
*My dear Redeemer took me in*

# Ten

⊶⊷

WITH A GOURD DIPPER THE OLD WOMAN FILLED A KETTLE FROM a wooden bucket, then hung the kettle over the flames on a chain dangling from a crane. A pot hanging below a second crane gave off a mouthwatering aroma.

She asked over her shoulder, "Did you meet a stranger on the road? Riding a dun horse?"

"Yes."

"At first I thought you was him coming back." The old woman straightened. "Will you drink some coffee?"

"Coffee would sure taste good."

"That young jake showed up here yesterday around dusk. Wanted a bed for the night. I turned him away."

As the water came to a boil, Gram Burns ground coffee and put it into a stoneware pot. She lifted the kettle off its hook with a forked stick, tipped it using a pot holder, and filled the pot. She turned her deeply lined face toward Gideon. "You ask him where he spent the night?"

"He told me he stayed on a farm up a hollow four or five miles from here. He said he paid for his lodging by splitting some wood."

Gram Burns snorted. "He didn't stay on no farm. He slept out in the woods, and not too far from here. He was back again this morning, nosing around. I sent him packing."

"How did you do that?"

"A rifle ball smacking into a tree next to your head sends a pretty strong message." The old woman narrowed her eyes at him. "You call

73

yourself a sheriff? You should have arrested him when you had the chance."

"And what law did he break?"

"No doubt he has broke a whole book of laws. Just look at him and listen to his palaver, and you can tell."

Gram Burns's suspiciousness made Gideon's own mistrust of the traveler seem mild. "You can't arrest a man for asking for lodging or for sleeping in the woods," he said. *Not even*, he thought, *for playing loose and fast with the truth when addressing the sheriff*. On the other hand, a person could possibly be arrested for endangering someone else's life with a firearm.

The old woman fetched the pot and poured the steaming coffee into two mugs. She lowered herself onto the bench across from Gideon. "I like my coffee perishing hot and devilish strong. If that don't suit, water yours down from that jug."

Gideon found the coffee just the way he liked it. He looked around the cabin. Carved horn spoons and wooden butter molds hung on the walls. Pumpkin rinds and apple snits lay drying on a rack near the fire. Bunches of dried plants were tied to square-headed nails driven into the ceiling beams. His eyes stopped on something brown sitting on a wooden chest among a scattering of small objects: the owl's severed foot.

"So the judge killed himself," the old woman said. "How'd he do it?"

"He shot himself. He used a shotgun."

"Guess he wanted to make sure."

"And I want to find out why," Gideon said.

The old woman stared at him. "Why are you here talking to me?"

"I want to look at events from his past. I want to learn about anything that could have made him decide that life wasn't worth living anymore."

"What is it you want to know?"

"Your son—my father-in-law—told me that you saw the Reverend Thomas McEwan hang."

She continued to stare at him.

He felt flustered at having broached the subject so baldly. "I just wondered—the hanging—if it might be in some way connected with Judge Biddle killing himself."

"Yes, I saw them hang the reverend." Gram Burns brought her mug to her lips. She studied Gideon through dark eyes—eyes that reminded him of True's. "Bet there was a thousand folks in Adamant that day." The wrinkles at the corners of her eyes deepened. "Afterward, some wouldn't talk of it, as if they hoped that would make it all go away. But the reverend didn't want anyone to forget what they'd seen, nor what he had done. And he'd want me to tell you about it. Yes, I believe he would."

She rose and refilled their mugs, then eased herself back onto the bench. "I'll tell you the whole story," she said. "And I'll tell it to you straight. But there's some things you need to know, you bein' a stranger in this place."

She took a long sip of the coffee and held it in her mouth for a while. Gideon found himself doing the same, wondering if its bitterness was necessary for the tale.

"I was born down in Adams County. My pa was the restless sort; he always figured the land was better in the next valley over, or the one after that. He didn't prefer having neighbors too close at hand.

"We come up here to Colerain County in seventy-five. 'Course, it wasn't a county back then. It was a wilderness. There was game everywhere—deer and bear and turkey and elk. Indian paths went through here. It was the Indians' traveling territory and hunting ground. You can bet they didn't like the settlers moving in. They wanted to put an arrow in you, or brain you with a tomahawk or a club—or, if you were a woman or a girl, carry you off and make you a squaw.

"We was here for a while, clearing off this land. Then the war

came. We had to leave in seventy-eight. They called it the Big
Runaway. You heard of that?"

Gideon nodded. The Big Runaway had taken place during the
War of Independence, when British officers led Indian raids against
settlements on the frontier, causing a great loss of life and forcing
people to flee to more settled areas south and east.

"I was ten years old then. We stayed away most of a year, but as
soon as things quieted down, we came back.

"I grew up on this place. I didn't get sick and die, like two of my
brothers and three of my sisters did. I got married and started having
babies of my own. I married a good man, Ezekiel Burns. He was
steady, put his mind to his work, didn't drink or chase other women.

"When we heard they were putting up an ironworks over to
Panther, Zeke went and got himself a job. We loaded our flitten in
the wagon, and the children walked alongside, the two that was old
enough. I carried the baby. That would be David, your wife's pa." She
looked over the rim of her mug at Gideon.

"Please go on."

"We got one of the cabins they put up—the same one Davey
lives in now. My husband, he helped cut the stone they used to build
the furnace and the ironmaster's house. When they finished building
the big house, I went to work there.

"Mr. Thompson—the ironmaster—he was from down
Philadelphia way. Just as much a stranger as you, y'might say. He was
a sharp dealer and a good manager. His business grew. The ironworks
prospered.

"When we lived at Panther," the old woman continued, "we
went to the church in the village. Presbyterian. The Reverend
McEwan preached there. A sturdy red-headed man, in his fifties, as
tall as you, maybe even a little taller. Strong as an ox. And fiery! Apt
to blow up at little things—men drinking or gambling or swearing,
women spreading gossip and lies. Then he would preach a sermon
that would have Christianized the Old Boy himself.

"His daughter, Rachel, was a pretty girl, small and dark. She must've took after her ma, who died when Rachel was young."

Gram Burns abruptly stood. "I have left us run out of coffee. Let me make another pot." Gideon objected that he was fine, but the old woman shushed him. As she made the coffee, she rambled, "It'll be a long hard winter, you can tell so, by how many acorns the oaks has got and how the hickory nuts are falling like hailstones." She poured boiling water, swirled the coffee in the pot. "The groundhogs are fat as pigs. That's another sign we'll get walloped by the snow and the cold. I hope you got your wood in."

She brought over the pot and refilled their mugs. "Want some rum in yours?"

"All right. Yes." The old woman's coffee could use sweetening. Gram Burns got out a jug and poured a dollop of dark rum into each of their mugs.

She settled onto the bench again. "Where was I?"

"The preacher's daughter."

"Rachel."

"How old was she?"

"Marryin' age, early twenties. The girl had some schoolin'; she was well spoken, not rough like me and mine. A stranger, too, you could say, but she didn't hold herself too good to nurse a sick neighbor, or put up food from their garden, or join in a quilting or a husking bee.

"All the young men were sweet on her. But I think they understood she was above them. The two men who really wanted her, and who courted her, were the ironmaster and the judge.

"In the big house, we heard all the stories. Mr. Thompson tried to give Rachel a gold ring and a silk dress, but she refused them. He proposed marriage; she turned him down. All along I think she had her cap set for the judge."

Gram Burns looked down into her mug. "It was good to get on at the ironworks. Zeke and I, we had bought this place from my folks. I buried two children here; we had our share of terrible lean years. At Panther, the work was regular. We made sure we didn't owe the company store, and managed to save some money. We could've left there and come back to this farm any time we wanted.

"So I had some independence. I was older than Ad Thompson by a few years. Only once did he put his hands on me." She raised fierce eyes to meet Gideon's. "You wouldn't credit it, looking at me now, but I was once a woman that would turn a man's head. When Mr. Thompson took hold of me, I slapped him hard across the face and yelled out so the others would hear—'You touch me again, I will have the law down on you!'

"He let go and never bothered me again." She lifted her chin. "He trifled with more than a few of the women who worked for him. Some fought him off, others didn't. He pestered my daughter-in-law, but she wouldn't have none of it, either. True worked in the big house before she married you. What has she said? He ever try anything on her?"

Gideon felt his face heat up. True had never mentioned anything about the ironmaster taking advantage of women. But he didn't want to get sidetracked, didn't want to stop the old woman's story. "You were telling me about Rachel."

"No, I was telling you about the ironmaster." Gram Burns stared at him, then drank from her mug again. "At the time you are interested in, there was half a dozen of us working in the big house. Mr. Thompson even had him a nigger butler, name of Harvey. Black as that kettle on the hearth. Such airs he put on, and him no more'n a slave. I can't tell you what become of him, maybe he bought his freedom or maybe Mr. Thompson sold him off, but I know for a fact he don't work there anymore.

"Mr. Thompson's brother Nat lived there, too. Nat was a few years younger than Ad. They were close, them two, thick as thieves. Nat was a sturdy fellow with blond hair that he wore long and washed every other day. Fancied himself quite the ladies' man. That made another pair of hands you had to watch out for.

"Nat sometimes took the iron to Pittsburgh. Back then, they cast the pigs in ingots shaped like a U to fit over a mule's back. He'd head out leading a string of mules, with a gang of men to help him. Sometimes my husband went along, but Zeke knew I didn't like him going off like that, so he tried to avoid it.

"When Nat came back, he'd be full of stories about how he'd pleased some rich woman in bed, or won a pile of money betting on a horse race, or whipped some man twice his size in a fight.

"As well as spouting such hogwash, he drank. It seemed like every other word out of his mouth was an oath. He didn't care for real work. Sometimes he drove the ironmaster's carriage—drove it fast as Jehu when Mr. Thompson weren't with him.

"One fall, right around this time of the year, the Reverend McEwan hired Nat to work on a barn he was building. We all laughed at that; we didn't think it would go too well. Mr. Thompson had sent Nat over to the reverend, saying he ought to lend a hand. Which that was odd, on account of the ironmaster hadn't forgotten how the preacher's daughter had thrown his proposal back at him, and I expect he grudged the reverend for favoring Judge Biddle as well—by then, you see, Rachel was engaged to marry the judge.

"Nat said the work didn't agree with him. He'd come home of an evening and brag on how he had slacked off whenever the preacher turned his back. It weren't long before they got into it. We heard that the reverend knocked him down—which Nat no doubt richly deserved, with that mouth of his. But no charges were filed, and it seemed to blow over. Nat even went back to work for the reverend. Then one evening he didn't show up for supper. Didn't come home the next day, either.

"Some figured Nat had lit out for Pittsburgh. Others reckoned he'd gone back to Philadelphia. Then some women said they were walking past the parsonage, and on the other side of the hedge they saw the reverend and Nat fighting. That turned out to be the last time anyone saw Nat Thompson alive."

Gram Burns inspected what was left in her mug, took a last sip, and set the vessel down.

"They found Nat's body buried in the garden at the parsonage. The Reverend McEwan was charged with murder and put on trial. Judge Biddle presiding." The old woman's eyes were unfocused; she nodded slowly to herself. "The reverend confessed. The news got to Panther real quick. A cry went up from folks gathered down at the company store. I was out sweeping the porch on the big house, and I heard them people from all the way down there. I tell you, there was a lot of sympathy for the reverend. Everyone felt sorry for him, even knowing what he'd done."

With a groan, the old woman hitched herself up from the bench. She shuffled to the cabin's door and opened it. Outside, the ground was white. In the dirty light Gideon saw Maude standing in the pasture with her tail to the wind and an inch of snow on her back.

Gram Burns shut the door. "You'd catch your death, riding out in this. You'd best stay the night. True will know why you didn't come home."

She went to the hearth, swung the kettle away from the fire, and dished out two bowls of the stew whose fragrance had, for the last hour, been making Gideon's stomach rumble.

"Sam Bainey, down the holler, he's married to my girl Peg," Gram Burns said. "Killed him a buck last week and brought me a haunch and the neck meat."

Other than saying a long and complicated grace, the old woman didn't speak during the meal. Afterward, she sent Gideon out to feed the animals. The snow came down hard, icy needles that stung his face. The hay was dusty and stemmy, but it was all the old woman had in her barn. He wondered how she got her hay in; probably her daughter and son-in-law helped her.

Inside, he found her seated on the bench, staring at the fire, her cup—and his, warming on the hearth—filled with rum. Taking the cup and sitting on the other bench, Gideon sought to get Gram Burns back to the story. All he had to say was "The Reverend McEwan . . ."

"Come the day of the hanging," she said, "Mr. Thompson told us we should all go and watch. Said it would be a lesson to us. So we packed lunches and walked in to Adamant.

"Gigs and wagons was all over the town, and horses tied to trees. The crowd covered the ground outside the courthouse; you could've walked on the people's shoulders. When they brought the reverend from the jail, someone yelled 'Hats off!' He went along in front of the cart that carried his coffin; him, the sheriff, and a preacher from another church in town. Two men marched behind them, one beating a drum and the other playing a fife.

"The reverend had on black smallclothes and white stockings. They obliged him to carry his own rope, with the noose slung around his neck. When he got to the gallows tree, he climbed up on the cart. His face was pale and sweating, but he smiled like he didn't have a care in the world. He looked out over the crowd and spoke. His voice was strong. He quoted from the Book of Lamentations: 'The Lord hath despised in the indignation of His anger the king and the priest.' He said that he had become swollen with pride and had let hatred rule his heart, which led him to commit a terrible sin. For this, the Lord had covered him with shame and laid him low with sorrow, so that he might finally see the glory of God and be raised up again through his son Jesus Christ."

The flickering light from the fire reflected in the old woman's eyes. "The reverend spoke of the fires of Hell but said he would not be burning in them, for he had repented his sins and received God's grace. We should all of us do the same, he told the people. He quoted from the Bible again: 'Though your sins be as scarlet, they shall be white as the snow.'

"They offered him a hood, but he shook his head. The sheriff fixed the noose and drew it tight. The reverend looked up, a smile on his face, like he could already see the angels coming to carry him to glory. The sheriff looked to Judge Biddle for a sign. The judge was staring at the ground, shaking so hard it seemed he must fall down dead himself.

"I couldn't watch, and turned my face away. I happened to look at the ironmaster, who stood not far off. He had a smile on his face—that tight, upside-down smile he likes to wear.

"They whipped the horse and drove the cart out from underneath the reverend. Out of the tail of my eye I seen him jerking and kicking at the end of the rope. People cried out, and some turned and ran. But Mr. Thompson stood there smiling as he watched the reverend die."

The fire crackled, and the wind hummed in the chimney.

"Rachel's brother arrived in Adamant the next day. He and his sister buried their father, and then they left. Far as I know, they never came back here again."

The old woman looked at Gideon with her sharp eyes. "Now you know about the preacher's doom. A sad enough tale, like so many in this world. Does it help you any?"

"I'm not sure." Gideon got up from the bench and stretched his legs. He found himself standing by the small wooden chest on whose top rested a scattering of bright creek-polished stones, some small animal bones, and the root of a plant, ivory-colored and split into two legs so that it looked like a little misshapen man. He thought it must come from *der buschabbel*, the mandrake plant. Folk down home believed the *buschabbel* had great magical powers. Hexes used it in casting their spells. You had to dig it out of the ground with care; if you just pulled it out, its scream would drive you mad.

Also sitting on the chest was the owl's severed foot. Gideon picked it up. It was shaped like an X, with two toes in front and two in back, each toe tipped with a curved, needle-sharp talon. The toes were clenched shut, leaving between them a small hole that an eye could peer through. He held out the foot to Gram Burns. "Can you look through that hole and tell me anything? Anything that would explain why the judge killed himself?"

He was surprised—downright shocked—to hear such a thing come out of his mouth.

"What's the matter? My story ain't good enough for you?" Gram Burns shook her head. "I don't have the power to look into the past. Just memories, same as anybody else." She took the owl's foot in her bent and wrinkled fingers. She looked at it for a moment, then held it up between herself and the firelight. She leaned her head forward and looked through it.

Quickly she set it down again.

*O may we all remember well,*
*The night of death is near*

# Eleven

—∞—

A T TIMES THE OLD WOMAN'S SNORING WAS REGULAR, LIKE TWO vigorous men ripping boards with a pit saw. At other times it was as random as a hog rooting through slop. Between bouts of snoring Gram Burns twisted and turned on her cornhusk mattress, filling the cabin with rustling, crackling sounds.

Gideon lay awake on his own pallet. Troubling images flashed through his mind. He pictured the red-haired preacher Thomas McEwan standing on the cart, the horse pulling it out from under him, the condemned man writhing and kicking at the rope's end, the ironmaster smiling cruelly as the preacher strangled to death—and Judge Biddle being forced to watch.

His thoughts flipped to the ironmaster's despicable treatment of women. He imagined True being molested by the powerful man who employed her. What if Adonijah Thompson had overpowered her, raped her? Gideon couldn't bear to imagine it. Would his feelings toward True change if he learned that such a thing had happened? He squirmed on the hard bed. True hadn't been a virgin when they made love that first time. Well, he hadn't been either. But what if she had willingly submitted to the ironmaster's advances? Or worse?

He lay on his back staring up into the darkness. He ground his teeth together. Could True have had designs to marry into the iron-master's status and wealth? Should he ask her about any relationship with the man? But what could that do, other than shame her or bring back awful memories? If she'd wanted to tell him anything, she would have done so. And if Adonijah Thompson had indeed raped

True Burns, or any other woman, should he be arrested? What was the statute of limitations for rape?

He sat bolt upright and wiped the sweat from his face. He reminded himself that he loved his wife. She was the dearest person to him in the whole world. He tried to convince himself that past miseries and pains should be forgotten. If you forgot things, if you thrust them from your mind, they lost their power to affect you. Shouldn't he just try to forget about Judge Biddle's suicide, put it behind him? And, if he was rational about it, shouldn't he banish from his mind his *memmi*'s murder as well? As if he ever could.

When he could no longer bear the old woman's snoring or the feverish unspooling of scenes inside his head, Gideon got up and pulled on his boots. Outside the cabin, the snow still fell. He stood on the doorstep, listening to the hissing of millions of flakes as they swirled down out of the black sky. He heard, far off, the howling of a wolf, then more voices joining in, the mournful wailing of the pack punctuated with deep, guttural barks. You never heard wolves anymore in the Dutch country. In Colerain County they were common. He stood in the cold until he began to shiver. Then he went back inside. He wrapped himself in the quilt and finally slept.

In the morning Gram Burns said little. She had a distant look on her face, as if she were exploring some lost world inside her head. Maybe she'd gone a bit *narrisch* over the years—no doubt it was easy to go a little crazy when you lived by yourself and grew old alone. Look where solitude and memory had taken the judge.

He thanked Arabella Burns for his breakfast, saddled Maude, and left the cabin. The sky was just beginning to lighten. He rode toward Adamant on an unmarked track. The snow had stopped, but the sky was still leaden. No animals showed themselves in the forest, nor birds in the air.

The farm folk were all indoors, like beasts gone to lair. Smoke issued from the chimneys of the houses and cabins he passed. Yet this must be but a temporary pause in the laboring. It was still October, the twenty-seventh day of the month; crops needed to be brought into barns, animals slaughtered and their flesh smoked or salted, apples and potatoes and turnips and carrots laid away in barrels of sand, fuelwood cut and split, pine boughs and cornstalks banked against the weather sides of dwellings.

He mulled over what True's grandmother had told him. And he wondered what she had seen when she peered through the owl's foot. He had asked her about that, twice—once right after she'd put the thing down like it was on fire, and again this morning, and both times she had refused to meet his eyes or to answer.

Worry grew in his brain like ice invading a pond. After his *memmi* died, he worried that every time he opened the door to a room, every time he walked around the corner of the house or the barn, he would find someone he loved lying there murdered.

He got back to town by midday. The snow was melting, turning the streets into mud. At home, when he pulled open the door, True flew into his arms.

"Did you miss me?" she said.

"Of course I missed you."

"I didn't miss you *much*," she said, grinning back at him. "I took a hot brick to bed to keep my toes warm, since I didn't have your big feet for that."

David lay bundled in a quilt on the floor, napping. "Can we leave this little man by himself for a while?" Gideon said.

In the bedroom he and True threw off their clothes and came together. She made him lie back on the bed while she straddled him. He rose to kiss her shoulders, her neck, her breasts. She kissed him on his cheeks and eyes and mouth, holding his head in her hands as she commenced the slow rise and fall; pausing, caressing, murmuring, drawing out their lovemaking until all thoughts had flown from his head—then the rushing tumbling release, their eyes locked together as with a sharp cry she fell forward onto his chest.

He held her against him and pulled up the quilt to cover them.

He wanted to shield her from anything that might threaten them in this uncertain and dangerous world. He wanted to protect her from bad things that might have happened in the past. He knew that both were impossible, foolish wishes. He held her close.

David woke and began to burble. Gideon and True looked at each other, rose, and dressed. Gideon ate some leftovers and put an apple in his pocket. He hugged True, kissed their son, and left.

★★★

At the jail he found Alonzo at the desk, rolling a rifle ball back and forth across its surface.

"Nothing has happened here for two whole days," Alonzo said, a note of complaint in his voice. "The town is too quiet."

"In our business, it's good to have quiet." Gideon yawned. "In fact, I could do with quiet most all of the time."

"Take a look at this." Alonzo laid a newspaper clipping on the desk.

Gideon picked it up. The article described a new pistol that had been designed in Paterson, New Jersey, by a man named Samuel Colt. It employed the percussion-cap system of ignition and was a repeating firearm with a revolving cylinder.

"Not in production yet," Alonzo said, "but the time is coming. This new gun will be much better than those antiques we're still using. Less chance of a hangfire. And five shots! And you can carry along an extra cylinder, fully loaded."

"The commissioners have already refused us the money to have our guns changed to percussion locks," Gideon said. "Why would they buy us new firearms?"

"Well, let me tell you something: a merry day it will be, when the outlaws all have percussion and we're still shooting those horrid old flintlocks."

At the moment, it seemed to Gideon that modernizing the armory was one of the smaller problems he faced.

"Speaking of guns," Alonzo said, "a man from the bank came by. The judge's estate passed probate. You need to go sign some papers, then you can take possession of all them things the judge willed over to you. Lucky feller. Though I guess you already took care of the horse and dog." Alonzo cast the rifle ball across the desk again. It made a droning sound. "I suppose they'll be auctioning off the rest of Hiram's stuff. Did he own any rifles? I am always on the lookout for a good tack-driving squirrel gun."

"The judge favored shotguns."

"He didn't shoot squirrels?"

Gideon shook his head. "He would only shoot flying game. More sportsmanlike, or so he said."

Alonzo scoffed. "Well, I bet he never et squirrel backstrap. Nor fried brains, neither." He shot the lead ball across the desk again, trapping it in his hand. Then grunted and dropped the ball into his vest pocket.

★★★

Gideon made his way along Franklin Street to Judge Biddle's house. It felt strange to knock and then be let inside by the judge's housekeeper while knowing that Hiram Biddle was no longer there to welcome him.

Mrs. Leathers had been cleaning. She held a polishing rag in her hand.

"I'd like to ask you a few questions," he said. "Can we go in to the kitchen?"

She nodded, went into the room, and sat down on the edge of a chair. Gideon pulled up a chair opposite her.

"Mrs. Leathers, how long had you worked for Judge Biddle?"

"Let's see. Going on twenty-two years."

Her answer disappointed him. He had hoped she'd been employed by the judge in 1805, the year the Reverend McEwan had been tried and executed, and could fill in a few more details about the incident. She certainly looked old enough for that, although her perpetually dour expression made it hard to guess her exact age.

"Did he ever talk to you about the past?" he asked.

Mrs. Leathers looked at the rag in her hands. "We didn't speak of such things. He was the judge. I was just his housekeeper."

"I realize you were not working for him in 1805, but do you recall a trial that year in which the judge sentenced a preacher to hang?"

"Heard of it. Don't remember much about it."

He tried a different tack. "Was there anything new in the judge's life lately? New acquaintances, new friends?"

"You're the only one he had much to do with, these last few years. Now and then he would invite the headmaster, Mr. Foote, for a meal and drinks. And sometimes Mr. Foote would send a note, and Judge Biddle would go over to the academy of an evening."

"Anything different or odd happen in the days leading up to the judge's death?"

"Well, not too odd, I guess." She changed her position in the chair. "A window got broke, there in the kitchen. A hawk chased a mountain pheasant into the glass." Gideon knew that "mountain pheasant" was what some locals called a grouse. Mrs. Leathers continued, "I was outside beatin' on a rug and seen it happen. The pheasant was killed outright. Broke its neck. I shooed the hawk away. The judge told me to hang the bird down cellar, save it to cook later." She shook her head at this daft bit of instruction. "It's still down there, I expect. Probably rotted by now. Oh, and a tramp stopped by a night or so before the judge . . . before he passed away."

Tramps occasionally visited the better homes in Adamant to ask for food or small sums of money. Complaints arose if they were too persistent. "Can you tell me anything about the tramp?" Gideon asked.

"Older man." Mrs. Leathers wiped her polishing rag along the arm of the chair.

"Did you recognize him?"

She shook her head.

"What took place?"

"I gave him some food, and he left." She balled up the rag, shook it out again. "I ought to get back to work, Sheriff. The bank wants this place neat and tidy so they can sell it." She looked down. "After that, I have to find a new job."

"If I hear of anything, I'll let you know. And if you remember anything else that you think might shed light on why the judge committed suicide, would you tell me?"

He went in to the study, found the floor scrubbed and freshly waxed. The chair in which the judge had died had been cleaned and placed back under the desk. Gideon drew it out: a good walnut chair with a gentle curve to accommodate the back. No damage to it, the charge of shot having apparently spent itself in Judge Biddle's chest. He sat down in the chair and looked around the room. It appeared as if nothing tragic or violent had happened here. He regretted not coming back immediately after the judge's death and just sitting in the room and thinking, before Mrs. Leathers had a chance to clean up and put things back in order. Maybe something would have come to him then.

On the walls were framed lithographs of dogs on point, still lifes of dead partridges and pheasants, a luminous scene of men in a sneak boat on a river beneath a full moon with the sheen of old ivory, the men kneeling low and holding their shotguns expectantly as the boat drifted toward a raft of sleeping waterfowl.

Beneath the prints stood a bookcase. Gideon took out one of the books: *Instructions to Young Sportsmen, with Directions for the Choice,*

*Care, and Management of Guns.* The judge had loaned this book to him, after Gideon had, for the first time, quickly accepted Hiram Biddle's offer to go grouse hunting. He put the volume back and got out another, *Pteryplegia: Or, the Art of Shooting-Flying.* That one he hadn't read yet. Gideon loved to read; his reading had helped him pick up English quickly when he was younger. First he had read his uncle's books, mostly about natural history, then those of a neighbor—until his father forbade it, declaring that reading was a waste of time better spent mending harness or sharpening tools or fixing fences.

He thought he might bid on some of the judge's books when the estate went to auction; maybe he could get the whole lot for cheap. The title page of *Pteryplegia* stated that the book had been printed for J. Lever, Bookseller, Little Moorgate, London. Date of publication, 1767; price, one shilling. The book had come from England, like the judge's shotgun. Had Hiram Biddle crossed the ocean and traveled there at some point? If so, he had never mentioned it.

As Gideon returned *Pteryplegia* to the shelf, his eye fell on four identical volumes, leather-bound, and without titles embossed on their spines. He picked out the first of the books and blew dust off its top edge. Its binding crackled as he opened it.

On the first page was inked: YEAR OF OUR LORD 1802. Gideon opened the book at random. In the judge's familiar script he read:

April 7. Enjoyed a morning on the banks of Panther Creek, & conclude that love is no exclusively human affliction. Thro' my glass watched 2 male grackles attempting to impress a half-interested female. Both males perched near her, with heads upraised & bills pointed skyward. The sun's brilliance painted their breasts with green & purple iridescence. One & then the other of these gaudy suitors drew in his head, fluffed out his feathers, & "sang" in the most discordant voice imaginable.

This was the judge's journal. Gideon paged ahead. He read entries recording the weather, outings, social events, philosophical thoughts.

July 9. I like to walk among the tombs, it is a melancholy pleasure yet I enjoy it. Reminds me that I am mortal. I ask myself: Is there a hereafter? Truly, there must be; it cannot be that we are to end when this tenement of clay becomes no longer inhabited. If so, what motive could have caused our existence?

August 12. How thick the shafts of death fly about us! High places, & riches, & good health seem to offer no shield or panoply against the Great Destroyer. John Cutler dead today after a week of the bloody flux; others in his family ill. "Prepare to meet thy God"—these words are too lightly said & too lightly thought of.

Sept. 27. Taking my leisure in the hills, I stopped in a birch grove at dusk. The trees' yellow leaves, strewn on the ground, made it appear that a patch of sunlight still bathed the earth, tho' the sun had dipped below the horizon. Standing in the half-light, I felt low & wretched. How sad, to be alone in the world. Would that I had a wife. Must I be solitary all my days?

The words of a callow young man, not the mature, seasoned jurist Gideon had known. He recalled the date of birth, 1773, to be incised on the judge's gravestone. In 1802, Hiram Biddle would have been almost thirty years old. Unmarried at that age, it was understandable that he felt frustrated and insecure.

Gideon wondered if it was proper for him to be peering at the judge's personal thoughts. He closed the journal and put it back on its shelf. Before killing himself, Hiram Biddle had used a book to hold down the written copy of his will on the desk. Gideon didn't recall anything about the book, other than that it had been put away, no doubt by Mrs. Leathers, between the time when he left to go tell the state's attorney about the judge's suicide and when he and the coroner, Dr. Beecham, returned for the judge's body.

He got out the next journal and skimmed through it. He read more vignettes describing the changing seasons and life in Adamant more than thirty years in the past. In autumn the judge wrote of hunting, compiling the numbers of woodcock and grouse he bagged. There were entries about marriageable women met at dinners, parties, church functions. This young lady was "too finicking, too much concerned with an appearance of propriety," while that one was "mercenary" and "would be a shrewd housewife but no doubt a demanding one." Another, with the weird given name of Birdelia, was jolly but hardly attractive, "mannish," the judge wrote, "& it seemed as if, in her construction, her legs had been turned upside down, such that the thickest part occurred just above the foot, which itself was not dainty."

With a smile, Gideon closed the volume on the poor thick-ankled Birdelia.

The journal for 1804 carried on in much the same vein. He paged through it until a name jumped out at him.

July 10. Adonijah Thompson, the ironmaster, cuts a striking figure, having an aristocratic bearing, and projects great energy & firmness of purpose. About my age. Quite forward in his manner, given to boasting about his achievements, grand plans & aspirations. Said to be litigious. Met him whilst taking the noon meal with companions at the White Deer Inn.

Gideon had never heard of the White Deer Inn. Had it burned in the fire that destroyed the old courthouse?

Mr. Thompson took a chair at our table & joined in our conversation, which concerned the county's settlement. He told of an occasion, soon after he arrived in this place, when he was inhabiting a cabin upon the site of his future ironworks. Engaged in chopping wood, he heard a turkey calling. He said "I could tell it was not a real turkey," & gave the "cut-cut-cut" call of a young turkey separated from the flock, which caused the other patrons to pause their forks & peer toward our table. Thompson stated that the longer he listened, the more certain he became that the calls did not come from a turkey but rather were being made by an Indian, no doubt for the purpose of enticing him in to an ambush. He therefore took up his rifle, went round behind the cabin, & moving quietly, circled thro' the woods. Hearing the calling again, he spied an Indian crouched behind a log, painted for war & coated with rancid bear grease.

The ironmaster explained, with undue relish, how he sighted his rifle on his foe & "dealt him the death he would have given me." Certainly he was justified in protecting his life & property, but the cruel delight he took in relating how he slew the redskin left a taste of ashes in my mouth. He said he turned the savage over with his boot & found he was "not much more than a boy." He smiled and stated fervently "If you kill 'em young, you needn't deal with 'em later on."

On July 11 the judge wrote of men scything grass in the fine summer weather, building the sweet-smelling hay into ricks and filling their barns with it. Then on July 12, the ironmaster's name appeared again.

Ad. Thompson here today on a fine grey gelding. The ironmaster sat the horse beautifully, & I was struck with the grand picture he and his steed made. He said he wishes to sell the horse, which he purchased down state, & served up a compliment by denominating me "one of the few men in these parts who would appreciate such an animal." He asked $50—a not inconsiderable sum, but I had heard of this horse, & knew for a certainty that the ironmaster had given $100 for him.

His offer caused in me a feeling of unease. Why should he wish to sell the horse so cheaply? I admit I was tempted, for cannot a man buy & sell at any price he chooses? But perhaps I will soon be seeing the ironmaster in court. Not wishing to compromise myself, I thanked him & explained that I was not in a position to purchase the horse. "What," the ironmaster replied, "you do not wish to own this fine piece of horseflesh?" When I demurred again, he wheeled the gelding about, & it walked away like a catamount stalking its prey. And the man seated upon him—nay, the man who was one with him in all his movements—had a bearing that was equally regal &, one might almost say, equally predatory in aspect.

*Within Thy circling pow'r I stand,*
*On ev'ry side I find Thy hand*

# Twelve

—∞∞∞—

THE LIGHT IN THE STUDY HAD BEGUN TO FADE. MRS. LEATHERS brought in a taper and lit a cut-glass lamp.

Gideon thanked her.

"Mrs. Leathers, on the morning when I found the judge, after he killed himself, there was a book holding down the judge's will. When I came back with the coroner a little later, the book wasn't on the table anymore. Did you put it away?"

"Well, I did come back in here." She colored. "I . . . I wanted to see if he was really dead." She looked off to one side. "Foolish notion. I suppose I did put a book away. It looked like the one you've got there."

Gideon nodded. He saw that Mrs. Leathers had begun to look askance at him, perhaps having realized that he was prying into the judge's affairs. He waited until she left the room, then resumed reading. He figured that the fourth and last of the leather-bound volumes, still on the shelf, contained entries for 1805—the fateful year when the Reverend Thomas McEwan would murder Nathaniel Thompson and the judge would sentence him to death.

Had the judge been reading that diary on the night he killed himself?

Gideon decided to finish sampling the 1804 book before getting out that final volume. He scanned entries on summer storms and "the peltings of the pitiless rain," a magnificently antlered elk that the judge had seen while bird hunting, the marble fireplace of some acquaintance "beautifully & elaborately chizzled in relief, with flowers & leaves." Then the name Thompson caught his eye again.

Dec. 11. It becomes crystal clear why Ad. Thompson on July 12 last offered me his fine grey gelding, purchased at $100 according to general report, for the favorable price of $50. Today court convened to hear a lawsuit bro't by Robert Wheeler vs. Adonijah Thompson, Robt. being the eldest son of Hugh, widower, who d. intestate this past March. At his death Hugh Wheeler owned a productive farm of 290 acres. This spring Wheeler's heirs asked the county to commission an inquest so that they might fairly partition the farm. The Court named Sheriff Bathgate & six jurors to convene a board of inquiry, which in due time fixed the worth of the estate at $16/ac, for a total of $4,640. The jurors, men of standing, & possessed of sound business acumen, concluded that dividing the farm would lessen its overall value. They proposed that the property be sold in its entirety, & the returns divided amongst Wheeler's heirs. The Court so approved.

Subsequently, Mr. Thompson purchased the farm at auction, paying $7.60/ac, or $2,204, less than half the price the board of inquiry had estimated the property should bring. Now Robt. Wheeler complains that Thompson influenced the jurors to value the land high, thus encouraging the heirs to sell, knowing that he could then in all likelihood acquire the farm at a significantly reduced price. One juror testified that the ironmaster approached him with an implied offer of a reward—the word "bribe" was never mentioned—but, being a man of high moral fortitude, the juror refused to violate his oath & overvalue the farm. Nevertheless, the majority of the jurors fixed the value at $16/ac, with Sheriff Bathgate testifying that, to his knowledge, nothing untoward had taken place.

Clearly the land is worth more than the $2,204 that Thompson paid for it. Robt. Wheeler appealed to the Court to let the purchase price be returned to the ironmaster, & allow the family to work out a division of the acreage amongst themselves such that those who wish to continue farming can do so, & pay the others their fair share.

Before I deliver'd my ruling, I saw the ironmaster glance scornfully at Robt. Wheeler. As I spake the words "It is the verdict of this Court," his face assumed that peculiar inverted smile he often displays; seeming to believe, I must assume, that I would find in his favor. However, I found for Wheeler, there being no need to hurry the matter, & the integrity of the board of inquiry having been brought into question.

What a stench in the land, were it to be bruited about that I had been influenced by the offer of a fine grey horse! Upon hearing the verdict, the ironmaster stared straight ahead, his face a frozen mask. Leaving the courtroom, he announced to Wheeler, in a manner calculated to be overheard, "You may hold on to that farm for the time being. But do not expect to sell your crops to the ironworks, nor grind your corn at my mill."

Gideon sat back in the chair. So the enmity between the judge and the ironmaster did have its beginnings in court. This must have been the case that Davey Burns mentioned when Gideon and True and David visited her family in Panther this Sunday past.

He scanned the rest of the 1804 entries and found nothing notable. He got out the volume for 1805. Its top edge was not dusty, as the journals for the three previous years had been. Nor did its spine crackle when he opened the book.

He paged through the better part of a year's worth of mundane entries—the depth of snow at Easter, a harvest of sponge mushrooms found under elm trees in May, a pianoforte concert, the death of a judge in a neighboring county "who is now as but a clod of the valley"—until an exclamatory sentence stopped him.

Sept. 4. The Lord has blest me! It being Saturday, I determin'd to ramble in the woods near the iron plantation. On my way I passed the Presbyterian church & parsonage, where, engaged in weeding a flower bed, was a young woman. She straightened as I came up, & I stopped & removed my hat. Tho' a bonnet shaded her face, I could see she was exceedingly beautiful, with dark hair, eyes lively & bright, & a countenance that bespoke an active mind within. She proved well spoken, neither immodest nor reserved but open & intelligent in her speech. As we conversed, she blest me with a smile, which called up in my bosom emotions most pleasurable. I confess I stammered, & lost my train of thought, something which never occurs in court! A man came out of the parsonage, tall & robust, with reddish hair & a florid complexion. He was the pastor, Thomas McEwan; she, his daughter Rachel.

Gideon stared at the page. He was both charmed by the judge's description of his meeting this beautiful young woman—and haunted by the knowledge that this was the opening scene of a terrible tragedy. Not one of these people had any idea of what must happen in the coming months: that the preacher would commit murder and go to the gallows; that the daughter would lose her father and leave Adamant forever; that the judge would have his hopes shattered and his life misdirected onto a sad and lonely path.

Sept. 5. The Rev. Tolliver is close friends with the Rev. McEwan despite that they cleave to different denominations. My pastor describes his colleague as "a Presbyterian of the old school," & speaks glowingly of Rachel, saying she is devoted to her father. Her mother died some years ago, so Rachel cooks & manages the household. She is thrifty, & possessed of good sense. The Rev. T. suggests it would be entirely proper for me to attend church at Panther on Sunday next; he smiled, & patted me on the shoulder, then hinted that Rachel might welcome the advances of a judge, "a pillar in the community & a marriageable man who could provide her a fine home." I felt no small degree of embarrassment at how quickly this Episcopal divine had divined my interest & intent in this matter.

Gideon smiled at the judge's pun. He missed his friend. In the next week's entries a lovesick young man mooned over the woman he had recently met.

Sept. 12. Arr. in Panther before service & took a seat in back. Rachel sitting in the front row. Her father read from the Book of Ruth, & based his sermon on the words Ruth spake to Naomi: "Entreat me not to leave thee, or to return from following after thee. For whither thou goest, I will go: and where thou lodgest, I will lodge also." He spoke with surpassing eloquence, his message being about faith, love, & steadfastness. I thought it a most propitious subject, & noted that he directed what I could only interpret as a welcoming gaze toward me several times during his discourse. After the service, the Rev. stood by the door greeting the congregation. He shook my hand with warmth & vigor, & asked if I might repair to the parsonage to partake in the noon meal; which invitation I accepted with no little alacrity! As I stood in the yard, looked back & saw the ironmaster, Ad. Thompson, whom I had not noticed in church. He shook hands I think rather perfunctorily with the Rev., then turned and strode away.

Enjoyed a sumptuous dinner that Rachel prepared, 2 kinds of meat & 3 vegetables followed by apple pie. I scarcely tasted the food, so entranced was I to be in her presence. After the meal I convers'd at length w. the Rev. McEwan concerning the Expedition of Discovery commanded by Capts. Lewis & Clark that has been sent forth into the Louisiana Purchase. He told me in great detail about papers & articles he has read describing mineral, botanical, & zoological specimens that the explorers have sent back, including a "prairie dog," not a canine at all but a fossorial rodent, which Pres. Jefferson rec'd alive in a box. The preacher then changed subjects abruptly, speaking of the war in Europe & the effrontery of the tyrant Napoleon declaring himself Emperor of France. The Rev. described Bonaparte as "a beast who has murdered countless civilians" & "a perfect demon in league with Satan." His face grew livid & he began to rant; but Rachel calmed him with a soothing hand on his arm & a whisper in his ear. Sitting down, she gave me a smile that caused such a pleasant emotion in my breast that I felt I "walked in climes of bliss."

Gideon looked up. The knocker on the front door of the judge's house was banging. He heard the door open, the sound of voices, then heavy footfalls coming down the hallway.

Alonzo burst in to the study. "You must come at once!"

*If this be death, I soon shall be*
*From ev'ry pain and sorrow free*

# Thirteen

"HAMMERTOWN," ALONZO GASPED AS THEY RAN DOWN THE STREET. "The Guinea Hen. Doc oughta be there now . . . Face looks like a horse kicked it."

He came to a wheezing, bent-over stop and waved Gideon ahead. Gideon put on a burst of speed.

The man lay on a table in a back room of the saloon. A folded coat pillowed his head. Beneath a blanket the man's chest slowly rose and fell. Dr. Beecham, normally placid and friendly, gave Gideon a glare as if he were the cause of this trouble. The doctor held the man's wrist in one hand while taking his pulse with his other hand. The man's face was turned away from the door.

"Pulse is weak and irregular." Beecham motioned Gideon around the table.

When he got a look, Gideon sucked in his breath.

The man's eyes had vanished beneath a blackened, grotesquely swollen brow. Bloody saliva roped down from his lips.

"They found him half an hour ago," the doctor said. "Must've laid in that alley last night and all of today. It's a wonder he didn't die of exposure."

"Does anyone know who he is?"

"I doubt his own mother would recognize him." Beecham felt carefully over the man's skull with his fingertips. His fingers stopped in one area, then withdrew.

A woman brought a basin of water. The doctor dipped a cloth in the water and touched it to the man's lips. The man did not stir. The

103

doctor cleaned caked blood off lips, cheeks, and chin. The water in the basin turned pink. The doctor parted the shredded lips and began cleaning out the man's mouth. Teeth fell clinking against the basin's edge.

Beecham said he would have the man taken to his house. Alonzo, who by now had arrived at the saloon, found four men to help. Beecham directed them to carefully slide the patient onto a second blanket. "Try not to jar him," he said. Three men to a side, they carried him from the room. Gideon gripped the blanket tightly. The doctor reached in between him and the next man and steadied the victim's head.

Outside, it was almost night. A voice whooped from another tavern. A fiddle sawed out a tune. Revelers sang a drinking song. Gideon and the others bore the unconscious man across the bridge and up the hill. At the doctor's house they eased him onto a bed.

Beecham turned to Gideon. His ruddy face was solemn. "Along with the contusions and a broken cheekbone—maybe two broken cheekbones—he has a depressed skull fracture. With an injury like that, if a person don't revive within a few hours . . ." He lifted his shoulders, let them fall.

Gideon picked up one of the man's hands, then the other. They were limp. Clean, the nails well kept, the knuckles undamaged: the man must not have had a chance to use his fists in defense. He wore a white shirt, flecked with dried blood, and trousers held up with suspenders that had slipped off his shoulders. His pockets were turned inside out. Gideon smelled the bite of urine on the trousers, along with something that tickled his nose. He shook one of the pocket linings above his cupped hand. Flecks of pale sawdust drifted onto his palm.

"Alonzo," he said, "please go and check at the boardinghouses. Ask if anyone didn't sleep last night in his room or didn't show up for breakfast this morning. Someone who works in carpentry, or maybe at the sawmill."

The doctor told Gideon that the man had been found by a boy, who followed his dog, which apparently followed its nose. The man lay beneath a heap of trash, covered over with boards.

Gideon stated the obvious: "Left for dead."

Beecham sat down in a chair. "With that skull fracture, I doubt he'll make it."

"Can you operate?"

The doctor grimaced. "It's difficult surgery. I don't have the instruments to do it right. Never even seen it done."

"Surely there's something . . . ?"

"Maybe you fancy yourself a surgeon, sheriff?"

"I didn't mean to criticize."

The doctor sighed. "All we can do is wait."

★★★

Gideon met Alonzo at the jail.

"It's likely a fellow staying at Shaw's," Alonzo informed him. "Name of Yost Kepler. Works at Latimer's. His landlord hasn't seen him since supper yesterday."

They took the man's jacket to the boardinghouse. Boston and Luella Shaw both nodded when they looked at the jacket. Lighting the way with a candle, Mr. Shaw led them up the stairs. The room was in an attic under the roof's slant, a cramped place with one small window in the gable end. Gideon figured it would be hellishly hot in summer and miserably cold in winter. A few items of clothing hung from nails driven into the wall. On a small table next to the bed lay a razor rolled up in a towel, a deck of playing cards, and a stack of letters addressed to Yost Kepler, General Delivery, Adamant, Pennsylvania. The return address was a place called Womelsdorf, Near Reading, the latter being a sizable town in Berks County north of Gideon's old home.

"What can you tell me about him?" Gideon asked the Shaws.

"He's been with us since April," Boston Shaw said. "A pleasant enough fellow. Pays his rent on time, keeps his room tidy, and talks polite at the table."

"He works at the sawmill?"

"He clerks. Sometimes he's in the yard, stacking boards and such. Been there since he came to town."

"Does he have any friends?

"I don't know anybody who didn't like him, because, like I said, Yost is a pleasant fellow."

"Close friends, among the other boarders?"

"I wouldn't say any in particular. No enemies, neither."

"Does he drink, go out to saloons?"

"Sometimes he will go out of an evening," Shaw said.

The name Yost Kepler was clearly German. Gideon asked, "How is his English?"

"You can tell he's Dutch. But it don't get in the way," Shaw said. Then added with a sheepish smile, "Kind of like yourself, Sheriff."

"What about his family?"

"The ones who write to him? Sometimes he spoke of his parents. An older brother is taking over their farm. Yost being one of the young 'uns, why, he had to make his own way. He talked now and then about traveling, heading west. Illinois, or some such place. Mentioned he might join the army. But first he wanted to work for a while, save some money."

"Does he ask you to hold his wages, or does he deposit them in the bank?"

Shaw shook his head. "He never asked me to hold money for him." He added, "He has a nice gold-plated watch that he likes to get out of his pocket; it has his initials inside the lid."

There had been no watch in Yost Kepler's pocket when Gideon inspected the unconscious man earlier.

Gideon looked under the thin straw-filled mattress and in the pockets of the clothes hanging on the wall, but did not find the watch or anything else. There was no other obvious place in the room where a person might hide cash or valuables.

Gideon picked up the letters. "I will take these," he said.

***

In Hammertown Alonzo showed him where Kepler had been found. The lantern cast long shadows on the rubbish, from which issued a sharp, sudden rustling.

Alonzo leaped back. "Snake or rat, I want nothing to do with you!"

"He was covered up with these boards?" Gideon said.

"So we are told."

Gideon peered about. Two roughly parallel lines, mostly effaced by others' footprints, led in to the alley from the street about ten paces away. He followed those drag marks—made by the victim's bootheels, he figured—to where they vanished in the general scuffed-over environment of the street. The alley itself was too littered and the lantern too weak for anything else to be revealed.

"Let's come back tomorrow," he said.

A few squat candles lit the interior of the Guinea Hen. Shavings lay on the plank floor. Bare spots were tacky with spilled beer. Three men seated at a table turned and stared, a drinking bowl between them, tobacco smoke clouded above.

"Too bad, that boy gettin' his head bashed in," the saloonkeeper said. He was stooped over, with an upper lip like a parrot's beak and a patch of white off-center in his black hair as if he'd bumped into a flour sack. "He going to die?"

Gideon thought, *We are all going to die.* Then he said, "The man's name is Yost Kepler. He works at Latimer's Sawmill. Do you know him?"

The saloonkeeper pushed out his lower lip. "That would be a Dutch moniker, wouldn't it?"

"I would say yes."

"There's a Dutch boy comes in here now and again. Though I don't recall seeing him last night."

Gideon talked to a serving woman and got the same story.

They moved on to the next block. A saloon called The Horse was the only establishment in Hammertown that agreed to serve Negroes—men who worked in the tannery or the livery or drove wagons. No one in that place, keeper or customers, had any notion or recall of Yost Kepler.

They entered a door beneath a sign showing a crudely painted crown atop a whiskey jug and the name HOUSE OF LORDS. The proprietor had small close-set eyes and a broad gash of a mouth. Stingy with his words. Finally Gideon pried out of him that a Dutch boy from the sawmill sometimes wet his whistle there.

"Did he come in last night?"

Using both hands, the saloonkeeper pushed back his mop of greasy hair. He gestured with his chin. "Ask her."

The waitress was tall, chubby, and fair-haired. She wore a stained apron over a frayed dress. "I know who you mean," she said. "*Yost.*" She said the name slowly, as if trying it out. "Set over there last evening." She indicated a table.

"Did he drink much?"

"His friend kept filling his glass."

"What were they drinking?"

"Mule. Our best."

Gideon knew that the best mule-kick this establishment offered was the local rye whiskey diluted with water and beefed up again with tobacco juice and burnt sugar.

"This friend, was he someone you recognized?"

"Never saw him before in my life."

"What did he look like?"

She scratched at the corner of her mouth. "Medium size, neither short nor tall. His face was plain as buttered bread. Clean-shaven.

'Bout the same age as the Dutch boy, twenty or so. Talkative, a regular blatherskite." She frowned. "Cheap, too. The whoreson didn't leave a tip." She held a wooden serving platter against her chest. "I recall he was wearing a vest. Very fancy it was. Had a pattern on it, like leaves—no, like pickles. Green pickles. The vest being red."

"Can you recall anything else?"

"A while back, maybe two weeks ago, I seen the Dutch boy with another fellow—that one was big and ugly, with broad shoulders, strong looking. I think he had dark hair and maybe a pocked face." She shrugged. "But that's not who he was with last night."

"Yost and his friend, the talkative one with the red vest. Did they leave here together?"

"I couldn't say."

"Did you hear anything that Yost and this fellow said? Any names, or where they were going next?"

She shook her head. "I didn't hear nothing. Tell me, is that boy going to die?"

"God willing, he won't die," Gideon said. Then he considered the goblin's face Yost Kepler would wear for the rest of his days if he lived.

*Our life is ever on the wing,*
*And death is ever nigh . . .*

# Fourteen

———∞∞∞———

THE GRAY BLANKET LOOKED LIKE A BARREN HILL AFTER WINTER'S snow had melted away. Gideon wished the blanket did not have to be removed, that it could stay in place, concealing the terrible truth that lay beneath.

Murder had been committed in Adamant.

The doctor lifted the blanket.

The corpse lay stripped and washed. The arms rested along the sides, hands palms up, fingers curling inward, the skin white as church paint. The face with its ruined mouth and brutal brow seemed barely human.

"We'll know better after the autopsy," Dr. Beecham said, "but for now I'd say the cause of death is the depressed skull fracture." He indicated the side of the head near the crown, where he had clipped away blond hair to reveal bruised skin and a sunken area perhaps an inch in diameter.

"What kind of weapon did that?" Gideon said.

"A blunt object. A club, maybe a heavy bottle or a jug? Whatever it was, it barely broke the skin."

Gideon reached out and touched Yost Kepler's shoulder. It was cold.

*You didn't deserve this. Your family doesn't deserve this.* Then he blinked and drew back a little, remembering how he himself had used a heavy pistol to club the Tattered Man on the side of the head. Had he fractured the man's skull? To this day, he didn't know whether the Tattered Man had lived or died. But Gideon had lashed out at his assailant in self-defense. And he hadn't gone on beating him and beating him.

Purple yellow-edged bruises covered Kepler's torso. They reminded Gideon of the *jonijumbubs* in his mother's garden—flowers that True called heart's ease.

There would be no easing the hearts of Yost Kepler's kin.

"The ribs are broken in a number of places," the doctor said. "Organ damage? An intriguing question, whose answer will be revealed by a thorough dissection."

Gideon looked at Beecham. He could almost imagine the doctor rubbing his hands together in anticipation of getting out his scalpel. He turned back to the corpse and focused on the flowerlike bruises. Each had a slightly lopsided but decidedly triangular shape. "I wonder if these were made by a bootheel."

The doctor peered at them. "Could've used their boots on him."

"Maybe just one boot. If you look close, it appears that one corner of the heel didn't bruise the skin. They're all pretty much like that, all those marks."

With pencil and paper, and using a ruler, Gideon measured and drew an accurate picture of several of the bruises. The doctor stood watching, unshaven and bleary-eyed after having sat with his patient through the night. Kepler had died at five in the morning.

"Why don't you get some sleep?" Gideon said.

Beecham glanced at the clock in the corner. An expectant, cheerful look came to his face. "Fish will be here soon. You can help, too, you got the stomach for it."

Gideon thought about what he might gain from watching the doctor open up the corpse and cut out the organs and peer at them. Slice them up, too, probably. And the last thing he wanted to do was to rub elbows with the Cold Fish. "I'll wait and read your report," he said. "I have an investigation to see to."

He found Alonzo leaning against the wall at the entrance to the alley where Kepler had been found.

"A lovely spot," Alonzo said. "Which I poked around some already."

The boards used to cover the victim stood propped against the wall. The alley was strewn with broken crates, sodden newspapers, coffee grounds, rotten fruit attended by yellowjackets.

They rooted about in the trash. "Where was he lying?" Gideon asked.

"Over here. His head was up against this crate."

Gideon got down on his knees—a bit cautiously, with all of the yellowjackets buzzing around. "Look here." The ground was soft. He pointed at several marks in the dirt. The indentations were triangular, and they lined up behind broader indentations that could have been made by a boot's sole. Gideon got out the piece of paper on which he had sketched the bruises on Kepler's torso. "I think that when we find a man wearing a boot with only half a heel, we will have found our murderer."

They continued sifting through the refuse. Gideon held up a heavy brown-and-tan crock, its handle broken off. "This could have been used to hit him on the head."

"Could've been," Alonzo said. He commenced whistling, then suddenly stopped and said emphatically, "Sheriff, I think we have looked here long enough. We need to go talk to people. Ask them questions while they may still remember something." He paused. "If you want my honest opinion."

Gideon fought down a smile. Alonzo was never reluctant to share his thoughts. After Gideon had been made sheriff, one of the county commissioners pointedly suggested that Alonzo, the brother of the commissioner's wife, would make an excellent deputy: He could read, and he knew Adamant and Colerain County like the back of his hand. He had been working as a house builder, a job that did not satisfy him. He knew lots of practical things. A bachelor, he could work long hours if needed. Gideon had to admit that Alonzo had proven a good choice. He shaved only sporadically, went weeks without washing his person or his clothes, belched and farted rather too freely, and talked about guns too much. But however quirky Alonzo might be, however dull-appearing and slovenly, he was an observant, perceptive man.

Gideon straightened and brushed his hands off on his trousers. He picked up the broken crock. "We'll drop this off at the jail. Then we'll start asking around."

***

Over the rasp of the up-and-down saw they spoke with Kepler's fellow workers at the sawmill. Kepler had no enemies that anyone knew of. The boss called him "a dependable lad, always on time and done what he was told."

They stopped people on the street, went into shops, quizzed clerks and layabouts and tradesmen and hostlers, men and women, and no one knew anything about the attack, nor anything about the victim or the potential attacker, either.

At suppertime they spoke with the Shaws again and interviewed their five other boarders. All of them had stayed in on the evening of the assault, four of them playing whist in the parlor while the fifth read Washington Irving's *Tales of the Alhambra*. None of the men could tell them anything of note. Although sobered by their housemate's death, none appeared ill at ease or aroused Gideon's or Alonzo's suspicions in any way.

***

Next morning on Burying Hill the clouds seemed close enough that Gideon thought he might reach up and grab some of their wool. Mr. and Mrs. Shaw had trudged up into the mist with him, and the foreman from the sawmill. No one else. The preacher's words, the same ones that had been read at the judge's burying, slipped through

Gideon's mind, which dwelt instead on a rhyme he had read in the *Wesleyan Methodist*: "All living things that fly or leap, Or crawl or swim or run or creep, Fear Death, yet they can find no spot in all the world where Death is not."

At the jail Gideon read through the letters he had taken from Kepler's room. They were all in *Hoch Deutsch*, High German, *Pennsylfawnisch Deitsch* being a dialect and not a written language. He found the letters somewhat difficult to parse out. Not because the handwriting was bad, but because he hadn't read German or even thought in it for a long time, except sometimes in his dreams or when a certain word or phrase popped into his head.

The letters told him that Kepler's parents had been neither angry nor disappointed at their son's removal to a new place. In fact, several passages suggested that Yost had been looking the area over and that other family members might follow if and when he established himself.

Gideon got out a sheet of paper. He took a quill and used his penknife to trim it to the proper angle, slit the end, and chisel the nib. He uncapped the inkwell.

Should he write in German or English? If the Keplers knew only German, no doubt they could get someone to translate if he wrote in English. And he doubted that he could do a decent job of putting his thoughts into *Deutsch*; two years had passed since he'd written anything in that language.

He did not consider himself German or Pennsylvania Dutch, but simply an American. Some people in Colerain County dismissed him as the proverbial dumb Dutchman, as more than a few might have judged Yost Kepler.

He went to dip the pen, then held off, remembering his last day on the farm. He felt again the heat of his father's glare. His *dawdy* had reached out with both hands and taken hold of his arms above the elbows, gripping them hard enough to hurt. He put his face two inches away from Gideon's.

"You will not leave us," he said in *Deitsch*.

"I will leave if I want to," Gideon retorted in English.

"I should have taken you in hand years ago." His father's eyes burned. "Ever since your mother—" He bit off his words. "This English you have learned . . ."

"A man needs English to be a success."

"*Pah.* You have all that you need right here. You don't have to go any farther than Lancaster to get whatever you want."

"*Lancaster.*" Gideon spat out the word like it was the sourest bottom-of-the-barrel kraut.

"This will be your farm," his father said urgently. "It will come down to you in the course of time."

"Give it to Friedrich. He wants it, I don't."

"You are the firstborn."

Gideon shrugged—hard to do with iron hands clamping his arms.

"We have farmed this land for eighty years," his father said.

He knew that anything he told his father would not be listened to. He did not want to farm. He hated farming. Plowing, sowing, cultivating, reaping, threshing—the same chores year after year on the same patch of land. Spreading manure, that most aggravating of tasks, fork the stinking shit into the wagon, dig it out again with the hook, scatter it over every inch of ground. Haying on the hottest summer days, with the sweat running into your eyes as they darted to the heavens and watched the gathering clouds, the knot in your stomach: *Will it rain?* He thought he resented the never-ending fact of the work even more than the backbreaking rigor of it. And what was there to liven such an existence? A market day, a butchering, an auction. Trooping off to church every Sunday to listen to the humbug pastor in his robes and ruff, elevated above the congregation in the pulpit, the sounding board at his back directing his predictable *Deutsch* words to the same set of vacant benumbed faces.

His father shot a glance toward the hilltop graveyard. "Our people's bones are in this ground."

Gideon almost wilted. "*Un mei memmi's*," he choked out. Tears sprang to his eyes. He would not let himself cry. He had always wanted to cry over what had happened to her, but he had never been able to let down his guard enough to do it. Anyway, he was damned if he'd weep in front of his father. In the absence of that release, he felt rage build in him. *Why didn't you protect her? Why haven't you turned over every piece of shit on this god-damned place to find the one who killed her?*

He struggled against the pinioning grip. He searched for what he imagined might be the worst insult he could throw into the old man's face. "The people in their graves on that hill," he blurted, "they wasted their lives in this shit hole."

The explosion against the side of his head knocked him down. He lay with his mouth open, tasting dirt. He hunched up, waiting for a boot in the *arsch* or the ribs; his father rarely stopped with one blow. But this time no more blows came. Gideon heard a curse, then hard footsteps receding.

He worked himself up to a sitting position. Gradually the barn righted itself. The house beneath the big sycamore swam back into focus.

He struggled to his feet. His ear and the whole side of his head pulsed hotly. A high-pitched ringing filled his head. He staggered to where he had hitched Maude to the post. He leaned his cheek against the saddle, smelled the sun-warmed leather. Then he freed the reins, put his foot in the stirrup, and hauled himself up. A wave of dizziness almost toppled him. As he listed sideways, he felt Maude shift that way to put herself beneath him.

Friedrich came out of the barn. He reached up and placed a hand on Gideon's arm. Two years separated them. They were both tall and broad-shouldered, although Friedrich had dark hair like their father's while Gideon's hair was sandy yellow like their mother's.

Gideon had gotten her regular features and good looks. Friedrich had a rawboned, long-jawed face like their *dawdy*. The neighbors and aunts and uncles had always pampered Gideon, but it was Friedrich they respected. He wondered if Friedrich had seen his father knock him down. He decided he didn't care.

"You could stay," Friedrich said. "You've always been a good mechanic. You could go into business, open a wheel shop—we can make over the old hay barn, we don't use it so much."

He must have known his words were in vain. His *Deitsch* words. Beneath those words, a note of relief?

Gideon shook his head, sending a rock of pain battering back and forth between his temples. He turned and took one last look at the house where he had found her. Friedrich had not seen their mother lying bloody and defiled on the floor—Gideon had made sure, he'd gone out in the yard and grabbed his younger brother and held him while screaming for someone to come help. When his sisters showed up at a run, he had begged them not to go inside the kitchen, either.

He shook Friedrich's hand off his arm. A hurt look came to Friedrich's face. Gideon had clucked to Maude and ridden out of the farmyard.

★★★

In the jail, he sat staring at the quill in his hand and the sheet of blank paper on his desk. The letters Yost Kepler had received from his family lay in a stack to one side. Surely Kepler had corresponded with his kin, written back to his parents and brothers and sisters. Since the day Gideon left Lancaster County, he hadn't sent a single letter home. His family had no idea where he had gone. They didn't know that he had crossed the Susquehanna, that he had narrowly escaped being robbed and killed in the Seven Mountains. They did not know that he had become a deputy, then a sheriff, a husband and the father of a son.

He should write and at least let them know he was alive. Now, though, he must pen a different letter.

In English, in a plain, straightforward way, he told the Keplers that their son had died from a blow to the head received during what appeared to be a robbery. Yost had been buried in Adamant with proper Christian rites. The expense of coffining and burying him would be deducted from the sixty-two dollars and eighty cents in his bank account, and a draft for the remainder of the money would be sent to them. If the family wished to have a marker put up over the grave, they should inform him, and he would advise as to cost. He wrote that, as sheriff, he would do everything in his power to apprehend and bring to justice the person or persons who had committed this despicable crime.

How to do that? For the moment, he had no better strategy than Alonzo's: Keep talking to people. Keep folks thinking about what they might have seen or heard, don't let them forget what had happened to Yost Kepler down in Hammertown.

He counted the letters he had taken from Kepler's room: an even dozen of them. He would keep them on file, wait to hear back from Kepler's people, then package the letters and return them to the family. He tapped the edges of the sheets against the desktop to square them up. Something caught his eye, scrawled in pencil on the back of the bottom-most letter:

*J Burns*

One of True's brothers—one of the jaybirds? He frowned. Why would Kepler know any of them? He turned the sheet over and read through the letter again. Nothing special, just a message from home telling who in the neighborhood was getting married, how high the corn was, the sow had pigged, Cousin Mary's baby was colicky, that sort of thing. He checked through all of the letters and found no other penciled additions.

Just that one *J Burns* scrawled on the back of a single sheet.

The serving woman at the House of Lords had described the

young man who had drunk with Yost two nights ago as medium-sized, clean-shaven, with a face as plain as buttered bread; talkative, a whoreson who hadn't left a tip. She had never seen him before; he was a complete stranger. Certainly that man had to be his prime suspect. But the woman also mentioned another companion with whom she had seen Yost a couple of weeks earlier. That one was big and ugly, strong looking, with dark hair and a pockmarked face. To Gideon it sounded a lot like True's brother Jesse. He would find Jesse, maybe learn something from him. Maybe—the thought jolted him—Jesse was somehow involved in Kepler's death.

The serving woman had said that Plain as Buttered Bread wore a red vest. The vest had a pattern on it like pickles. What would it look like if you emptied a crock of pickles onto a red tablecloth?

Something nagged at his brain. In the Panther Valley, on the road to True's grandmother's house: the traveler he had met. Talkative. From a town with a strange name—Chinclaclamoose, it sounded like an Indian name—a town Gideon had never visited, a settlement even farther out in the sticks than Adamant. His name: George, George something . . . a country, wasn't it? Yes. George England. The man had lied to him, given false information about where he'd spent the night. True's grandmother had blacked him a scoundrel through and through.

He closed his eyes and tried to put himself back on Maude under that dull and threatening sky. He mentally called up the dun horse the stranger had ridden. It was long-bodied, he remembered that. It looked strong and fit. About fifteen hands. A very good-looking horse. He tried to recall the rest of their conversation. It shouldn't be too hard, it was only the day before yesterday that he laid eyes on the man, even though it seemed to Gideon as if a much longer span of time had passed—could that be because he had ridden so far, and talked so long with True's grandmother, and then spent hours reading intently in the judge's journals of the past? Gideon thought about the dun horse again and the man who looked like he could ride that horse very well. The man was of medium height and weight, clean-shaven, with a dirt-smudged face. The man had sniffed the air and commented on the weather. Said he was riding to Adamant and then asked about jobs in the town. "Safe travels," Gideon had said when their conversation ended, and "I hope you find Adamant to your liking." In his mind's eye, Gideon saw the dun horse step forward, start to go past. The young man had touched his hat brim in salutation. Gideon had seen something else. What was it? He pressed the heel of his hand against his forehead. A red feather stuck in the fellow's hatband? No. Lower down. Peeking out from behind a missing button on the coat. That's what it was: Beneath his overcoat the stranger had been wearing a red vest. If it had a green pattern on it, Gideon hadn't noticed.

If the stranger had assaulted Yost Kepler, then he'd done it on his very first night in town. A night when he knew that the sheriff of Colerain County was miles away in Panther Valley.

He set a new sheet of paper on the desk. When he finished writing, he called to Alonzo. "Please take this to the newspaper and have them print it on some handbills. I think we can afford fifty of them. Get them to add pointing fingers or stars to draw attention. These bills we will post around town—in the hotel, the post office, the freight depot, boardinghouses, livery stables. Put some up in Panther, in that store they have there. Also in the saloons in Hammertown. Especially down in Hammertown."

WANTED FOR QUESTIONING!

IN A CASE INVOLVING *assault* AND *murder*

GEORGE ENGLAND

A MAN IN HIS *twenties*, CLEAN-SHAVEN, OF MEDIUM HEIGHT AND BUILD

MAY BE WEARING A *red vest* WITH A *green design* ON IT

AND RIDING A *dun horse*

STATES THAT HE IS A RESIDENT OF CHINCLACLAMOOSE

REPORT ANY INFORMATION TO:

GIDEON STOLTZ, SHERIFF

*The moment when our lives begin*
*We all begin to die*

# Fifteen

⬦⬦⬦

THE TALL, BROAD-SHOULDERED FIGURE SLIPPED THROUGH THE saloon's rear door a moment after Gideon walked in at the front. Rather than wade through customers, Gideon stepped back out the front entrance and took off running. Three buildings down, he rounded a corner and saw the broad-shouldered man angling across a street.

"Jesse!" he yelled.

The man stopped, looked back over his shoulder, and slowly turned.

"Brother Gideon," Jesse Burns said.

"It's good to see you."

"I didn't think a man of the law would tell such a bald-faced lie," Jesse said. "I know, you've just been itchin' to find your favorite brother-in-law and buy him a drink."

"I could do that."

They went back to the House of Lords and took a table. The clientele on this Saturday night was noisy and rough-looking. Sheriff Payton's stance toward the various tippling establishments in Hammertown had been to largely leave them alone. If they paid their liquor taxes, and if nothing too violent or immoral took place, he paid little heed to what went on down there—the arguments and fisticuffs, the petty thefts, women peddling their favors. But you could not ignore something as vicious as Henry Peebles gouging out an eye and chewing off a thumb—and certainly not a beating that caused a man's death.

Jesse ordered whiskey and a beer. Gideon asked for sweet cider, figuring he shouldn't drink on the job.

"Have you seen the bills we are putting up?" he asked. He pointed at one that Alonzo had tacked to the wall in back.

Jesse tossed down the shot, followed it with a gulp of suds. He wiped the back of his hand across his mouth. "I seen 'em."

"I wonder if you can help us. The man we are looking for sat drinking with Yost Kepler in this tavern on the night when Kepler was beaten and left for dead."

Jesse shrugged lazily.

"Have you heard anything about what happened that night? Have you seen anyone like the man described in the bills?"

Jesse's head went side to side. "All I heard was that the Dutch boy got knocked on the head, poor fellow. I don't know nothin' about the one you think done it."

"Do you know anyone who goes by the name of George England?"

"You don't listen too good, Brother Gideon. I just told you I don't know nothin' about that one."

"I'm told that Yost Kepler came in here to drink now and then. Did you know him?"

"Can't say I did."

Gideon stared into Jesse's eyes. "Are you sure?"

Jesse looked at his beer.

"I think he may have known you," Gideon said.

Jesse glanced off to one side and tipped his mug again.

"Where do you work these days, Jesse? In case I need to talk to you."

"Kind of hard to find me. I ride around scoutin' for timber. The ironworks always needs wood for coaling. The furnace burns through better'n five thousand cords a year and the forge another three thousand. I find the trees, somebody else tracks down the owners and asks if they want to sell."

"You must be all over the county. You must meet a lot of people."
Again the lazy shrug.

"You must turn your charm on many, many folks," Gideon said.
"Why do you think Yost Kepler wrote your name down on a piece
of paper?"

Jesse had been raising his beer mug. It paused for a moment in its
upward arc. As he placed the mug against his mouth and drank, Jesse's
dark eyes searched Gideon's. When he finished, Jesse set the empty
mug down on the table, hard.

"I have no fucking idea," he said. He wiped his hand across his
mouth again and returned Gideon's stare with defiant eyes.

Gideon was footsore and frustrated. He and Alonzo had spent the
day tramping all over town putting up posters and fruitlessly asking if
anybody had seen their suspect, George England. Gideon scowled
back at Jesse. Jesse folded his arms and smirked.

Gideon laid money on the table and left.

★★★

The next day, after church and the noon meal, Gideon went to Judge
Biddle's house. Mrs. Leathers was not there. Gideon had a key and let
himself in. He collected the shotgun in its case, and the judge's journals,
and took them to the jail, locking the shotgun in the closet that served
as an armory. He said hello to Alonzo, who was out back splitting stove-
wood. Then he sat down at his desk and opened the journal for 1805.
He found the page he had been reading when Alonzo summoned him
to come look at the young man found beaten and lying in an alley in
Hammertown. Now Gideon prepared to immerse himself in the world
of a different young man, a man deeply, blissfully in love—and perhaps
as doomed, in his own way, as Yost Kepler had been.

Sept. 16. I have learned that Ad. Thompson courted Rachel
this summer. The Rev. Tolliver told me this, not to shock me,

but, I come to believe, to warn me. At first, I admit, I found the news repellent, for I disdain to tread in any man's footsteps, but the more especially in his. Yet the Rev. T. assured me that the ironmaster did not progress far in his suit before Rachel spurned him, tho' her father was perhaps not displeased that his lovely daughter had caught the ironmaster's eye, Mr. Thompson being a wealthy man & a favorable match for any woman, or so it would appear. The Rev. McEwan was inclined to consider the offer of marriage that the ironmaster tendered, but when he saw how firmly Rachel was set against the match, I am told, & I do believe, he at once deferred to her wishes.

Sept. 19. Again to Panther for Sunday service, again happily accepted an invitation to dine at the parsonage, after which Rachel & I went strolling by the creek. The sumacs are donning their scarlet raiment, foretelling the autumn colors that soon will paint these hills. Rachel picked a bouquet of wild gentians, & I desired to tell her that their blue was but a faded wash compared to the blue of her eyes, but my lips would not form the words. She smiled, as if perceiving what went unexpressed, & placed one of the flowers in my buttonhole. I chose that opportunity to take the fair hand that held the bloom, raise it to my lips, & kiss it.

She blushed, but remov'd not her hand from mine. Never before have I experienced such joy, such unalloyed bliss, as it were a Seraph had condescended to brush her wing against my heart. Upon our return to the parsonage her father spoke jovial to his daughter, noting that her face was flushed—perhaps the day was warmer than it seemed! Rachel smiled and said she would go inside & prepare some Lemonade. After she departed, the Rev., with no small amount of pride, ushered me outside and showed me a barn he is building, to accommodate a cow and horse, the cow for fresh milk & cream, the horse so that he may take his ministry into the hills to reach those who cannot come to church. He wished me to especially note the frame of the barn, whose timbers he had squared himself, & pointed out the mortise & tenon joints, the members pinned together with square pegs driven into round holes—not a nail in the entire structure. A party of men from the church helped him stand the frame up. He has hired a man from the iron plantation to continue the work. However, the Rev. pronounced him a lamentable worker, "lazy, saucy, & profane." This fellow is Nat Thompson, the ironmaster's brother.

Gideon read through more entries describing Hiram Biddle's courtship of Rachel McEwan: "The scenes which have been presented in my life's drama have been full of Joy & Happiness, & more has been crowded into this one little month than has often passed before me in a year." It appeared that the young judge had a hard time getting up his nerve to propose marriage. Gideon recalled how he had barely gotten his own proposal out of his mouth when True flew into his arms, planted a kiss on his lips, and said "Yes, yes, yes!"

Oct. 10. The Most Blessed Day of my life! After church met with the Rev. in his study & rec'd permission to ask Rachel for her hand in marriage. When I knelt before her, without hesitating she replied, "Of course I will marry you." Her father shook my hand & pounded me on the back, gave us his blessing & best wishes for a long & fruitful union.

Oct. 12. (Writ. the morn after) Friends & neighbors filled the parsonage to celebrate our betrothal. The Rev. Tolliver present, having rode over from town with me in my gig, also a number of guests from congregation & iron plantation. Rev. McEwan spoke most movingly of how he was giving to me his most beloved treasure in all the world, & how he knew I would honor her and be kind to her. He quoted from Genesis, saying,

"I have given my maid into thy bosom." I stumbled through some remarks about my Great Good Fortune, & Rachel allowed me to kiss her, which caused the people assembled to huzzah & call out their wishes for long life, good health, &c. The tables groaned with food, but no wine or whiskey in evidence, not even applejack or bounce. My father-in-law (dare I so name him?) is perhaps one of those Stiff & Formal Clergymen that I somewhat fear. I myself believe that Temperance is a glorious affair—if not followed too intemperately. A memorable levee, nonetheless. A fiddle was produced. Rev. McEwan called out "Praise the Lord in the cymbals & dances, praise Him upon the strings & pipes!" & soon people were clapping & dancing. Our jubilee lasted well-nigh till dawn.

*On slipp'ry rocks I see them stand,*
*And fiery billows roll below*

# Sixteen

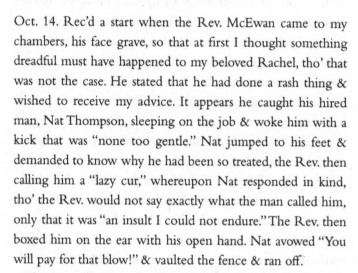

Oct. 14. Rec'd a start when the Rev. McEwan came to my chambers, his face grave, so that at first I thought something dreadful must have happened to my beloved Rachel, tho' that was not the case. He stated that he had done a rash thing & wished to receive my advice. It appears he caught his hired man, Nat Thompson, sleeping on the job & woke him with a kick that was "none too gentle." Nat jumped to his feet & demanded to know why he had been so treated, the Rev. then calling him a "lazy cur," whereupon Nat responded in kind, tho' the Rev. would not say exactly what the man called him, only that it was "an insult I could not endure." The Rev. then boxed him on the ear with his open hand. Nat avowed "You will pay for that blow!" & vaulted the fence & ran off.

The Rev. asked were he in Serious Trouble. I replied that the fellow might well file charges for assault, at which the Rev. blurted out: "No man should have to tolerate what he called me!" Tho't to myself that, when wronged, our Redeemer says we must turn the other cheek, but replied only that if Sheriff Bathgate were to pay him a visit, to tell him exactly what Nat said, & if it were that Disrespectful, the sheriff might not support a charge—tho' I thought such advice somewhat more Hopeful than Assur'd, knowing the sheriff's consideration for the ironmaster & his kin. Strongly advised that the Rev. look for a different man to hire. He thanked me for my time & bade me good day.

Oct. 16. Rachel & a friend of the family, a widow named Mrs. Whitehill, came here, as my beloved wished to look over my house, where we will be domiciled together as husband & wife. Tho' neither large nor grand, the house is ample for a single man, & would be sufficient for a married couple, at least at first. Seeing my wife-to-be somewhat distracted, I took her air to be one of disapproval, & so, opening my heart, told her of my long conceiv'd plan to build a finer residence more suitable of a judge's dignity, for which I have already purchased a large lot near the courthouse. My beloved, however, seemed not to hear, or understand, or, I feared, to share in this dream of our future abode, saying only, rather absently, that my present house would be more than adequate, but if I wished to build a larger one, that would be fine also. At which point I became certain that something was terribly wrong.

When Mrs. W. went off to inspect the kitchen, I took the opportunity to ask my dear Rachel what was troubling her. Admit I was somewhat reliev'd to learn that it was only her father & his Rashness she was fretting over, not any misgivings concerning our selves & our imminent Matrimony. Nat Thompson has come back to work on the barn, & she fears more strife between him & her father. Said Nat was contrite, so the Rev. assigned him to finish shingling the roof, not wanting to go clambering around on the rafters himself. She said she worries how her father will fare, once she has left his household. I understood her to imply that she mollifies her father when his temper gets the upper hand. No doubt her sweetness & good sense have saved him considerable trouble & embarrassment in the past.

Oct. 19. At the parsonage found the Rev. in a black humour. He greeted me briefly, then retired to his study. Rachel made tea, & sat across from me at the table, appearing quite anxious & beside herself. Upon my prompting, she revealed that another row has occurred between her father and Nat. It seems her father rived a great many shingles, & stacked them next to the barn, directing Nat to finish nailing them to the roof, to assure that the frame be got under cover before the heavy rains of autumn commence. When the Rev. went outside several hours later, he found Nat cracking hazelnuts & eating the nutmeats, having done no work at all. He roared at Nat, calling him "good for nothing," & the hired man, ungovernable wretch that he is, answered impudently that he was not a servant to be ordered about—cared not a straw for the preacher or his barn—the old man could Go to the Devil for all he cared. The Rev. M. had gone out of the house carrying a maul, intending to rive more shingles, & R. told me that in his fury he struck Nat with it.

"Dear God!" I said, & expressed fear that the Rev. had injured the man. But Rachel stated that her father said that tho' Nat fell down in a heap, he jumped back up again very spry & shoved past the Rev., who then fell himself, striking his own head against the chopping block. The blow dazed him, but he insists he saw Nat go running off thro' the woods. My beloved now fears that Nat will come back & work some harm—set fire to the church or parsonage. I said I doubted it would come to that, but I would not be surprised if he brings charges for Assault, as striking someone with a deadly weapon is a serious & actionable offense. I told my betrothed in all honesty that I could not possibly shield her father should this matter come before me in court.

Oct. 20. Again to Panther, the Rev. meeting me at the door & asking me in to his study, where he told me essentially, tho' in greater detail, the same story R. related yesterday. My only advice was that he be scrupulously honest about the incident, should he be brought up on charges. He seemed shamed, & agreed that "honesty is the best policy." My reason for visiting had been to bestow upon my beloved the ring my father had given to my mother upon their engagement, a thick gold band beautiful in its simplicity, which I had resized to fit her slender hand. She kissed & thanked me, but much of the luster of the occasion was dull'd, owing to our mutual apprehension regarding the affray between her father & the hired man. Nat not having been seen since, people are saying very publickly that the Rev. killed Nat & hid his body. Would that the knave had never set foot on the parsonage.

Oct. 22. A Flood has washed away all!—the Rev. McEwan's good name & his Freedom!—I can scarce see this page or hold my pen, know not whether it be night or day—

I was in my chambers when horses & waggons arrived in a great hubbub. Sheriff Bathgate & the State's Atty. Mr. Sewell rushed in, & Ad. Thompson, who shouted, "The preacher has killed my brother!" I acknowledged having heard rumours to that effect, but considered them to be no more than idle gossip. I informed the sheriff and Mr. Sewell that I had spoken with the Rev. & he assured me that Nat had gotten up after their scuffle & run off. The ironmaster insisted, quite heatedly, that the Rev. had struck down his brother & Killed Him in Cold Blood. I made to reply, but Sheriff Bathgate cut me off. He stated that witnesses have come forth & he feels he must investigate. He called in to my office two women & a man. The women were Edwina Hendry & her daughter Flora; the sheriff instructed them to tell me exactly what they had told him.

Mrs. Hendry said this past Monday, in the late forenoon, she & her daughter were walking past the parsonage when someone called out to them from behind the hedge. It was Nat Thompson; he parted the shrubbery & invited Flora to share some hazelnuts. He said, "Old McEwan hired me to put a roof on his barn, but I would rather take my ease & eat these filberts." At that moment Mrs. Hendry heard a door slam at the

parsonage. She said Nat rolled his eyes & stated "Now I'll catch
it" & let go of the shrubbery. Mrs. Hendry admitted she could
not see clearly thro' the hedge, but heard the Rev. shouting &
Nat answering back. The Rev. cried out "You will lie dead at
my feet!" Mrs. Hendry said she saw something rise & fall &
heard a heavy dull thump. She and her daughter were scared &
ran away. Flora Hendry confirmed what her mother had said,
adding that, as they hastened away, she looked back over her
shoulder several times but saw no one leave the garden.

I thanked the women for coming forward with that they had
seen. I told the sheriff & Mr. Sewell that the Rev. McEwan had
already informed me of the fight, & that Nat had risen after
receiving the blow & run off into the woods adjoining the
parsonage on the other side. The sheriff then produced his next
witness, one Samuel Lingle, a teamster. Lingle stated that he
had attended a social event, some gentlemen playing cards, on
the next night—not the night of the day when the Hendry
women said they had seen the Rev. & Nat fighting, but the day
after that. Lingle was returning home after midnight, in the
light of the full moon. As he passed the parsonage he heard the
sound of digging &, curious as to why someone would be
working so late, peer'd thro' the hedge. He saw a man in the
garden digging with a spade—a tall man wearing a dark night-
gown & white nightcap. At which point the man in the night-
gown raised his head & appeared to look toward the hedge, so
Lingle quietly let the branches close & went on his way. The
sheriff asked Lingle if he recognized the man digging in the
garden. "I'm pretty sure it was the Reverend," he said.

My heart gave such a lurch, & my knees grew weak. I pushed
aside a feeling of dread, & said that digging in one's garden at
night hardly constituted grounds for an accusation of murder:
Do not farmers work their fields by moonlight & drovers push
their cattle to market? I reminded Ad. Thompson of the

Severity of his charges against the Rev. & advised him to retract them immediately. The ironmaster gave me a cold stare, & repeated his accusation that the Rev. had killed his brother, stating he would not be satisfied until the garden was dug up & we see what is found there. He added, & his words stung me: "Would you stand in the way of Justice, simply because you are engaged to marry the preacher's daughter?"

The sheriff and State's Atty. wished to proceed directly to the parsonage. I rode in the waggon with them and several others, whilst the ironmaster followed on horseback. A drear day, & my tho'ts as Bleak as the Grey Clouds that pressed down upon us. I prayed that the Lord watch over us & keep us from all harm—a most futile wish, as I was soon to find out. I planned to be the first to the door, & prepare the Rev. & my beloved so they would understand that I in no way suspected the Rev. of this Crime. But when we were almost arrived, Thompson spurr'd his horse ahead, charging up to the door just as the Rev. opened it, & cried out that the Rev. had murdered his brother, & the Judge—in that, to my Horror, meaning I, Judge Biddle—had declar'd he would see to it that the Rev. paid for his Crime!

I leap'd from the waggon, remonstrating that "This base Accusation has nothing to do with me!" & further asserting to the Rev. that I was sure he would want the investigation to proceed, so that the vile slandering of his name be stopped. Just then Rachel came to the door, & tho' I told her to fear not, all the color drained from her face. I told her to return inside, saying, "I swear to you"—as I so, in retrospect, wish I had not—"I swear to you that this will all come to naught."

The Rev. professed he had nothing to hide & urged the sheriff to look in the garden, the barn, the house, wheresoever he wished. The sheriff had brought along men & spades. We all trooped around the parsonage & into the garden, to where a patch of earth appear'd to have been newly turned over. Sheriff Bathgate commenced digging, as did his deputies. A light rain fell, pattering on the dead leaves lying on the ground, causing me to shiver and clasp my coat around me; but when, after digging down some little ways, they came upon packed earth— soil that had never been disturbed—I felt my chill lift. I was about to Close these Horrendous Proceedings, when Ad. Thompson took Lingle by the arm & asked where he had seen the Rev. digging. The teamster pointed off to one side. The ironmaster seized a spade from one of the sheriff's men. Pushing aside some branches & clots of dead grass, he commenced to dig.

I turned to the Rev. & apologized for this Great Imposition & explained again how my hands were tied, procedures must be follow'd & Justice done. I assured him that all would be well, & tomorrow this would seem like nothing more than a bad dream. It was then, O Blessed God!, that one of the deputies recoiled and cried out.

I rush'd to where they were digging, the Rev. stumbling forward beside me. His face had taken on a ghastly pallor. As the spades bit into the earth—No! I cannot describe the Horror that seized me at the sight of those chalk-white fingers, an ear filled with dirt, & mud-caked yellow hair! O Holy Savior, shield us from Satan's pow'r! The Rev. sagged, & I took hold of his arm.

The men lifted the body from the ground. The face was black with dirt, yet it could be seen that the nose was broken, crushed almost flat. The scalp was split on the side of the head, & the bone of the skull showed through the dirt encrusted rent. The ironmaster gave out an anguish'd Howl as he knelt and brushed at the muddy clothes. "My dear brother!" he wailed. He pointed out his brother's initials sewn into his shirt. He lifted one of the corpse's hands & scuffed away the dirt, revealing a copper ring. He said that as long as he could remember, his brother had worn such a ring on the last finger of his left hand. He shouted at the Rev., "Look what you have done!"

The Rev. raised his face toward Heaven. He cried out to his God, who knew he had struck Nat down in his Wrath, but—& here he fix'd on me his wide & staring eyes—truly, he swore, "The man was still alive when last I saw him!" At this there came a shriek that near curdl'd my blood, & I turned to see my dear R. bent forward at the waist, her hands covering her face. Would that the Heavens had split open then & a Bolt of Lightning come crashing down to strike all of us dead. I held her, & she fainted away. Her father reached out, took his daughter from my arms, & bore her toward the parsonage.

Sheriff Bathgate waited outside at the door, & the Rev., returning to the threshold, held out his hands. "The Lord will decide my fate," he said. They put him in irons & led him away.

But it is not God who will decide the fate of the Reverend Thomas McEwan. It is I, Judge Hiram Biddle.

*Heav'n, earth and hell draw near,*
*Let all things come*

# Seventeen

⬥

S O ABSORBED WAS GIDEON BY THE ACCOUNT OF THE EXHUMING OF
Nat Thompson that only slowly did he become aware of his
thumb digging painfully into his jaw. In the fading light, sitting at his
desk in the jail, he squinted at the words on the page. Words written
by a hand that had remained surprisingly controlled and legible even
as it recorded a life-shattering event.

To discover that someone you know has killed another human
being. To realize that you must judge, and almost certainly condemn,
the father of the woman you love. Gideon shook his head at the
monstrousness of the situation.

He put the journal in a canvas sack and set it by the door. He
moved about the jail, checking that all was in order. The front room
held a desk, several chairs, and a couch on which Alonzo slept on
those nights when a prisoner was housed in one of the cells—Alonzo
should be here soon with supper for Henry Peebles, a jovial enough
chap, at least when he hadn't been drinking. Opening off of the front
room was the storage closet where Gideon had put the judge's shotgun. He gave the heavy lock a tug to make sure it was secure. Inside
the closet, in addition to firearms, were handcuffs and leg irons—
including restraints that doubtless had been used on the Reverend
Thomas McEwan.

Alonzo arrived. Gideon said goodnight to him and left. Outside,
the sky was gray. Tomorrow would be the first day of November, and
the days were getting markedly shorter. The wind came hunting
down the street, stripping leaves from the trees in town and forest

alike. The land was closing down, tightening in on itself. Soon it would lie drab and lifeless.

At home, he fed Old Nick—which was how he still thought of the dog, despite True's dislike of the name. He sat on the rickety back steps as the dog polished off his meal, then came over for some attention. Gideon rubbed the setter behind his ears, in the sweet spot between his shoulder blades, and on his broad, white-blotched chest. He felt that the dog looked at him in a puzzled way. Could he be longing for his master, whom he would never see again?

Inside, True gave him a sultry smile. "Your dear son is asleep," she said, brushing her lips across his. "If you can manage to be quiet, he might stay that way."

Later, as they lay beneath the quilt, part of him wanted to tell her what he had read in the judge's journal. Another part of him did not want to expose her to the calamity that had befallen Hiram Biddle and had, in the end, perhaps caused him to end his life. He thought, too, of the letter he had sent to the parents of Yost Kepler. He imagined them breaking the wax seal and unfolding the sheet, reading it or getting someone else to read it to them, and the cries of anguish and streams of tears it must cause, the scenes that would invade those poor people's minds as they imagined—as they were incapable of not imagining—the murder of their son. The world would never be the same for them again.

As it had never been the same for him. He peered back in time yet again and saw his mother lying on the kitchen floor. He had gone over in his mind so many times the way she'd been tormented and killed. He wished he could tell Kepler's kin that they were not alone in their misery and their grief.

Someday he would tell True about his mother. And not simply that she'd been raped and murdered, but all that she had been to him. Not just a mother but a friend. She had shielded him, when she could, from his father's anger. She encouraged him to attend to his schooling, to read books and learn English. She had talked to him about grand and important things, like families, and God's love, and the beauty of a winter sunset or a single flower from her garden, and what he could make of himself if he worked hard and lived by God's commandments and tried to become the best person he could be.

He grieved at how the love given him by his mother so often got shoved aside by the fact that she'd been murdered. She would not want to be remembered for that, but rather for how she had loved and lived.

In his letter to the Keplers, Gideon had promised to do all that he could to find the person or persons who had taken their son's life. Yet even if he did track down this George England, or apprehend some other suspect, could he actually link that person to the young man's slaying? Sheriff Payton had said that if a crime was not solved within a few days, if no witnesses came forth, no stolen articles were found, no confession obtained—then the thing might remain a mystery forever. Already five days had passed since the attack on Yost Kepler. And time was racing ahead.

Time. He saw its thoughtless ravages in the rotting logs of a failed homestead, in the mossy stones that lay between fields, piled there by hands that no more would wield a scythe or steer a plow, embrace a wife or comfort a child. Hands that had belonged to a person now gone, perhaps already forgotten, here in a place where settlers had lived for not much longer than sixty years. Even as he felt soaring joy and deep love when he looked upon True and David, he also felt a numbing sadness.

"What are you pondering? You look so sorrowful," True said.

He was unsure how to answer. "I am thinking about how we are punished for loving."

"How is that?"

"We fall in love, with life, with other people, with our kin. We love the land, and galloping on a horse, or singing hymns, or watching the clouds pile up in the sky, we love our dear wives and children—" Tears welled up in his eyes, and he shook his head. "I don't know what I'm talking about."

She laid her hand on his chest.

"We love these things so much," he said, "that we can't bear to think of being parted from them. When we see others torn away from life, by disease, or confusion of the mind, or the cruel actions of others . . ." He stopped, could not go on.

"We must believe on God," True said, "on his plan for us and the everlasting reward that he promises." She caressed Gideon's chest. "Is it the judge? Or the poor boy who was murdered?"

"Both." And his *memmi*. Always his *memmi*. He saw for the thousandth time her ravaged body lying in its own blood. He longed to tell True about her, but he was mute. He could not form words to get past the pain that had vexed him for so long. "I can't be a sheriff," he said.

"Of course you can. You're good at what you do."

"The things I see, they wound me."

"Part of why I love you," she said.

"I muddle along, I daydream, and my thoughts freeze me in place."

"But not too bad, for a dumb Dutchman."

He looked at her mischievous eyes.

Her gaze became serious. "All of those thoughts prepare you for what you must do next." She cupped his cheek in her hand. "Don't let this wear you down. Don't forget how much we have—our life together, our dear child. They are blessings from God. Of course the world can be cruel and sad. Of course we're all born to die. But don't let that take the joy out of those other things."

In time, they rose from the warm bed, put on sleeping gowns and wool stockings. True boiled potatoes and served them with salt pork.

She nursed David while Gideon reread last week's newspaper. This coming week there would be a new paper with new stories in

it, including one about the murder of Yost Kepler. Might he have
solved the crime by then?

He and True returned to bed, taking David with them. True and
David slept. Gideon lay there smelling the clean sweet scent of mother's milk, listening to the quiet breathing of his wife and child. With
every breath, he thought, we are brought closer to death. He closed
his eyes, slowed his own breathing, and tried to imagine himself sinking down into the bed. But he could not sleep.

He got up, went in to the other room, and added wood to the
fire. He wrapped himself in a blanket and drew a chair close to the
hearth. He opened the judge's journal.

Oct. 23. Sick at heart following events of yesterday & today.
The State's Atty. avers he will try the Rev. for Murder in the
First Degree, opening the way to a sentence of Death. I believe
Voluntary Manslaughter is more fitting, or at most Murder in
the 2nd, yet this is Mr. Sewell's decision to make & clearly he
takes into account the alleged purposeful burying of the victim,
& the statement of the Hendry women, who will testify that
they heard the Rev. say to Nat "You will lie dead at my feet!"

This morning the Rev. sent a message asking to see me. I had
to force myself to climb down thro' the trap-door into the
dungeon. The cell was cold & dreary, with its low ceiling of
hewn logs, dirt floor, & stone walls exuding dampness. I found
the Rev. kneeling in prayer. Mercifully the sheriff has removed
his irons, giv'n him candles, a rug, and a cot with warm bedding.
I told him the trial is scheduled to begin in two weeks. He
asked after R., & I told him she scarcely speaks, just stares at the
floor as if she sees nothing. The Rev. groaned, & passed a hand
across his face. "My poor child."

He told me again that he clearly remembers Nat jumping to
his feet & running off after receiving the blow from the maul.
The Rev. himself then tripped & fell and struck his head on

the block. He states that R. found him lying on the ground &
helped him to his feet & in to the house, where she gave him
a tincture & put him to bed. But of this he retains no memory,
nor of anything else between the time his head hit the block &
the afternoon of the following day. He does not even remember
going back out to the barn the next morning &, over R's stren-
uous objections, finishing shingling the roof. He then wondered
aloud whether Nat died somewhere in the woods, & he then
found the corpse, bore it back to the garden, & buried it before
his memory returned.

I pointed out to him the discrepancy in the time. The teamster Saml. Lingle testified that he saw someone digging in the
garden on the night of the day following the fight, & the Rev.
said that his memory had returned by that afternoon. Nor did
I believe he could do something so complicated & not recall it.
To which he replied very glum that he must tell me of some
other matters. He stated that he had always been of "a Wrathful
Nature" & struggled mightily to control his temper for many
years, that endeavor guiding him to the ministry to make
amends for some of the things he had done. Twice he was
expelled from schools for getting into fights in which he badly
hurt another student—fights that he picked, following an argu-
ment or some insult or slight.

A hot temper is one thing, I replied, & the Assault upon Nat
Thompson is a most serious matter. But what he was now
charged with is something premeditated & complex: locating a
dead body, transporting it over some distance, & concealing it
by burying it beneath the ground—all of which actions imply
a Cogent & Calculating Mind.

Here the Rev. sat trembling, staring down at his hands. He
told me that once, while in seminary, he woke in the morning
to find that he had broken his hand in the night. He held out
his right hand for me, & spread its fingers, of which the middle

& ring are visibly crooked; a doctor set them, he said, but they never healed proper. That night he had dreamt that someone was breaking into his room, & struck out with his fist. Believing he had driven the intruder off, he went back to sleep. In fact, he had hit the Door so hard that he broke one of its panels as well as his fingers. Another time, & this only a year ago, he went to bed troubled because he had not returned an Anvil that a member of the congregation had lent him, & which he needed back to shoe his oxen. The next morning at Sunday service the man thanked him for returning the anvil; this puzzled the Rev. greatly, as he believed the anvil was still in the shed attached to the parsonage. He hurried home & found the anvil gone. Next to where it had stood was a sledge. The last he had seen the sledge, it was sitting outside the shed. When they transported the anvil to the parsonage, it had taken both the Rev. and his friend to lift the anvil on to the sledge, which was then drawn to the parsonage by an ox.

His voice breaking, the Rev. stated that he must have got up out of bed, put the anvil on the sledge, & while still asleep dragged this great burthen down the road no less than 3 furlongs to his neighbor's farm. There he set the anvil back on the block where it was kept, dragged the sledge home again, & got back in bed. Of this he remembered nothing! When the congregation found out, they laughed & teased him about being a great strongman & Walking in his Sleep.

The Rev. look'd at me with a panick'd expression on his face. He lowered his face & wept, saying, "It is a terrible guilt that I bear. O Great Jehovah, have Mercy on my Soul!"

*But now I am distressed,*
*And no relief can find . . .*

# Eighteen

⸺∞⸺

Oct. 24. At the service in Panther a deacon spoke briefly, then called for prayers. Some in the congregation asked God to reveal the Truth of what had happened on the grounds of the parsonage. Others beseech'd the Lord Almighty to protect the Rev. from Satan & his Evil Snares. Overall a fatalistic, gloomy atmosphere, with tears streaking many faces. Ad. Thompson was not present, nor my betrothed. As I left the sanctuary, the people looked at me thro' eyes filled with pity and regret, as if they saw not a Judge, but the Man beneath the outer shell—a pitiful man whose heart must verily be torn asunder.

At the parsonage found my love seated in a chair with a quilt across her lap. When I took her in my arms, she began to weep bitterly. After a while she quieted, & I knelt before her & took her hands in mine. She said to me, "Promise me you will protect him. He could not have done this wicked thing." I was wracked with indecision. Should I tell her what her father reveal'd to me yesterday—his past episodes of uncontrollable rage? Surely she must know of his penchant for walking in his sleep. Should I tell her he had all but admitted, to himself & to me, the strong possibility—nay, the likelihood—of his Guilt? I still harbored a hope, albeit faint, & lessening with every hour, that some shred of evidence would appear & exonerate him. Finally I said I was certain the Truth would come out, & that we must accept the Truth whatever it be.

She began to weep again most disconsolate. There seemed nothing more for me to say, other than that her father was being comfortably kept in the gaol, & her brother might arrive at any time, as I had dispatched a rider with a letter to him. It was with a Heavy Heart that I made my way back to Adamant.

There followed two weeks during which the judge made only a few terse, impersonal entries in his diary as he prepared to preside over the trial of the Reverend Thomas McEwan, charged with murder in the first degree for killing Nathaniel Thompson. Gideon could barely make himself continue reading, knowing as he did how all of this would end.

Nov. 10. How Wretched a Man am I, to sit in judgment upon my beloved's father! Would that I could cast off my judicial robes, & never face this or any other legal decision again, & that by so doing the Lord would return my dear Rachel to me, serene and blithe as she was on that day not long ago, when we walked along the Stream, & gathered blue gentians, & I kissed her innocent hand.

But Time revolves on its Wheel, & I remain the Judge of this county, & so will endeavor to set down, in hopes of seeing some way thro' to the end of my task, the events of today.

The Courthouse full to overflowing, with a large crowd standing outside. R. sat behind the bench where her father, shackl'd in irons, was seated. The Rev. McEwan earlier declar'd he would represent himself during trial. This was not a wise course, & I so advised him in private & once again during conference before the trial began, but he refused to be swayed. Further, the Rev. requested that only a judge—I and I alone!—should hear his case, & not a jury.

The State's Atty. has not listed R. as a witness, nor has her father indicated he will call her. It is just as well. Spare her that grim duty, for how could a daughter's testimony, however Truthful, however Exact, hold sway over what we heard today!

The prosecution's first witness was one Micah Carson. He identified himself as "a friend of the deceased" who, on numerous occasions, had accompanied Nat Thompson to Pittsburgh & various other destinations to sell iron. Carson testified that Nat told him about going to work on the Rev. McEwan's barn, & related the incident in which the Rev. kicked Nat when he found him sleeping, called him a "lazy cur," & when Nat objected & answered back, the Rev. "flew off the handle" & boxed him on the ear. Mr. Sewell had the witness make clear this was the first time the Rev. struck Nat, & not the later, more serious Assault. The Rev. did not cross-examine.

The Hendry women both repeated almost verbatim what they said in my chambers on the day the body was found, incl. having heard, on Oct. 17, the day of the assault, the Rev. threaten Nat Thompson's life—"You will lie dead at my feet!"—at which an audible murmur came from the gallery, & R. hung her head. Again the Rev. elected not to cross.

Sam Lingle took the stand. Appeared very uneasy, looking down & shifting in the chair. He stated that on the night of Oct. 18, he had seen in the moonlight a "good-sized man" digging in the parsonage garden with a spade. He testified that the man seemed to be filling in a hole with dirt & tramping it down—which is more than he had described before, at least in my hearing. When prompted by Mr. Sewell, he said, "I am pretty sure it was Rev. McEwan." The accused raised no objection to this clearly speculative statement, nor did he elect to cross.

Sheriff Bathgate then testified that Ad. Thompson had come to him, worried because his brother had failed to return to the ironmaster's residence, where he was domiciled, for two consecutive nights. The sheriff said he had spoken with the

Hendry women & Lingle, & described how the party of deputies, along with Ad. Thompson & myself, went to the parsonage where the corpse was unearth'd from the garden & identified as that of Nat. Thompson. The sheriff then desc'd the wounds on the corpse's face and head. Again no cross by the Rev.

Mr. Sewell called the ironmaster to the stand. Spoke very calm & direct, not obviously venomous, yet with a grim smile playing upon his visage. He describ'd Nat & his nature (painted his brother as an Upright Being, if somewhat Slothful at times, & with a Wild Streak as many a young fellow will have), how he had failed to come home, rumours of his demise at the hands of the Rev., how he had then alerted the sheriff—& so on up to the discovery of the body & subsequent identification of Nat's clothing & ring. After Mr. Sewell finished, & it was time for the Rev. to conduct cross—he simply shook his head. The ironmaster sat there on the witness stand, all smug & self-righteous, his arms crossed over his chest, & I had to remind myself that Ad. Thompson is not on trial here, the law must remain impartial & consider the evidence presented & Nothing Else.

It being the defense's turn to bring witnesses, I turned the trial over to the Rev. I had tho't he might change his mind & call his daughter to testify, at the very least to her father's probity & high character, but perhaps the Rev. wished to shield R. from cross-examination, for he simply stated that he himself would constitute the sole witness for the defense.

Rising unsteadily, he came forward & mounted to the stand. After swearing upon the Bible, he described, in as much detail as he could summon up, the "scuffle"—for such did he call it—between himself & Nat. Then said Most Emphatick that he did not hit Nat so hard that he couldn't leap back up again & run off, which the Rev. saw Nat do in the moment during which he himself fell, before striking his own head against the chopping block. Said he did not know what happened after that, as he was unconscious for some span of time—a few minutes, perhaps somewhat longer, until his daughter reviv'd him. But as to the testimony of Sam Lingle, that on the next night he saw the Rev. digging in the garden—the Rev. declared "Before God Almighty, I have no memory of burying a corpse, either that night or at any other time."

Mr. Sewell can be rather combative with a defendant, but during his cross he treated the Rev. gently. He asked if the accused possessed a long dark robe & white nightcap. The Rev. said he did own such garments. The prosecutor then led the Rev. thro' the events culminating in the fight between himself & Nat, asking him if he said to the deceased, as Mrs. and Miss Hendry had testified hearing, that "You will lie dead at my feet." The Rev. stared down at his lap & nodded. I directed that he answer the question, the witness then saying meekly, "Yes."

An undercurrent of whispers swept thro' the courtroom. My poor beloved began to sob—but could I go & comfort her? I could not. Cries of "Have mercy on a Christian gentleman!" & "He is innocent!" rang out. Such reactions arise from emotion & sympathy toward a respected, beloved figure. With every fiber of my being I wish for the Rev. McEwan to be innocent, but I am a Judge, & cannot be swayed by pity, nor hatred, nor self benefit, but can only look at the facts in any case & judge them as fairly & honestly as I can, with God as my witness.

I brought down the gavel & the uproar subsided. Mr. Sewell had no further questions. It being late, I adjourned till tomorrow.

Now I am alone in my study. These words I have written by the light of two candles. As I sat recording the day's events, trying to bring order to my Agitation, to the Utter Misery in my mind, the candles burned low. Suddenly, at the same moment, both of them guttered out.

A chill ran down Gideon's spine. *True saw this.* When the two of them lay drowsing in bed on the night of the day when he had discovered Hiram Biddle's body, True had envisioned two candles guttering and going out, and two people arguing and in pain. Had she somehow perceived the anguished thoughts that must have gripped the judge's mind as he read this passage in his diary—before he loaded his gun, set it on the table, picked up the poker, and pressed the trigger?

Did she really have second sight? He told himself again that there could not be an unglimpsed world that paralleled the real world in which people lived and breathed.

Shaken and confused, he lowered the judge's journal to his lap. In his mind's eye he imagined a youthful Hiram Biddle penning these words: a young man who seemed to have a wonderful life ahead of him, who had finally found a woman worthy of his love, and she in love with him—only to have his dreams utterly shattered. Then in a blink of an eye, the judge finds himself old and gray, alone in the world, and he sees with piercing clarity how his life has been so bitterly diminished.

Gideon felt his throat close as his own personal hellish vision came again. He fought against that image and pictured his mother alive and happy, saw her warm smile, conjured up her soft words and merry laughter and loving touch. Then her visage darkened and her features twisted. He saw her writhing in agony with each blow of the knife. He heard her screaming in pain as a whirlwind of evil overwhelmed her and carried her away.

He held his face in his hands. He longed for the hot rushing release of weeping. But try as he might, he could not let the tears flow.

*With a hard, deceitful heart*
*And a wretched, wand'ring mind*

# Nineteen

∞

THE FINAL ENTRY IN THE JUDGE'S JOURNAL BORE NO DATE. GIDEON noted that the penmanship had gone slack and imprecise, though the thoughts and observations recorded by Hiram Biddle remained cogent.

It is finished. After court conven'd & almost before the spectators had taken their seats, the Rev. stood & said he wished to make a statement. He turned to the gallery, wherein his daughter sat. He said he had looked into his Soul and found there Anger & Defiance toward God. In his Sinful Pride, he had placed himself above his fellow men, upbraiding them & at times treating them cruelly. The Rev. stated that he had set himself up as a Judge, & now he himself would be judged.

He said that when he went back to his cell yesterday, he reviewed in his mind the attack he had made upon Nat Thompson. He also hearkened back to several incidents in the past when, at night, tho' sound asleep, he got up out of his bed, & walked about, & did things that required dexterity and great strength. Later, he had no memory of those doings.

He said he remembered that on the morning after the night when Sam Lingle saw someone digging in the parsonage garden, he awoke to find his robe on the floor, lying in a heap at the foot of his chair. He always took care to hang it neatly on the back of the chair before going to bed. Calling it "a Sign from Above," he said he could come to but One Conclusion

Only: He must have risen in the night, left the parsonage, gone out searching in the woods, & there found the body of Nat Thompson, the victim of his violent temper. He then carried the corpse to the garden, buried it, covered the spot with grass & branches—did all of those things in his sleep.

A commotion swept thro' the gallery. I saw R. weeping & being held by Mrs. Whitehill; it pierced my own heart to see her bro't so low. The Rev. turned to the people. Standing straight and tall, he thunder'd at them, bade them look upon a man who could recite the Commandments given us by our Lord, yet who had failed to follow those Commandments himself, including the most important one, Thou shalt not kill.

He reaffirmed his belief in the Lord our God, Maker of Heav'n & Earth, & His Son Jesus Christ. A base sinner, he commended his soul unto God. He cried out then, "I plead guilty to the murder of Nat Thompson!"

A man rushed outside shouting the news. Thro' the door came a swelling of voices—cries & wails—a wild lament. The ironmaster sprang to his feet & bellow'd "An eye for an eye!"

I pounded the gavel. I had not expected events to tumble so rapidly to a close. I was not prepared to sentence the Rev., had been considering what a just sentence would be, should a conviction result, & whilst the penal code specifies Death by Hanging for the crime of willful murder, & the Rev. admitted to telling the deceased that he should "lie dead at my feet"—yet I felt the evidence pointed to his having struck the man in a fit of rage rather than in a cold & calculating manner. But all my considerations were for naught.

He turned to me, the father of my beloved, that most unfortunate man, & said forcefully that he did not wish to Languish in prison. He begged me to sentence him then & there. He cried out, "And let the sentence be death!"

Again I let fall the gavel, struck it down again and again, until it dawn'd in my grieving brain that all in the courtroom had fallen silent, & were sitting there watching me, watching my pain'd and futile blows.

As I passed sentence, as the words I spoke made of my heart a stone, the Rev. smiled radiantly, seeming to exult in his doom.

This evening, alone in my chambers, sick at heart & with no desire to eat, or even to rise from my chair, I heard the door open. Rachel came in, a lanthorn in her hand. I confess I had been too much of a Coward to have gone to comfort her after the verdict & sentencing. Now her face was wild; her hair undone. Setting down the light, she took hold of both my hands, kissed them feverishly & press'd them against her bosom. She told me I was sending an Innocent Man to the gallows. I sought to reason with her, telling her that her father had confessed, that he took a man's life with malice aforethought, & concealed the body, a capital offense. "In this the Law is specific," I said. "I have no say in the matter, truly I do not."

I tried to take her in my arms, but she struck my hands aside & drew back, crying out that if I truly loved her, I would go with her now & set him free! She brought out a purse, said the sheriff could be bribed, he would listen to me, he would say the Rev. overpowered him, broke gaol & escaped. I told her that even were the gaol house door flung open & the way clear, her father would not flee, for he knows that what he did was grievously wrong. To redeem himself before God, to expunge this great sin, he is ready to accept his punishment.

I caught hold of her again, & immediately she grew still & looked upon me in such a cold & icy way that I fell silent. She said that I was their last hope, that I and I alone could protect them from the Evil that has come to ensnare them. When I did not reply, she removed herself from my hands. "No," she said, "I see that you will not save us." She took from her finger the ring I had given her & placed it on my desk. Then she turned & walked away.

It is finished

There were no more entries in the book, only blank pages. Staring into the fire, Gideon thought about how True had somehow seen this final, bitter conflict. He thought of what True's grandmother had told him, about the hanging on that long-ago day in Adamant, how the crowd had parted for the preacher and the death cart. He could almost hear the murmur of voices, the squeal of the fife and the beating of the drum. The old oak would have held the last of its withered leaves, through which the wind must have keened. In his mind's eye he saw the cart driven out from under Thomas McEwan, the preacher kicking at the end of the rope, Adonijah Thompson watching with his cruel smile. And he saw Hiram Biddle bowed down with anguish as, in his official capacity, he witnessed Thomas McEwan forfeiting his life.

Gram Burns had said that Rachel and her brother buried their father and were never seen again.

Alonzo had said that people claimed "the judge was never the same, after he sent the reverend to hang."

Hiram Biddle must have gone over this story in his mind again and again as the months and the years flowed past. But why had the judge decided now, with thirty years gone by, that life no longer could be borne? Was it simply the long and finally crushing accretion of grief and guilt? Or had there been something else, some triggering event that pushed him to take that final, irrevocable step?

He thought again of their last hunt together. At its end, the judge calling him "Gideon" and giving him his day's take of game. Of agreeing to go hunting for ducks on the morrow—and then changing his mind.

*He must have known I would find his body*, Gideon thought again, and felt again a flush of resentment that Judge Biddle should have laid this burden on him.

Why didn't he at least leave a letter? Why didn't he explain?

*Remember you are hast'ning on*
*To death's dark gloomy shade*

# Twenty

———∘∞∘———

OLD NICK'S BELL WENT SILENT. GIDEON CLOSED IN. HE SPIED THE dog, crouched and quivering. He heard the grouse's querulous *pert-pert* call and the thunder of its wings, which, even though he was expecting it, still made his heart jump. The bird came thrashing out of the thicket in swift flight. The judge's shotgun leaped to Gideon's shoulder. The swarm of shot stopped the grouse in midair like a huge invisible hand.

Gideon called "Fetch!" and the setter broke point, dashed ahead, and picked up the fallen grouse. He came padding back, wagging his tail. Gently he laid the bird in Gideon's hand.

Gideon pouched the grouse and set about reloading. As he worked with powder and shot, he stared out into the brush, hoping he might see, for just a moment, an erect, sober-faced, gray-haired man.

But he was alone. He was using the judge's dog and gun. He felt that in a small measure he was carrying something forward, something that went beyond simply enjoying sport or procuring game. It was a way of letting the land seep inside him, work its magic on his soul. A way of honoring his friend.

And he was taking a rest. The investigation into Yost Kepler's murder had stalled; a week had rushed past since the young man was found unconscious in that stinking alley. Yesterday, Monday, Gideon and Alonzo had again walked all over town, going door to door, questioning everyone they met—and learning nothing. This morning Gideon told Alonzo to stay at the jail in case anyone came in

157

with information on the whereabouts of George England, or reported having seen or remembered something from the night when Kepler was attacked. But Gideon held little hope that this would happen. So he toted the judge's gun and game pouch to the livery, with Old Nick whining and tail-wagging along beside him. He hitched the gelding Jack to the judge's shooting brake and drove out of Adamant into the cutover lands.

He hunted the creek bottom through brushy second-growth woods where only a few remaining leaves twinkled gold and red on the tree branches. Old Nick pointed two more grouse. Gideon missed one and killed the other. He didn't see any woodcock; maybe the flights were ended, though it was only the second day of November. Finally he called Old Nick in. He sat down against a tree, and Old Nick lay next to him. Gideon put his hand on the dog's back, and the red setter thumped his tail against Gideon's leg.

His sleep had been troubled the night before. In a dream, Old Nick had turned on him. A huge wolfish creature, he came snarling and slashing with his teeth. Gideon fended off the attack, the bites searing his hands, blood spurting from the wounds. He kept pushing Old Nick away only to have the beast surge forward and slash him again. He felt himself weakening as the dog pressed home its attack, tried to break through his defenses and tear out his throat. With the last of his strength Gideon seized each of the dog's jaws in his hands and, with a loud cry, wrenched them apart and tore the head asunder. The judge appeared then and placed his hand on Gideon's shoulder. Beneath a yellow moon they took up spades and buried the dead dog. Tipping dirt into the hole, Gideon saw that it was not Old Nick in the grave but his *memmi*.

He had jerked awake, gasping and soaked with sweat. True had been shaking him by the arm. "Gideon, Gideon, it's all right."

He breathed in the cold clean autumn air and leaned back against the tree. Its rough bark poked him through his shirt in a reassuring way. He closed his eyes and napped for a while. When he woke and stood up, Old Nick roused himself as well, stretching out his lanky front legs, his back legs one and then the other, and giving a little whine.

True had continued to press him to give the dog a new name, since Old Nick was what some people called Satan so as not to have to speak the Evil One's name. Gideon had no idea why Judge Biddle should have bestowed such a baleful moniker on this good-natured setter.

"Maybe she's right and we should change your name, *hund*," Gideon said to the dog. He slipped the judge's shooting bag over his shoulder and picked up his friend's gun. It was already past noon; time to return to town and act like a sheriff again.

"Come on, Dick." Gideon clucked his tongue, and the setter heeled beside him.

As they neared the wagon, Jack neighed a greeting. Gideon took off the gelding's nosebag and put it into the wagon's bed along with the shotgun and the shooting bag. He motioned with his hand, and the dog—Old Nick, Old Dick, what did it matter?—jumped up there. The setter sat and regarded Gideon, his tail whisking back and forth. Gideon took one floppy feathered ear in each hand. No slavering jaws gaped, no fangs came slashing. The setter appeared to grin. He licked his new master on the chin.

★★★

The sour-faced woman inched through the doorway as if the prospect of entering a jail filled her with dread. Gideon rose from his chair. "Hello, Mrs. Leathers," he said. He had been on the verge of going home. The day was almost ended: another day with no progress made toward finding the man who called himself George England, the man who wore the fancy red vest. Gideon offered to take Mrs.

Leathers's coat, but she shook her head. He arranged a chair, held her elbow as she lowered herself into it. He drew up his own chair and sat.

The judge's housekeeper tilted her head forward and peered down the passageway to the cells. People were always interested in the cells, Gideon had noted. No doubt they wondered what it would be like to be confined there, looking out at the world from behind bars.

Mrs. Leathers returned her gaze to him. "I got to thinking about something that happened a day or so before the judge did himself in. It probably don't mean nothing."

"Go on," Gideon said.

"Remember I told you a tramp came to the house? Knocked on the side door like they will, and asked for food?" She tucked her skirts about her legs. "The judge was in the dining room, and he heard the knock. He came in to the kitchen, opened the door, and invited the tramp inside. Told me to feed him and put some provisions together for him to take along.

"After the old tramp finished eating, and while I was fixing him a bundle for the road, the tramp asked the judge if they could talk. They went in to the judge's study."

"Did Judge Biddle know the man?"

"I don't think so."

"What did this old tramp look like?"

"His face was brown and weathered, dark as a walnut hull. His beard was white. His eyes were pale blue. I remember how pale they looked against his face."

"How big was he?"

"Not very tall. Thin, and bent over. Walked with a limp. He had a stick that he leaned on, which I told him to leave it in the kitchen before he went in to the study. Made him take his boots off, too, I wasn't about to have him tracking dirt all over my clean floors."

"What were his clothes like?"

"Old duds, with rips and tears. His boots were cracked and had holes in 'em. His hat was dark brown. Low crown with a broad brim, wavy, like it had been rained on a good many times. And with a buck tail."

"A buck tail?"

"You know, pinned to it, like hunters will sometimes wear. Tail off of a deer. White, 'bout a foot long, dangling down off the brim in back."

Gideon had never seen a hat decorated like that.

"When I had the bundle of food ready, I went down the hall. I stood outside the door for a bit, so as not to interrupt in the middle of a conversation." Mrs. Leathers's hand went to her collar; her fingers smoothed the fabric. "I weren't eavesdropping," she said. "That ain't my way."

"Of course not. What did you hear?"

"It weren't what I heard, so much as what I *didn't* hear. There was no one talking in that room. Scared me, so it did. I wondered if the old tramp had attacked the judge, knocked him out. I rapped at the door. After a bit, the judge opened it. I said the food was ready, and the old beggar followed me down the hallway. In the kitchen he put his boots back on, and that silly hat, and took the sack of food. He picked up his staff, winked at me, and left." She sniffed. "Didn't even thank me for my pains."

"Anything else?"

"I stayed in the kitchen cleaning up. When I went to say good-night to the judge, he was just sitting in his chair."

"Did he say anything to you?"

"No, he didn't. And he didn't get up. Which that was a bit odd, because the judge always saw me to the door and wished me a good evening. He was a polite man, a gentleman. Many today are not polite. They are rude and profane. They never bother to thank you even when you do something for them."

"Let me get this correct," Gideon said. "This was one day, or maybe two days, before the judge shot himself?"

"Yes. Because the judge didn't have his hunting clothes on, which he did on the night that he . . ." She frowned. "It was the evening before the day when you and him went hunting. I remember now, I had just brushed out his green waistcoat and trousers and hung them on the wardrobe in his bed chamber, so they'd be ready for him to put on come morning."

"Did the tramp say anything to you, Mrs. Leathers? His name, where he was from or where he was going?"

"Nary a word. Didn't thank me. Just winked at me." She scowled. "Winked at me, saucy-like, and then he left."

*I'm a long time travelin' here below,*
*I'm a long time travelin' away from home . . .*

# Twenty-One

⟨∗⟩

GIDEON SEARCHED THE WALL FOR THE HANDBILL ALONZO SAID HE had posted. It wasn't there. Gideon had brought several extra bills with him, and he found a place to tack one up amid the hand-lettered signs for rooms to let, horses for sale, social events, tinkers' and carpenters' services.

In the Panther Emporium were shelves with jars of hard candy and patent medicines in bottles of various colors and sizes and shapes. Bolts of cloth sat on other shelves. On the floor slumped an opened bag of coffee beans, along with sewn-shut sacks of cornmeal and flour. Smells of leather and sharp cheese tickled Gideon's nose as he approached the store's counter.

The man who stood behind the counter had a fleshy face whose features seemed to have been tugged in different directions. A bulbous nose angled to one side; a thick-lipped mouth dipped toward the man's chin. The eyes slanted down at each corner, and one seemed slightly larger than the other and situated lower in the face. The storekeeper's ears were huge, with fleshy dangling lobes. Gideon realized he was staring, with no small amount of fascination, at a face that would certainly be remembered—would never be described as "plain as buttered bread."

The storekeeper frowned. "Who in the Sam Hill do you think you are," he said, "marching in here and putting up your bill like you own the place?"

"I am Gideon Stoltz, the county sheriff."

"The Dutch Sheriff, eh?" The storekeeper inspected Gideon for a long moment. "You don't look like no sheriff to me. Do you even shave yet? And where's your badge?"

Gideon pointed at the badge worn very obviously on his coat.

The storekeeper scoffed. "Anybody can pin a hunk of pot metal on his chest and claim to be the law."

Gideon placed one of the handbills on the counter in front of the man.

The storekeeper used his forearm to shove it off onto the floor.

Gideon bent and picked it up. He set it on the counter again, reached out, and took hold of the storekeeper by one pendulous ear. He pulled the man's head down until his face was six inches from the bill.

"God damn . . . !" the storekeeper said in a whining tone.

"Read the handbill," Gideon said. "If you please."

"All right, let go my ear!"

"Read it."

The storekeeper's eyes bulged as he read. "All right, I read it. Now let go, will you?"

Gideon released the man's ear.

The storekeeper straightened and rubbed his ear. "You didn't have to do that," he said.

"The bill does not the best description provide," Gideon said, "but I wonder if you have seen anyone who might answer to it."

The storekeeper kept rubbing his ear. He stared at Gideon, the look on his face a mix of resentment and apprehension. His eyes shifted down to the paper again. "Your man," he said, "what's his eye color?"

"I don't know."

"Long or short hair?"

Gideon shrugged. The stranger had been wearing a hat when he'd encountered him in Panther Valley, and Gideon hadn't noticed anything about his hair. He realized that he had not asked this very obvious question of the woman who had served the suspect while he sat and plied Yost Kepler with whiskey at the House of Lords.

"What color hair?" the storekeeper asked.

Gideon had no answer to that question, either.

The storekeeper sniffed. "Well, Mister Sheriff, your handbill could describe, oh, about ten hundred gents."

Gideon felt properly deflated.

"The vest your man had on? Red with a green decoration? I sell one like that. Red cotton with a green paisley pattern." The storekeeper opened a drawer, reached down, and set a neatly folded vest on the counter. "Got five of 'em left."

"Did you sell one to a young fellow with a dun horse?"

"Don't recall that."

"How many have you sold?" Gideon asked.

"I ordered a dozen before last Christmas. From J. B. Harper Clothiers of Philadelphia. That paisley is the latest thing. A stylish and well-made vest. These are what's left. You want one, I'll give you a good price."

So. Apparently at least seven men on the ironworks or in the nearby countryside might own such a vest. Gideon decided to open up another line of inquiry. "Have any strangers come in here lately?"

The storekeeper breathed out audibly. "Well, of course they have. Strangers come in here all the time. I bet you a baker's dozen of men I have never seen before set foot in here every month."

"The ones who get hired at the ironworks—where do they live?"

"In the boardinghouse, or with families, or in the logging and coaling camps. You're not talking about real permanent residents. A lot of 'em stick with a job of work for a couple months, get a stake together, and move on."

The shop's door opened and a woman came in; Gideon glimpsed her out of the corner of his eye. The woman hung back, apparently waiting for him to finish his business.

"I am also looking for a different man, an old man," Gideon said to the storekeeper. "His clothes are ragged and torn. He has a white beard and pale blue eyes, and a face lined and darkened by the sun.

He walks with a limp and carries a staff. And he wears a hat with a white buck tail pinned to it."

The storekeeper shook his head. "Sorry, but I can't help you. Nobody like that has been here. I'd surely remember if they had."

"All right. That bill I posted, I want it to stay on your wall and not get taken down or covered up. I am investigating the murder that happened in Adamant last week, and I want people here in Panther to be on the lookout for this man, who is a suspect in the killing. Also, if you or anybody else sees an old tramp with a buck tail hat, I want to know about it as soon as possible."

When Gideon turned to leave, he saw that it was True's mother who had entered the store behind him. Before he could greet her, she gave him a slight nod and flicked her head toward the door. He took it to mean that he should wait for her outside.

A few minutes later, she came through the door carrying a package. She placed her hand on Gideon's arm and steered him off to the side. They stood beneath a tree. She set the package down, looked around, then said, "I don't know if I should be telling you this, but an old man like that showed up at the big house a couple of weeks ago. He had a beat-up hat with a buck tail dangling down off the brim, like I heard you tell the storekeeper. Why are you looking for him?"

"I'm not really sure," Gideon replied. "An old man like that came and talked to Judge Biddle just before the judge killed himself. I wonder if there could be some connection."

"That old man was an odd duck," Mrs. Burns said. "He didn't knock or ring the bell, just opened the front door and waltzed right in. I was in the kitchen and heard him. He had a hunk of rat cheese in his hand, and he was nibbling on it; they sell cheese like that here at the store. The old man asked, 'Is Ad here?' Now why should an old jasper like that call the ironmaster by his nickname? Mrs. Glenny came in to the hallway then, she's the head housekeeper, so I told the old man he should talk to her." Mrs. Burns paused. "I was fixing the evening meal, it was a big roast beef, so I went back to work. I recall hearing something the old man said. He told Mrs. Glenny, 'Well, go fetch him.'"

"Meaning the ironmaster?" Gideon said.

"I suppose so, but I don't know for certain. Mrs. Glenny must have put the old man somewhere, maybe in Mr. Thompson's study, because I didn't see him again. Later she came in to the kitchen and told me I could go home for the evening. She said she'd finish making the meal and serve it herself."

"Does that happen often—you getting sent home and the housekeeper serving the meal?"

"No. It never happened before. Come to think of it, she sent the other girl home, too. When I came back the next morning, the old man was gone. I asked Mrs. Glenny about him, and she said it was nothing, I should just put it out of my mind." Gideon's mother-in-law shrugged. "So I did. Until I heard you in there, asking about an old man with a buck tail hat."

Gideon thanked her for the information.

She nodded, worry creasing her face. "Another thing. I can't swear to this, but a couple days later I might've seen that old man again. It was late, after dusk. I was leaving the big house, headed for home. And I saw, well, I saw this pale thing among the trees not far from the house. It might have been that old man, might've been that buck tail hanging from his hat. Or it might have been the tail of a real deer. Or something else. It kind of frightened me. I hurried on home, didn't see anything else. Gideon . . ." She looked him in the eye. "Might be best if you didn't let on to anyone that I told you this."

"Why is that?"

"I just wonder whether I could get in trouble, maybe lose my job for telling you something I wasn't supposed to."

"Don't worry. I won't say who told me."

\*\*\*

He left Maude tied in front of the store. The rail, which horses had stood before for decades, was almost chewed through in places.

He went to the boardinghouse, where the proprietor, a middle-aged woman, said she had seen neither a young man with a red vest nor an old man with a buck tail on his hat.

He continued along on the blue slag road. He smelled hay and manure from the stock barn, the fruity smoke from the iron furnace and the finery forge. The trip-hammer in the forge pounded deep and dull, like a giant's pulse. He stepped off the road for a team pulling a wagonload of charcoal. The teamster, striding along beside the six-mule hitch, cracked a long black whip above the mules' backs.

At the communal well Gideon winched up a bucketful of water. A dipper hung from a nail driven into one of the posts supporting the roof over the well. He rinsed the film of ash out of the dipper's bowl, plunged it into the bucket, and brought it up brimful. As he drank, he observed that his hand was shaking.

The coal wagon stopped near the furnace. The teamster hallooed, his voice carrying over the roar of the blast and the thumping of the blowing tubs. The teamster unhitched the lead pair of mules, led the mules around to the back of the wagon, backed them up, and attached the doubletree to hooks made out of old muleshoes projecting from planks beneath the load. The mules walked forward and drew the planks out, dumping the charcoal on the ground. The falling charcoal made a tinkling sound like broken glass. The teamster freed the planks and replaced them in the wagon. He hitched the mules back in front, and drove the empty wagon away. Workers began spreading out the lumps of charcoal. Other workers forked up charcoal from earlier wagon loads, dumped it into baskets, then lifted the baskets onto their shoulders and trudged up the ramp to the coal shed.

Gideon didn't see anyone who resembled the young man calling himself George England. He didn't see an old man with a buck tail hat.

He resumed walking.

The porch of the big house was neatly swept. He twisted an

ornate brass knob on the door, which caused a strident jangling within. The girl who answered wore a cream-colored smock over a blue dress. She was slim, with a budding figure. Her reddish-blonde hair was parted in the center and pulled back from a pretty face. Freckles dappled her cheeks and nose. She gave him a shy smile, and the little brown spots seemed to dance. Her welcoming expression made Gideon consider what True might have looked like when she was fifteen. Then he wondered with a cold distaste if the ironmaster had forced himself on this young woman.

"Miss," he said, "I am Gideon Stoltz, the county sheriff."

The girl's face brightened. "Then we're relations. You are husband to my cousin, True Burns."

"Yes, I am married to True. Well, I guess we are related then. I was just wondering, is Mr. Thompson at home?"

"He's at his office." The girl stepped onto the porch and pointed back the way Gideon had come.

Gideon nodded. "I left my mare tied up at the company store. Guess I'll have to walk back there again."

The girl's smile broadened, showing even white teeth. She was really very pretty. "I suppose you could set on that glider for a spell, or on the steps, if you cared to rest."

"Thank you," he replied. "That's a kind offer. May I ask your name?"

"Ginny. I mean Virginia. Virginia Ross, sir."

"Miss Ross, do you live in the house here?"

"I work here days. Nights, I go home. We live on the ironworks."

"Can you tell me, about two weeks ago, did an old man show up here? An old white-haired man with a weathered face? As old as your grandpap, maybe even older. Wearing beat-up clothes, with a walking stick and a pack on his back. His hat has a deer's tail pinned to it."

She gave him that radiant smile again. "Yes, he . . ."

"*Virginia.*" A tall, thick-waisted woman stood in the doorway.

"Yes, Mrs. Glenny?"

"I will take care of this gentleman. You can go back to work."

As the young woman withdrew, Gideon introduced himself.

"Pleased to meet you, Sheriff," the tall woman replied. "Drusilla Glenny. I have charge of the household here."

"May I ask you a few questions?"

"We are rather occupied today," the woman said.

"It should only take a few minutes."

The woman had a doubtful look on her face. Before she could say no again, Gideon stepped past her.

In the foyer a wide staircase commenced between a pair of carved newel posts. The newels, volutes, handrail, and balusters were of black walnut, polished to a high sheen.

"Please come with me," Mrs. Glenny said, pushing past Gideon.

Pier glass panels lining the foyer threw Gideon's reflection back and forth as he followed the tall woman down a hallway and into the kitchen at the rear of the house.

She made him stand waiting as she cleared some dishes from a table and put them in the sink. Wiping her hands on her apron, she turned toward him. "What is it you want to ask?"

In a casual tone, Gideon explained that he was looking for an old man, and went on to describe him—the pale blue eyes, the deeply tanned face, white beard, staff and pack, a pronounced limp, and the decorative white tail of a deer attached to his hat.

"Two weeks ago, you say." Mrs. Glenny chewed on her lower lip. "We do get tramps coming by now and then. We feed them here in the kitchen. But I can't say I've seen one like that."

"Miss Ross seems to remember the man. May I speak with her again?"

Mrs. Glenny cocked her head. "Let me think. You know, I believe I do recall an old tramp like that happening by."

"I wonder if this man may have lived here, in the ironmaster's house, some time in the past."

"That's quite unlikely. Tell me, sheriff, has this tramp caused any trouble? Is that why you're looking for him?"

Gideon thought quickly. "He asked for food at a house in Adamant, and afterward some silverware was missing."

"Well, nothing has gone missing here. I would certainly know it if something had been taken."

"Can you tell me anything about the old man? Anything he said?"

"Quite honestly, I do not remember much about him. As I recall, we gave him a meal. He was properly grateful. After that, he left."

"Did he mention his name?"

"No."

"Or where he was going?"

She shook her head.

"Did he ever come back?"

She looked at him sharply for the briefest moment, then replied: "No. I imagine he is long gone from here."

Gideon could tell that this cautious, close-mouthed woman would give him nothing of value. He did not want to alarm her, make her think he suspected who, against all odds, the old man might be. He nodded politely, thanked the housekeeper for her time, and did not allow himself to feel slighted when she let him out the back door.

***

The furnace bell clanged, calling workers to tap the crucible and cast the iron.

Standing off to one side, Gideon watched as they came jogging from all directions. Tall men and short, thick and thin—mostly thin, as the ironworkers seemed on the whole to be a gaunt and sinewy lot. He did not see a red vest, although it seemed unlikely that anyone would wear such a dressy item to labor in. Nor did he see a face like the one belonging to the talkative young man he had met on the road near Gram Burns's cabin. Some older men showed up, but the only one with a limp was Bet Craigie's husband, the old cockerel who had jawed at him about the Dutch taking over the state's government on the Sunday when he, True, and David had come to Panther to visit True's family.

★★★

Riding back to Adamant, he kept Maude at a quick amble—there was the Wednesday night sing at church this evening, and he knew True wouldn't want to miss it. He hadn't found George England at Panther. But perhaps he had discovered something of great and terrible significance.

*I'm a long time travelin' here below*
*To lay this body down*

# Twenty-Two

～∞～

FAW AND SOL AND LAW NOTES FLEW THROUGH THE AIR BEFORE THE voices launched into the quick staccato words:

> *Farewell, vain world! I'm going home!*
> *My Savior smiles and bids me come,*
> *And I don't care to stay here long!*

Gideon put his all into the singing. The music enraptured him, uplifted him.

> *I'm glad that I am born to die,*
> *From grief and woe my soul shall fly,*
> *And I don't care to stay here long!*

His soul took wing, his spirit rose higher and higher, seeming to untether itself from the griefs and cares of the world. It flew up and up, and a soft light shone all around him, a light that grew steadily more beauteous and peaceful, and he was with his mother at last, she was smiling at him, and all would be well, all would be well.

The song ended and the leader called out a different number in the tunebook, for a hymn called "Holy Manna," whose poetry, as Gideon sang it, seemed to reach between his ribs and wrap cold fingers around his heart:

> *Brethren, see poor sinners 'round you,*
> *Trembling on the brink of woe;*
> *Death is coming, Hell is moving,*
> *Can you bear to let them go?*

He couldn't bear to let her go. He had never been able to let her go. He felt again the familiar tension flow and harden across his shoulders like a stream freezing up in a midwinter cold snap. His voice cracked, he stopped singing. He almost dropped the tunebook. He saw his *memmi* again, her broken body and her twisted lifeless face, the vision that had lived inside him for years like some loathsome disease that could flare up and lay him low at any moment.

> *See our fathers, see our mothers,*
> *And our children sinking down;*
> *Brethren, pray and holy manna*
> *Will be showered all around.*

He looked at the rapt faces, the congregation whose members he didn't really know. Had they taken him in? The outsider elevated above them?

> *Is there here a trembling jailer,*
> *Seeking grace, and filled with fears?*
> *Is there here a weeping Mary,*
> *Pouring forth a flood of tears?*

He was the trembling jailer, the sheriff who had no business being a sheriff, the man stumbling about looking for answers to questions he barely knew enough to ask. All the troubling things he'd learned that day at the ironworks came flooding back. He thought of Hiram Biddle driven to kill himself just a day after the mysterious stranger, the old tramp, came to his door. He thought of the tramp walking into the ironmaster's mansion like it was his own home. He thought of the ironmaster, cruel and powerful and dangerous.

He stopped singing and sat there, trying to decide what to do next.

★★★

At home, after nursing David and putting him in his cradle, True came over to where Gideon stood in front of the fire.

She wrapped her arms around him from behind, kissing him on the back of the neck. "All right, what is it? What are you keeping from me?"

He turned to face her. "I rode to Panther today. In the company store I put up one of the bills about the man who is a suspect in the murder of Yost Kepler, the man I met on the road to your grandmother's house. The fellow who runs the store—"

True laughed out loud. "Mr. Briggs. What a face! Like an ape's. We used to go in there when we were little just to look at him. He'd bug his eyes out and jabber like a monkey to run us off."

"His face *is* very memorable. Though I thought he looked more like a dog than an ape—maybe a hound, with those big droopy ears." He took a breath. "Your Mr. Briggs was no help at all. But I did learn from someone else—well, I guess I can tell you who, it was your mother. She told me that an old white-haired tramp came barging into Mr. Thompson's house about two weeks ago. It appears that the same old man may have gone to see Judge Biddle, perhaps the next day, just before the judge killed himself.

"You know that I have been reading the judge's journals from the year when Nat Thompson was murdered," he continued, "and when the preacher Thomas McEwan was tried and convicted and then hanged for killing Nat. With Judge Biddle passing sentence." He took a deep breath. "True, I will tell you what I fear: Nat Thompson has come back."

True gasped. "It's his shade," she blurted.

"No. This was a flesh-and-blood man who went first to the iron-master's mansion and then, I think, went on to the judge's house."

True's voice was awed and tremulous. "It's a spirit, a wandering, troubled soul."

Suddenly David started crying.

Gideon said, "I am telling you that a man has shown up in Colerain County, apparently after having been away from here for thirty years. If this really is Nat Thompson, then he was never murdered, and a terrible miscarriage of justice took place in 1805." Putting the idea into words caused the force of what might have happened to finally hit him.

"No," True said, "this is a haunt, a spirit that will not rest easy in the grave. Nat Thompson was killed and buried, and his bones lie under the ground."

She went in to the bedroom and fetched David, now bawling.

"Everyone has long believed that Nat Thompson lies dead and buried," Gideon said when she came back. "But I wonder if that's really the truth."

True sat down in a chair and began rocking David. The child would not quiet. "If the old man is not a shade," she said, her voice catching in her throat, "if he really *is* Nat Thompson, then the iron-master has something wicked to hide."

"Yes."

"Do not cross him," she said.

"I have to investigate."

She looked away from Gideon and rocked David faster. "Adonijah Thompson goes to church every Sunday. He appears to be a respectable man. But he is evil through and through."

"Tell me."

"He does not believe that God's commandments or man's laws apply to him."

Instantly Gideon wanted to know whether the ironmaster had ever forced himself on her. "Did he do something to you?"

"The life I lived at the ironworks . . ." The firelight danced on True's face. Her eyes were opened wide, her breathing rapid. "Why would you ask me that?"

Gideon had never seen his wife look so upset. "Your grandmother told me that the ironmaster once laid hands on her. She fought him off. It seems he has a reputation for taking advantage of the girls and women who work for him."

"Am I not a good wife to you?"

"You are my dear and precious wife. You are everything to me."

"Do you not love and respect me, as a husband should?"

"Of course I love and respect you. But the ironmaster, you say he does not follow God's commandments, that he thinks he is above man's laws. I feel I need to know . . ."

"You need to know *nothing*." She opened her blouse and put David to her breast. The child stopped fussing and began to nurse. "Gideon, please, leave that man alone."

He knew he should break off this line of conversation. If he took the lid off this pot, everything could boil over and be ruined. But he couldn't ignore his duty. He touched True's cheek and gently turned her face toward his. "I love you, True. You're the best woman I could have married. But when I became sheriff, I took an oath to uphold the laws of the commonwealth. And I owe it to Judge Biddle to try to find out what may have happened here thirty years ago. Maybe we've been visited by a crazy old man. Maybe he's some kind of a sharp or blackmailer." He paused. "Maybe he really is Nat Thompson."

True held David tight. She resumed rocking him forward and back, forward and back. David clutched at his mother's breast and made discomfited mewling sounds. "It's Nat Thompson's shade," she exclaimed, "his unquiet spirit that will not keep to the grave."

Gideon shook his head.

"Swear to me you will not go to the ironworks again," she said.

"You're being ridiculous."

"Consider my wishes, for once!"

"I do consider your wishes," he snapped. "All the time. But I have a job to do."

"At least think of this baby." She rocked David faster. "Would you leave him fatherless?"

Gideon waved his hand. "If the old man is, as you put it, a shade—a *shpook*, as an ignorant Dutchman would say—then why would he do me any harm?"

"I'm not feared of Nat Thompson's shade, which you should not make light of, in any case. And you shouldn't mock me. Ignorant! You're the ignorant one. There are all sorts of things you don't understand."

"Then enlighten me, wife."

She glared at him.

"Of course there are things I don't understand," he said. "There are many things I don't understand." *I don't understand you*, he thought. He let out an exasperated sigh. He got up, went to the door, and grabbed his coat off the peg.

David lost the nipple. He began to wail. True pressed the child against her breast. She jumped up out of the chair. Clutching the howling child, she followed Gideon to the door.

"Gideon, please!" she said. "Leave the ironmaster be!"

*I am a stranger here below,*
*And what I am is hard to know*

# Twenty-Three

—∞—

HIS BOOTS RANG AGAINST THE GROUND AND HIS BREATH PLUMED white in the darkness as he climbed the hill.

Slowly the jagged edges of his anger dulled. He had expected True to be intrigued and excited about what he'd found out. Instead she'd been upset, irrational, asked him to shun his responsibilities and turn away from the whole situation. He found that ridiculous and unreasonable but still wished they hadn't argued. And he must not press her for details about her time in Adonijah Thompson's house. It might offend him to think about the ironmaster molesting her, but his own sense of outrage must be as nothing compared to how she might feel. This evening he had seen a precariousness in his wife that he had never known existed. Perhaps she had buried something from her past, perhaps not. He must not pry. He must try to be more sensitive to her feelings.

But the thing he would not do was to shirk his duty as sheriff. He would not walk away from the suicide of Hiram Biddle and the hanging of Thomas McEwan if any heretofore uncovered criminal acts could have triggered those events, even though they happened thirty years in the past.

At the top of Academy Hill he stood in the frost-stiff grass and looked out over Adamant. The pale limestone school building reared up behind him. Below, in the town, lights glowed faintly from a few windows, but more light by far came down from the starry sky. Burying Hill loomed large across the way. Far off, through the gap in the hills penetrated by the creek, bloomed a red glow: the furnace at the ironworks, its fiery heart reflected from the smoke above it.

"D'you see it?"

Gideon almost jumped out of his skin. A figure rose from behind shrubbery a few feet away.

"Low in the east, in the neck of Cetus." A shadowy arm pointed.

He looked in that direction. Above the horizon he saw a pale glowing smudge.

"Edmond Halley did not discover it, but he calculated its interval. The comet visits us every seventy-five years, give or take a few years. The last time it appeared was in 1758. The Seven Years War was raging in Europe; here in the New World, men were butchering one another during the French and Indian War."

"Halley's Comet," Gideon said wonderingly. "I read in the paper that it was coming."

The dark figure motioned to him. "Come on around, and you will find a comfortable bench."

Gideon made his way around the hedge.

The man standing before him was bundled in clothing, his head topped with what appeared to be a floppy Scotch bonnet. "You are the sheriff, Gideon Stoltz, if I do not mistake." The man stuck out his hand.

Gideon gripped it. The smaller hand shook Gideon's hand up, then down, then released it as the figure turned abruptly back toward the comet. The man said over his shoulder, "Horatio Foote."

"Headmaster Foote," Gideon said. "I've heard good things about your school. I'm pleased to finally meet you."

"Well met, indeed, beneath the hairy star." Foote gave out a high-pitched grating laugh. "In 1456, or so it is said, Pope Callixtus excommunicated the comet because he thought it was an agent of the Devil."

"What are comets made of?" Gideon asked.

"Ice? Rock? Certainly gaseous matter forms the tail. Kant argued that comets are composed of particles of 'the lightest material there is.'"

The headmaster sat down on the bench and motioned for Gideon to sit beside him. He drew out of his coat a telescope, expanded it, and handed it to Gideon.

Through the glass, Gideon viewed the comet as an elongated smear of light trailing a luminous, curving tail. "It's beautiful," he said.

"I spotted it last night. It will brighten as it approaches perihelion." The headmaster put out his hand for the glass. "Comets excite alarm among the ignorant, who call them 'malicious meteorites' and suppose that they foretell wars, famines, plagues, and such." Foote raised the telescope to his eye. "Tell me, what brings you up Academy Hill?"

"I wanted to look out over the town. To think about certain things."

"Such as murder." Foote clucked his tongue. "And suicide. No doubt it's this damned comet working its mischief."

"Mr. Foote, you attended Judge Biddle's funeral. I'm told you were his friend."

"Yes. We had drifted apart somewhat of late, not because of any disagreement, mind you—just two old men whose lives and interests were on separate paths." He lowered the telescope. "May I ask if Hiram left a letter explaining why he took his life?"

"He left a will," Gideon said. "Nothing else."

"So I heard. Hiram was a private man. He had known great tragedy, and all his life I believe he struggled with anger and regret. He may have thought he had overcome his past. I've often wondered whether that is truly possible."

"Mr. Foote, how long have you lived in Adamant?"

"I came here in aught one. Started my school in a one-room cabin—it's long gone, as I sold the lot and the one next to it to some people, who then put up the hotel. With the money they paid me, plus subscriptions from a number of citizens, I built the structure behind us.

"There are two other teachers besides myself," Foote continued. "Our students learn Greek, Latin, literature, history, mathematics, and the sciences. I teach them to be skeptical, also. You are seated next to a Connecticut Yankee, a man who is exceedingly skeptical."

"And exceedingly curious?" Gideon said.

Again the high-pitched laugh. "What would life be, without a keen curiosity regarding one's surroundings? The natural world is a continual delight to me. I'm somewhat less curious about the mind of man, as it has disappointed me many times in the past."

"I too am interested in the natural world," Gideon said, "and also in the mind of man. Why it makes him do so many strange and unwise things—things that may hurt him or other people, things that disrupt order and peace."

"You are a philosopher, sir."

"No, just a sheriff. The son of a Pennsylvania Dutch farmer." He paused. "Mr. Foote, did you attend the trial of the Reverend Thomas McEwan in November of 1805?"

"Thirty years ago. A mere thirty orbits around the sun of our small and rather insignificant planet," he said. "Yes, I was there. They held the trial in the old courthouse—a primitive space cobbled together out of a log structure and a frame addition, with a cranky old stove that finally burned the place down. I sat in the gallery both days. I listened to the witnesses giving testimony—Sheriff Bathgate, as I recall; Flora Hendry, an attractive young woman; Sam Lingle, a teamster, who saw the preacher burying the body of the ironmaster's brother at night; and, of course, the reverend Mr. McEwan himself."

"After the judge died, I found four journals in his study," Gideon said, "his diaries for the years 1802 through 1805. In them, the judge made many entries about nature, the weather, people he met. He described meeting Rachel McEwan and courting her. And he wrote a detailed account of her father's trial. The last entry was for November

11, 1805, the day the preacher confessed in court to murdering Nat Thompson, and Judge Biddle sentenced him to hang. There were no entries after that. It seemed as if the judge's examination of life ended on that day."

"Oh, I'm sure Hiram continued to examine life," Foote said, "though he may not have judged it worth recording."

"I know things were done differently back then," Gideon said. "Colerain County was even more remote and isolated than it is today. But I have a hard time imagining holding a trial so soon after such a crime took place."

"Yet it was common to do so, not only here but in other places as well."

"I wondered why the judge didn't recuse himself. After all, he would have to try the man who was supposed to become his father-in-law."

"Hiram always had, shall we say, an abundance of confidence in his own impartiality and judgment. And at that time, I suppose it might have been difficult or at least inconvenient to bring in a judge from elsewhere."

"It seems to me that Judge Biddle rushed to judgment in the case," Gideon said. "As if he lost control of the whole process. I think he let the Reverend McEwan convince him of his guilt."

"Wasn't the man guilty? As I recall it, the evidence was overwhelming. And, of course, he confessed to his crime. What an amazing set of circumstances and events! A fight, witnessed by passersby, that resulted in a man's death. The preacher striking down his victim, Nat Thompson, then burying the corpse in the middle of the night—also witnessed, by the teamster, Lingle. The Reverend McEwan sleepwalking, having no recollection of finding or burying the corpse—or so he said. Yet the situation resolved itself. It became completely understandable in the end."

Gideon looked at the comet. It seemed to have grown brighter, or perhaps the air had become clearer as the temperature fell. "I wonder about the preacher walking in his sleep. How can a man get out of a warm bed, wander around in the dark, find a body lying somewhere in the woods, carry it back, dig a hole in the ground, put the body in the hole, cover it with dirt, smooth out the spot and conceal it with branches and dead grass, go back to bed—and not remember any of those things?"

"At first," Foote said, "I believed that McEwan knew full well what he had done. He had struck Nat Thompson a terrific blow to the head. Maybe Nat was killed outright, or maybe he scrambled to his feet and staggered off, only to die later. Either way, the preacher hid the body and then buried it under the cover of darkness. He did all those things consciously and willfully. He then made up the story about falling and hitting his head, which caused a loss of memory and led to his supposed sleepwalking—in other words, he lied to make his actions seem less culpable. After all, he was a minister. What a thing for a man of God to have done!

"But if it was play acting," the headmaster continued, "then it was a most convincing performance. On the second day of the trial, I had no sense whatsoever that the broken, remorseful man standing there making his confession was being anything but truthful—completely and brutally truthful about his own flawed character and what he had done."

"The judge wrote that when they dug up Nat's corpse, there was more than one wound to his head," Gideon said. "The nose was flattened. 'Crushed,' is how the judge described it in his diary. Also, the bone of the skull had been exposed by what must have been a different blow. But before the trial, he also wrote that the preacher's daughter Rachel told him that her father had struck Nat 'a blow.' She didn't say that the reverend hit Nat twice. Anyway, it seems to me that striking a man hard enough to cause either of those two injuries would have dropped him like a stone. He would not have remained standing to receive a second blow."

Foote thought for a moment before replying. "I don't recall the testimony that clearly; it's been thirty years, after all. But I guess Hiram assumed that one of the injuries happened when Nat fell, perhaps hitting his head on a rock."

"That could explain the two wounds," Gideon said with a nod. He went on: "Mr. Foote, as a learned man, can you tell me whether people really walk in their sleep?"

"Indeed they do. The condition is called somnambulism, or noctambulism. It is well documented. Men—usually they are men, though there are female somnambulists as well—ride horses, climb up and down ladders, sing songs, write letters, do all manner of complex tasks. Their eyes remain open; they are able to see, and navigate their surroundings, and even respond to questions. Yet mentally, they are asleep.

"The Reverend McEwan had just been in a fight," Foote continued. "He was worried that he had badly hurt his adversary. He had suffered a serious blow to his own head. He had a history of getting up and doing things while asleep. If all of those suppositions are true, then I believe it's entirely possible that the preacher found and buried Nat Thompson while somnambulating—and did not realize he'd done it."

Gideon shivered and wrapped his arms around himself. The Milky Way stretched overhead, two broad bands of glittering stars arrayed against the inky sky. The comet lay below the galaxy, nearer to the horizon, where it seemed to pulsate against the blackness.

"From *Julius Caesar*," the headmaster murmured, "the great Shakespearean drama of betrayal and deceit: 'When beggars die, there are no comets seen; the heavens themselves blaze forth the deaths of princes.'"

Beggars. Gideon considered for a moment, then said, "Mr. Foote, what would you say if I told you that Nat Thompson may still be alive?"

*Through grace I am determined*
*To conquer, though I die*

# Twenty-Four

⊶⊷

THE ROOM OCCUPIED ONE END OF THE ACADEMY'S THIRD AND uppermost story. As the headmaster lit a lamp, he cautioned Gideon not to step on the box turtle asleep on the floor nor sit on the green snake coiled up on the cushioned seat of a chair. The lamp's strengthening glow revealed book-lined shelves, wooden leaf presses, gauze collecting nets, fishing poles, walking sticks, a battered flintlock blunderbuss leaning in a corner. From branchlet perches on the wall, owls with cruel curved beaks and hawks with speckled breasts stared down, their glass eyes reflecting the light.

"Will you join me in a drop of the creature?" Foote said.

The headmaster set out two chairs in front of the fireplace. Pouring from a thick columnar vessel, he filled a pair of tumblers and handed one to Gideon. Seating himself in one of the chairs, Foote raised his glass. "A product of the agricultural surplus of our fair community. I use it medicinally and for preserving specimens. I assure you that this batch has never pickled a foetus nor preserved a toad."

Gideon inspected the contents of his glass, took a cautious sip. The whiskey was strong but it went down smoothly. He was now able to get a close look at the headmaster. The man's narrow-bridged nose mimicked a beak. His blue eyes appeared shrewd and quick. From a head of unruly white hair, snowy sideburns extended down to cover a pointed chin. For some reason, Gideon felt he could trust this man he'd just met.

"Now tell me about this resurrection of a murdered man," Foote said.

Where to begin? "Just over two weeks ago, an old tramp came to Judge Biddle's door." Gideon explained how, according to the judge's housekeeper, Judge Biddle behaved oddly after meeting the tramp; how the beggar had also appeared at the ironmaster's house, where he walked in the front door, asked for "Ad" in a familiar manner, and where suspicious behavior ensued.

Foote listened intently, now and then sipping his drink.

"The day after he was visited by the old tramp," Gideon said, "the judge and I went hunting. He didn't say anything about the stranger who had shown up at his house. But I got the feeling that he wasn't himself. He was quieter than usual. Somber. I remember thinking he seemed hopeless, and sad. After the hunt, he gave me the birds he'd shot. And he called me by my forename. He had never done those things before. That evening, he killed himself."

The headmaster rose from his chair. He set his glass down on an ornate wooden display case whose glass-fronted compartments contained mollusk shells, crystals, fossils, Indian spear points, the empty-eyed skulls of birds and mammals. Foote muttered "*Solvitur ambulando*." He strode the length of the room, his hands clasped behind his back, canted forward so that Gideon feared he might topple. Before the headmaster collided with the far wall, he turned abruptly on his heel and retraced his steps. The area he trod was paler and more deeply polished than the surrounding floorboards. After a half-dozen transits, Foote returned to his chair, which he repositioned to face Gideon's.

"I suppose that it could be Nat Thompson," Foote said. "If so, most astonishing. And troubling."

Gideon sipped his whiskey. "What I don't understand is what really happened thirty years ago. Because a dead body definitely was dug up in the preacher's yard." He paused. "I wonder if any of the witnesses who testified at the trial are still alive."

"Flora Hendry, I mentioned her when we were outside—the poor girl died, I believe it was from scrofula, probably twenty years ago." The headmaster brushed a bony index finger back and forth across his nose. "Sam Lingle—he was no spring chicken. I haven't seen him for years; I doubt he survives. I might add that, as a teamster, he worked for the ironmaster and would have been prepared to say exactly what his employer told him to. The sheriff, Ben Bathgate, is long dead. I helped perform an autopsy on his body; his stomach was a fibrous mass, the liver much distended. After leaving office, he pretty much devoted himself to drinking." As if reminded of his own libation, Foote lifted his glass and took a generous swallow. "Have you heard about Bathgate? He was not an honorable public servant. Quite open to a bribe. In the end, that led to his being turned out of office."

Gideon drank from his own glass. The whiskey had begun to make him feel light-headed. "If the preacher was made to appear a murderer, if he was somehow made to *believe* he was a murderer, then I think Adonijah Thompson did it."

Foote lifted a snowy eyebrow. "Indeed, he has several possible motives. Animus toward Rachel McEwan for rejecting his proposal of marriage. And toward her father, for favoring Hiram Biddle as a suitor, not to mention handling the ironmaster's brother roughly."

"My father-in-law told me that Mr. Thompson had hated Judge Biddle for years. For winning Rachel's hand, but also because the judge ruled against Thompson in a case concerning a valuable piece of land."

"The Wheeler farm." Foote nodded. "If the old beggar really is Nat Thompson, that could certainly explain why Hiram . . ." He shook his head. "My poor friend. To learn that your life could have been far happier and more fulfilling. That through your own inability to see the truth, you destroyed a great love and hanged an innocent man."

"If the old tramp is Nat Thompson, I wonder why he went to the judge's house," Gideon said. "Did he want to mock him? Did he even know who lived there? Judge Biddle wasn't in that house back in 1805; it hadn't been built then. Or did he go to Judge Biddle out of grief and shame, determined to reveal the truth of what happened so long ago?"

"Do you think he knew about the trial and hanging?"

Gideon considered what he had learned of Nat Thompson, both from the thirty-year-old entries in the judge's journal and from the way the tramp had behaved, two weeks ago, at the judge's house and at the ironmaster's mansion: Nat's and his brother's closeness; Nat's argumentative, combative nature in the past; his slothfulness, his boasting, his saucy, entitled manner. A possibility began to take shape in Gideon's mind. He took another sip of whiskey, cradled the glass in his lap.

"Mr. Foote, consider this theory, this explanation of what Nat Thompson may have done over the last sixteen or so days. He comes back to Colerain County after being away somewhere for thirty years. First, he goes to Panther to see the ironmaster. But he doesn't sneak back; he walks right in through the front door and demands to see his brother. That suggests he wasn't part of any plan to trick the preacher and the judge back in 1805. Let's say he's down on his luck, wants to get his share of the profits from the ironworks. Adonijah Thompson is shocked to see his brother, and he's frightened, because the ironmaster knows what could happen if people find out that he caused a man to be unjustly hanged thirty years ago. I don't know what charge could be brought against him, but probably it would send him to prison for the rest of his life.

"The ironmaster grabs whatever money he has lying around, shoves it into Nat's hands, tells him, Get out of here, leave this place and don't come back. Maybe that was the arrangement they had thirty years ago, and Nat broke his promise not to return.

"Nat is angry because his brother won't give him the money he thinks he deserves—and, from his appearance, apparently needs. So he goes to the judge to see what his legal options are. He has no idea of the trick his brother played three decades ago. But he learns it from the judge." Gideon took another swallow. He thought of what the judge's housekeeper and his own mother-in-law had told him. "Could he have gone back to the big house to demand more money from his brother? To blackmail him?"

"And how would Adonijah Thompson then react?" Foote said. "Would he tell Nat to go into hiding again, until he could gather more money, a lot of money, to pay him off once and for all?"

Gideon stared into the fire flickering low on the hearth. "Or would the ironmaster decide he can never let his brother go again?"

***

True stood in the doorway to their house. When Gideon made to enter, she grudgingly moved aside. She sniffed. "You've been drinking. You went down to Hammertown."

"No. I went in the other direction entirely." He pointed a finger upward, smiled at his wit. Ach, the headmaster's whiskey was powerful stuff.

She put her hands on her hips.

"I walked around town," he said. "In case you didn't know, it's what a sheriff is supposed to do." Her frown deepened, and he regretted what he'd said. "True, honey, I went up on Academy Hill. The headmaster was out on the lawn, looking at a comet through his spyglass. Imagine, Halley's Comet has appeared in the heavens! Mr. Foote invited me inside. We went up to his rooms and had a drink. Well, maybe it was two drinks." He looked at her. "I stayed out too long. I'm sorry. You have every right to be cross with me."

Her face softened. "Gid, I was worried. I still am. I'm worried about the judge killing himself, and that boy getting murdered, and now you tell me that Nat Thompson may not be dead." She pressed against him. "Let's not fight anymore. Come, come to bed."

*O could we make our doubts remove,*
*Those gloomy doubts that rise*

# Twenty-Five

IN THE MORNING HIS HEAD ACHED. TRUE WAS LESS THAN SYMPATHETIC. She fed him breakfast, and he hoofed it to the jail.

With some misgivings, because it all seemed so improbable, he told Alonzo what he suspected about the return of Nat Thompson. Alonzo sniffed at Gideon's breath. Then he withdrew his head and turned his face so that his eyes, opened wide, regarded Gideon with an exaggeratedly surprised sidelong glance. "You're joking," he said.

"No, I'm not joking."

"Well. Time will tell."

"Perhaps it will, and perhaps it won't," Gideon said. "Anyway, please don't mention it to anyone."

"You don't have to worry about that."

Gideon had also asked Headmaster Foote not to say anything about their conversation; he didn't want word of his suspicions to spread. And he had no clear idea of how to proceed, or even how to find the old tramp, let alone the man with the dun horse and the red vest. He sat down at his desk and busied himself filing away papers that had accumulated over the past few days. He paid out a bounty on a wolf cape that a trapper brought in. He looked through a batch of notices from southern states describing escaped slaves who might be headed north. Finally it became impossible for him to stay at his desk.

He spent the rest of the day walking around the town watching out and talking with people. He went back to places Yost Kepler had frequented: his rooming house, the sawmill, the post office where he picked up his mail. He talked to mill workers, people in stores and on the street, and he learned nothing new.

In the evening he left True and David and went to Hammertown. He quizzed barkeeps and serving girls and women out strolling singly and in pairs and drinkers shifting between saloons. No one knew anything about the man who called himself George England. No one, save the serving girl in the House of Lords, remembered seeing anyone wearing a red vest. No one had met an old tramp sporting a buck tail hat. No one could tell him anything about the night when Yost Kepler had been assaulted. And no one seemed to care.

He plodded down the street in a funk. He went into the alley where Kepler had been found eight days ago. The alley still reeked of rotting food and piss and excrement. He stood in the shadows and thought hard, hoping some revelation, some new idea, would come to him. Sporadic rustling sounds issued from among the heaps of trash. A calico cat stalked past the opening to the alley, stopped, looked into it, then bunched its legs beneath itself and ran—Gideon knew he hadn't scared it, because it raced past his boots before disappearing into the darkness farther down the alley.

He stood there mulling over ways he might investigate Kepler's murder, how he might locate the old tramp, and in the back of his mind he asked himself why that cat had bolted. When he heard the sound of movement and a hiss of breath, he quickly ducked aside. He felt a glancing blow to his head, then pain exploded between his shoulder and neck. He fell to the ground and immediately rolled sideways as a club thudded hard into the dirt where his head had been.

He yelled, rolled farther, scrambled to his feet. He heard someone running away down the alley. Panting, he leaned against the rough wood siding of a saloon. Pain shot down his shoulder and arm and up his neck. He moved his arm, groaned out loud. He wondered if his collarbone was broken; he didn't think it was, but that part of his body practically screamed with pain.

He took a few halting steps in the direction his attacker had run. The only light in Hammertown glimmered in the street, leaking out from saloons' meager windows. The alley lay deep in shadow, the wall of a building on one side lit faintly by starlight. Suddenly he was filled with fear. He touched the muscle between his shoulder and neck. Pain flared again. His ear and the side of his head pulsed. He decided that the last thing he should do was to blunder ahead in the darkness and give his assailant another chance.

Who could have done it? People might not like the fact that a Dutchman had been put above them as sheriff, but he didn't think anyone would attack him for that. This came from his investigation. It was tied to his search for George England. Or for the old tramp. Someone wanted to hurt him. Maybe even kill him. He wondered how far the ironmaster's reach might extend.

He stumbled in to a saloon and, despite the star on his jacket, lay down money for a drink. He took the glass to a table in the corner and collapsed onto a bench with his back against the wall. A serving woman brought him a rag. "Something happen to you?" she said.

He took the rag from her and held the cloth against his ear; it came away bloody. "Someone hit me with a club. In the alley."

"Lucky you didn't end up like that Dutch boy," she said, then went on to the next table.

He glanced at the men and women in the saloon. Three Negro men drank together at another table—this was The Horse, the bar where colored folk might come and drink. He looked around and saw the place for the drab, lonely wasteland that it was. He had formed an understanding that there was no law that could stop anyone from doing anything. No law in Adamant, or Colerain County, or Pennsylvania, no law in the land could truly protect people. *We are each of us alone,* he thought bleakly. *We have only ourselves to depend on, and maybe one or two others. But no one can possibly defend us. Not sheriffs or judges. And nothing watches over us, no Almighty God looks down and keeps us from harm. How I doubt*, Gideon thought. *And he who doubts is damned.*

*Long in silence I have waited,*
*Long thy guilt in secret grown . . .*

# Twenty-Six

❦

THE NEXT DAY, DESPITE A SHOULDER AND ARM THAT STILL THROBBED with pain, Gideon saddled Maude and rode her to Panther. He checked at the store and was glad to see that the poster asking for information about George England remained on the wall. No, the storekeeper had not seen the man the poster described, nor any old man with a buck tail on his hat. "Guess you'll have to keep looking, Sheriff," he said in a sarcastic tone.

Gideon got some advice and directions from a worker at the furnace, then rode out of the settlement and followed a narrow wagon road into the woods. Here the trees had been cut for charcoal decades ago, and now a new generation of trees was being axed again to provide more fuel for the ironworks.

Where the wagon road entered a clearing, Maude tossed her head and sneezed. Gideon smelled the acrid odor, too. In the middle of the clearing stood a beehive-shaped mound thirty feet across and twelve feet high, with white smoke rising lazily from its top. Four men stood looking up at the smoke. Gideon noticed that the white smoke was interrupted by a faster-rising plume of bluish smoke.

Maude picked her way past chopped-off stumps and scattered treetops. As Gideon drew near, he heard his father-in-law say, "You got a mull."

Davey Burns stood next to a scrawny man whose head came barely to Burns's shoulder. Burns and the scrawny man gave Gideon a glance, then returned their attention to the smoke issuing from the mound.

The scrawny man took a shovel and, motioning for the two other colliers to follow him, climbed up onto the mound. Soot blackened the men's faces and clothing. Taking small, light steps, they shuffled their feet over the layer of dirt and leaves that covered the mound, all the while gently tapping the surface with the backs of their shovels. Gideon knew what they were doing: jumping the pit, trying to find and seal a breach where air was leaking in. The extra air was causing the fire inside to burn too quickly, which, if it continued, could turn the charcoal into worthless ash. It was dangerous work. If the covering gave way beneath them, the men could plunge into the smoldering charcoal and burn to death.

Davey Burns kept his eyes on the smoke. Gideon dismounted, knowing not to interrupt. When the bluish smoke turned white, Burns called up, "You got it. Now get your sorry asses down here."

He turned to Gideon. "This one should come to foot in a day or two. We get her done, and a half-dozen others, then we're finished for the year." His eyes were red and bleary. He rubbed them with the heels of his hands. "How'd you know where to find me?"

"I asked at the ironworks. And I followed the smoke."

Burns gave Gideon the smug smile he reserved for his Dutch son-in-law. "I seen the notice you put up in the company store. I can't read too good, so I had the storekeeper read it to me."

"The man the handbill describes, the one calling himself George England. Have you hired anyone by that name?"

Burns coughed, a deep, ragged hacking that went on for a while. He cleared his throat and spat. His voice was gravelly. "A young jake asked me for a job a week or so ago. He may have said his name was George. Can't recall his last name, or if he even gave one."

"What did he look like?"

"Light-colored hair, clean-shaven. It was his horse I noticed. A dun, damn good-looking animal."

"Did you hire the man?"

Burns shook his head. "Like I said, we're about done coalin' for the year. But I seen the horse again, at the stable, the one in Panther."

"How long ago was this?"

"Three, four days. Could be he got some other job."

"Why didn't you come tell me?"

Burns smiled and shrugged. "I do my job. Why should I do yours?"

Gideon was fed up. It was the closest he had come to getting a lead on the man with the dun horse. And it was just like Davey Burns not to help his Dutch son-in-law. "All right," he said. "I would like you to do me a favor. This evening, please ask your sons, as many of them as you can find, whether they have seen this George England with the red vest and the dun horse. Can you do that much for me?"

Davey Burns shrugged, then nodded.

Gideon footed the stirrup and swung up onto Maude. He suppressed a gasp at the pain that lanced through his injured shoulder. "I'll come by your house tomorrow morning."

"Make it early. I work for a living."

★★★

By chance, on the road back to Adamant, Gideon met Jesse Burns, riding a roan horse with a white-splotched nose and a hammer head—an animal just as ugly as its rider, Gideon decided. The roan flattened its mouth and fought the bit when Jesse jerked it to a stop.

"Brother Gideon," Jesse said. "You are like a bad penny, showin' up here, showin' up there."

"Just doing what the county pays me to do." Gideon gritted his teeth, both against his hurt shoulder and his annoying brother-in-law. "I told you earlier that I found your name written on a piece of paper in Yost Kepler's room. In the saloon, you denied that you had ever met him, but a woman at the House of Lords told me she saw you drinking with Kepler some time ago."

"That woman made a mistake."

"I don't think so."

"You calling me a liar?"

Gideon was exasperated. He wanted to learn from Jesse anything about Yost Kepler that might help him find out why the man had been murdered. He was sick and tired of Jesse's obstructive belligerence. He was ready to get down off of Maude and have it out with his brother-in-law, right there in the road. Even though he knew it would be the height of stupidity to fight Jesse, especially with his shoulder bruised so badly he could barely lift his arm. "Yes," he said, "I'm calling you a liar. A no-good, lickspittle liar."

Jesse's mouth fell open. After a moment, he laughed. "Have it your way, Brother Gideon. Yeah, I had a drink with that Dutch boy."

"For what purpose?"

"Business."

"What kind of business?"

"None of yours."

"Did you kill him?"

Jesse's mouth gaped again, and his eyes narrowed above his pocked cheeks. "Hell, no. By God, you're a suspicious bastard."

"And you, Jesse Burns, are as different from your sister as night and day. All you do is *schpeddle* me for being Dutch. You are as ill-mannered as a dog that no one has bothered to train."

Jesse grinned. "You plan on training me, Brother Gideon? Till you do, this here *doch* is happy to lift his mangy leg and piss on your Dutch foot." He took off his hat, bowed, and swept it low, then walked his horse past. The roan snaked out its coarse head and tried to bite Maude. Jesse laughed.

*I'll reprove thee, I'll reprove thee,*
*Till thy crimes exact are known*

# Twenty-Seven

———————

THE COMET POINTED DOWNWARD AS IF STREAKING TOWARD A collision with the earth. It held there fixed and otherworldly, its head and tail and the stars behind it slowly dimming as the sky brightened toward dawn.

It was Saturday, the sixth of November. Gideon rode alone toward Panther. He had decided to take Jack, whom the judge had willed to him. He wanted to rest Maude after riding her yesterday. And he wanted to see what sort of a saddle horse Jack might be. He knew that Hiram Biddle had ridden Jack on occasion, although mainly he used the gelding to pull the light wagon or the carriage.

Jack had a good reaching walk. Past the town's outskirts, Gideon asked him to speed up by touching his heels against the horse's sides. Jack kept up his stolid walk. He pointed his ears back at Gideon as if to say, "I don't think you really want to go any faster than this." Gideon clucked to the gelding and kicked him harder. To no effect. "All right, you." He got down and, with his pocketknife, cut a limber switch from a willow growing beside the road. When he got back on, Jack took off unbidden in a fast canter that was nevertheless easy to sit. Gideon grinned. "Good horse," he said. "You can slow down whenever you want."

Jack seemed to understand the calming tone of Gideon's voice, for he dropped back into a soft rocking-chair canter.

Gideon alternated cantering Jack and letting him walk down the road. The sky grew red in the east.

Gideon took stock of how he felt: excited and hopeful and a bit scared all at once. His encounter with Jesse still had him upset. True hadn't helped his mood this morning, either.

She'd woken him out of a sound sleep, gripping him by the shoulder. He barely managed to stifle a cry at the pain that caused—True didn't know he'd been hurt; on both of the last two nights he'd managed to get into his nightshirt without letting her see how bruised his shoulder was. "Gid, Gid," she cried out. She was almost weeping. "I had a dream." He took her in his arms. Her voice slurred. "I was in a dark place, a cellar or a cave, maybe a grave! And this thing, this face, came at me." She began to weep. "It was wrinkled and gray, full of disease and rot, and it came right up to me and I couldn't get away. It opened its mouth and showed me its teeth." She wept harder. "White teeth! Covered with blood!"

He tried to comfort her, assured her that dreams didn't mean anything.

"No, you don't understand," she said. "Of course a dream can have a meaning. That kind of dream *always* has a meaning." Her breathing was rapid. "If the teeth had been yellow, it would mean an old person will die. But these teeth were white. Like a child's! It means somebody young is going to die."

She looked at him with terrified eyes. Then she tore herself out of his arms and hurried off into the darkness to fetch David from his crib. All that had done was waken and upset the child. She'd come back to bed with a crying baby, at which point Gideon got himself up. He was disgusted and angry. "I didn't need to get woken up like that. For a bad dream." He shivered in the cold room. "But now I may as well stay up. I'm going to the ironworks today. Maybe I'll get lucky and make an arrest on the man who killed Yost Kepler."

"Don't go," she blurted. "Please, Gid. Come back to bed. Don't go to the ironworks. Nothing good waits for you there."

"What nonsense," he had said, then stalked off to the kitchen to start a fire and hunt up something to eat.

Now he rode Jack through the brushlands. The cold air made his eyes water. He slitted his eyes and pictured a visage perhaps not too different from the one that had plagued True's dreams: Yost Kepler's brutally beaten face. Then into his mind came the judge, head lolling, blood bearding the side of his neck. He got rid of that image only to be confronted yet again with the vision of his *memmi* lying bloody and violated on the kitchen floor.

Why did God watch silently over such misery? When his mother was killed, one of the neighbors said it must be part of God's plan. It hurt Gideon so much to hear that. Because why would God want anyone to be tortured and slaughtered like that? Especially a good woman like his mother. Why would God even let somebody be born, if that was how they were going to die?

*Because there isn't any God.*

Gideon tried to pull his mind back from that thought. It was like looking into an abyss.

The whole sky was now red. The road dipped into a low spot where cold mist lay. It climbed up again into clear air. Gideon's teeth chattered, and his toes felt numb. He reached down and touched the buttstock of the rifle in its leather scabbard, then felt for the pistol in his belt and the second pistol in his boot. He had brought wrist and leg shackles in a saddle bag.

He rode into the ironworks on the pale blue road. He stopped Jack outside the Burnses' cabin. Gideon's father-in-law emerged from the outhouse behind the dwelling. Davey Burns put a hand against the weathered boards of the privy, bent over, and coughed for a long time. He spat, then slowly straightened.

"Good morning," Gideon said.

"Yeah, it's morning," his father-in-law croaked. "Can't say it's any good."

"Did you find George England for me?"

Burns shook his head. "Nobody I talked to had heard of him or seen him lately. I doubt he got hired here. I checked with the hostler. Seems that dun horse might belong to the man you're looking for—leastwise he used the name George England. But the horse ain't at the livery. The man paid up and left a while ago. That's all I can tell you."

"*Gottverdamm,*" Gideon said under his breath.

His father-in-law mustered a smile. "Well, Sheriff Stoltz, looks like you wasted your time and the county's dollar coming all the way out here. May as well waste a little more and have some coffee."

Inside the cabin the burly man set out chipped floral-patterned cups that looked tiny in his hands. He got the pot from the hearth and poured. "What will you do next?" he said.

"I don't know," Gideon said. "Maybe the handbills will get some results." But with each day that passed, he felt it less and less likely that he would find the man. Maybe George England had seen the bills and fled. Gideon thought of the oddly named town, Chinclaclamoose, that England claimed to be from. It lay a long way west through thinly settled country. Perhaps too far to go on pure speculation.

Davey Burns remained seated as Gideon finished his coffee and stood. The big man coughed again and rubbed the back of his neck.

"You don't look well," Gideon said.

"Something's clawin' at me, that's for sure." He hauled himself up off the bench and put his coat on. They went out the door. Davey Burns set off down the road, his shoulders slumped. He stopped again, hacked, and spat.

Gideon looked around. The ironworks was a sprawling place. Could George England be working here somewhere, despite what his father-in-law had said? Could the old tramp be here, hidden away in a cabin or in one of the buildings?

Cocks crowed back and forth throughout the settlement. A cow bawled. A woman came out of a cabin lugging a bucket toward one of the wells.

Sunlight gilded the hilltops.

The side-angling light picked out a black horse on the road in front of the ironmaster's mansion. On the horse sat a rider, bare-headed and clad in black. The horse strode along the blue road. Clinkers of slag threw back the rising sun in brilliant spears and winks. As Gideon watched, horse and rider passed from light into shadow, becoming silhouettes against the dull frosted land. The horse broke into a trot, the rider posting rhythmically above its back. Then the rider sat deep and leaned forward and the horse took up a canter, the treble-beat of its hooves carrying through the air.

Davey Burns scrambled off the road and doffed his hat as horse and rider swept past.

The horse stretched out into a gallop. The rider crouched behind the horse's neck. The road made a wide arc, and the horse came on, thundering past the Burns cabin. Thirty yards beyond, the rider reined to a sudden stop, the horse's rump bunching and its hooves spraying slag.

The rider wheeled the stallion about and retraced his steps, the horse lifting its front legs high and seeming to dance on its muscular haunches. The ironmaster rode the stallion up to Gideon where he stood next to the gelding Jack.

Adonijah Thompson wore his hair clubbed back in a queue. Beneath a broad brow, his eyes were set deep in his skull. His cheek-bones were sharp and angular, with hollows beneath them, and prominent lines ran from each side of his nose to the corners of his mouth. His eyes bored into Gideon's.

The stallion huffed quick breaths, pink in the new light, and sidestepped, tossing his head. The ironmaster paid no need to the stal-lion's fidgeting. He hardly appeared to move in the saddle, and his eyes never left Gideon's.

"What is the sheriff doing at Panther?" His voice was deep and cold.

"I'm looking for a man who is a suspect in a murder case."

"What man is that?"

"He may be using the name George England. I heard that he

asked for work here, and that his horse was stabled for a while in the stock barn. He is wanted for questioning—"

"I saw the handbill you put up in my store."

"—in connection with the murder that happened in Adamant on the twenty-eighth of October." Gideon's heart hammered, and his mouth was dry. He imagined True subject to the unwanted attentions of this fearsome man. He took a deep breath, then spoke carefully. "Mr. Thompson, do you know—or do you employ—this George England?"

The ironmaster took his time before answering. "Not as far as I know. But I do not know the name of every person who works for me."

"Is it permitted for someone who does not work here to stable his horse in the ironworks' stock barn?"

"If there are open stalls, they can be rented." The ironmaster's stallion switched his tail and danced sideways. "You have been a frequent visitor here of late."

"I came here three days ago to post the handbill."

"You knocked on my door, also."

Gideon made himself return Thompson's stare. The ironmaster's eyes betrayed nothing: Adonijah Thompson's face appeared to have been formed from the same material that was smelted in his furnace and tempered in his forge. Gideon had not intended to raise the subject of the old beggar, but he thought it best to acknowledge what the ironmaster had said. "Yes. As well as searching for George England, I am looking for an old man, a tramp, with white hair and a beard, pale blue eyes, and a limp."

"Why do you seek him?"

He decided to repeat the lie he had invented for the ironmaster's housekeeper. "The man stopped at a residence in Adamant, where he was given a meal. Some silverware was reported missing."

"Nothing has gone missing from my house."

"So your housekeeper said. I wondered . . ."

The stallion surged forward, taking three powerful, barely contained steps.

Gideon stumbled back, and Jack snorted and threw his head up and stepped backward. Gideon held onto the reins, laid a hand on the gelding's neck.

"I have work to do, Sheriff." The ironmaster loomed over Gideon. "You are wasting my time as well as your own."

Gideon wanted to say that he had heard of the old tramp entering the house in a familiar way, demanding to see "Ad." But he reckoned the ironmaster would quickly figure out that Gideon's mother-in-law had told him.

Instead he said, "Do you have any idea who that old tramp could be?"

The flesh around the ironmaster's eyes tightened. With the slightest pressure on the reins and, Gideon knew, a straightening of his spine, Thompson caused the stallion to step backward. And again. The horse stopped with his weight gathered on his hind end. "I have no idea."

Gideon decided to end the conversation. He nodded and shrugged. "Yes, well. I guess I won't trouble myself too much over a couple of missing spoons."

The ironmaster stared down at him. Gideon thought about how he himself had been attacked in Hammertown. The longer he looked into those hard gray eyes, the surer he became that Adonijah Thompson was behind the assault—either he had sent someone on a murderous errand, or he had done it himself.

"If you or any of your workers should see the man who calls himself George England," Gideon said, "would you please send word to me?"

The ironmaster kept his baleful stare fixed on Gideon. "I need you to leave here right now," he said. The ironmaster turned his horse aside. The stallion, in all his power and grace, walked away down the road.

*Let's covet those charms that shall never decay,*
*Nor listen to all that deceivers say*

# Twenty-Eight

———∞———

GIDEON PUSHED BACK FROM THE NOON TABLE, FULL OF FOOD, finally warmed up after his ride to and from Panther on this chill morning. He felt deflated by disappointment—and subdued and undermined by fear.

"It didn't go so well," he told True. "I didn't find that man's horse at the ironworks' stock barn." He decided not to mention his confrontation with the ironmaster, which had frightened him badly, or anything to do with the old tramp.

"I'm not sure what to do next," he said.

True bit her lip. She looked like she wanted to say something—also didn't want to say it. The emotions warred on her face.

"There's another stable in Panther where that horse might be at," she finally said. "Mr. Thompson's." She reached out and took Gideon's hand.

"I'm not much of a sheriff," he said. "I don't always think of everything I should."

She squeezed his hand.

"True, I met the ironmaster this morning. He was out riding his stallion."

"I doubt he welcomed you."

Gideon let out a breath. "No. He pretty much ran me off of the ironworks." He raised his eyes. "He holds himself above everyone else, doesn't he?"

"Yes."

"Does he fear any man?"

Her eyes narrowed. "He fears men that are no longer men."

"Tell me," Gideon said.

"For years Mr. Thompson would go walking around on his plantation at night," True said. "To make sure everything was in order. You never knew where he might turn up. He saw all manner of things. Drunks staggering home late, trying to figure out which cabin they lived in. Women getting together with other women's men on the sly. Wolves slinking across the fields. They say Mr. Thompson can move as quiet as a wolf himself when he has a mind to.

"But he quit doing that a few years back, when he saw something that put fear in him. It was a ghost. The ghost of a man who died in the furnace." She looked defiantly at Gideon, as if daring him to deny that such a thing was possible. "The man's name was Calhoun. He was a filler—they work up on the bridge, dumping charcoal and ore and limestone into the stack when the furnace needs fed. Forty times a day—load after load of coal and ore and stone. My brother Jim, he was learning to be a founder then. He said Calhoun used to drink—kept a bottle hid somewhere, probably in one of the bins, and by the time his shift was over he was usually drunk. Jimmy was there that night. And Mr. Thompson showed up to check on things.

"It's loud up on the bridge," she continued, "a roaring that goes on and on. It's hot, and the light flickers orange and red. Jimmy was down below in the cast house, with the ironmaster watching him, and he called up for more ore. They heard the charging buggy rumble across the floor, and a scuffling sound as Calhoun dumped the load. Then a yell.

"Jimmy and the ironmaster ran up to the bridge. There was no one there—just the buggy half empty and Calhoun's rake lying on the floor and a scuff mark in the dust. Jimmy covered his mouth and nose in the crook of his arm and looked down into the throat. Mr. Thompson looked, too. There Calhoun lay, on top of the burden. His clothes had already burned off. Then his arms lifted up like he was begging God to carry him to safety, but in that heat he was already dead. There was a glow all around him as his whole body caught fire. Jimmy said his head exploded, went all to pieces in the blast."

She shuddered. "They rang the bell and kept on ringing it. Woke people up all over the ironworks. I remember how I came upright in bed. I was worried about Jimmy, I knew he was working that night. I was just a little girl then, but I tagged along when they all went running to the furnace.

"It took three hours for the charge to work its way down. By then, there was nothing left of Calhoun's body. No bones or nothing. They broke the crucible and ran the pour, filled the sow and pigs. The workers clumping around in their wooden shoes, sparks in the air like it was a precinct of hell. Ma took me on home. Some other women took Calhoun's widow back to her cabin. She was crying and tearing her hair. They tried to comfort her but it was no use."

True's voice was tight. "And what did Mr. Thompson do? He set one of the pigs aside. Sent word to Calhoun's wife that she could take that hunk of iron and bury it, put up a stone over it with her husband's name. He gave her ten dollars. The next day he turned her out of their cabin and sent her down the road. She ended up in Hammertown. She sold her body so she could feed herself and have a roof over her head. Then in the spring, when the creek was up, she threw herself in it and drowned.

"From that time on, Calhoun's spirit would not rest. Folks would see him at night, wandering around. One time Ma and I were coming back late from a church social, and there he was, setting on the edge of the well."

She looked at Gideon, a guarded expression on her face.

"Please, go on."

"He didn't say nothing, just smiled and beckoned us over, but we picked up our skirts and ran. He means to pull someone down into the water with him. He needs to quench the fire that burned him up. Or maybe he wants folks to die the same way his wife did.

"Mrs. Glenny told me that one night Mr. Thompson was out

patrolling, and he met Calhoun's haunt. The ironmaster tucked tail and ran. Mr. Thompson came in to the big house white as a sheet and whimpering like a child. Now he daren't go out after dark. I know, that's just another one of my ignorant stories. You think you married a simple girl who doesn't have a lick of sense in her head."

"I don't think that at all," Gideon said. He got up, went to True, and kissed her. "Thank you for telling me. Thank you for reminding me that the ironmaster has at least some weakness in him. That he isn't as hard as he appears to be."

"Oh, he's hard, all right." She shivered. "You'll go back, I know you will." She began to cry silently, her face against his chest. "I'm scared. I'm awful scared. But maybe you aren't. Be careful, Gid."

He gave her a long hug and another kiss. Then he stole into the bedroom, where David was napping in his cradle. He rearranged the blanket around the baby. David stirred and thrust out an arm with its perfect tiny hand. Gideon tucked the hand back under the covers. The child thrust it out again. Gideon smiled. He wondered what his son was dreaming about—he had such a serious, workmanlike expression on his little face. He kissed David gently on the forehead, said goodbye to True, and left.

*Let sinners take their course,*
*And choose the road to death*

# Twenty-Nine

⸙

RIDING MAUDE, GIDEON RETRACED THE ROUTE THAT HE HAD taken that morning. It was now the middle of the afternoon. Before leaving Adamant, he had shifted his saddle from Jack to Maude because Jack was not in good shape and Gideon did not know how far he might have to travel, and because he trusted his mare to take him wherever he needed to go. He had told Alonzo of his plans. Alonzo volunteered to go along, too, but finally agreed that he should stay behind, mind the jail, and keep the peace in town.

Dark clouds scudded across the sky, hurried along by a northeast wind. The wind hissed in the treetops. It felt like bad weather coming. But Gideon felt strongly that time was running out. Almost three weeks had gone by since the old tramp visited the judge. Yost Kepler had been attacked and left for dead eleven days in the past.

He followed the blue road across the ironworks. He looked toward the building that housed the office. Was the ironmaster watching him? The skin between his shoulder blades twitched. But the building was far enough away that he doubted he'd be recognized even if anyone happened to look out a window.

The ironmaster's mansion stood on a gentle rise. Tucked away behind it was a small hollow surrounded by mature pines, huge old trees with feathery green needles, trees that had been spared the ax and left standing to provide shade. In that hollow, True told him, lay the ironmaster's stable.

Like his fine house, Adonijah Thompson's stable was built of dressed fieldstone. As Gideon rode up to it, six horses stuck their heads over green-painted half-doors. They whinnied at Maude. All of the horses were blacks or bays. Not a dun among them.

A man and a boy came out of the stable. The man was sturdily built and bowlegged. The boy, slope-shouldered and with a large blunt head, made Gideon think of an owl.

"I want to ask you about a horse," Gideon said.

"We don't rent 'em," the sturdy man said. "These here are Mr. Thompson's personal riding horses."

"Very handsome horses indeed," Gideon said.

The man puffed himself up. "We keep 'em polished to a fare-thee-well. Are you here to inquire about Vagabond? You want your mare bred, you will have to talk with Mr. Thompson first."

"I don't want my mare bred. I need to ask you some questions."

"I know all about horses. I like 'em, can't say as I trust 'em, on account of some of them is always looking to kick you into next week. Been around horses all my life. You have any questions, ask away."

"I am looking for a dun gelding, a big, strong horse with a long back, looks like he could run all day and half the night. Do you know a horse like that?"

"That would be George's gelding."

The boy standing beside the man tilted up his moony head. "Edgar," he squeaked at the man, "you weren't supposed to tell."

Gideon looked more closely at the small male person, whose coarse features and wrinkled face suggested that he was, in fact, not a boy but a stunted adult.

The sturdy-built man reddened and thrust his hands into his pockets.

"Not supposed to tell?" Gideon said.

The man's mouth slacked open. He whipped his head from side to side.

"Why not?"

"Mr. Thompson said so," the owl declared.

Gideon tapped his badge. "Gentlemen, this badge identifies me as the sheriff of Colerain County. As citizens, you are bound by law to answer any and all questions that I ask you."

The sturdy man directed a vindicated expression at his smaller friend, who shook his head before lisping, "Mum's the word."

"I'm looking for the man who owns the dun," Gideon said. "In his early twenties, a talkative fellow. Calls himself George England. He may be wearing a red vest."

"That's George, all right," the sturdy stable hand said. "But it's *George*, not 'Chorch,' like you just said. He stayed with us last night. Slept up in the hayloft. You are so right, he loves to gab, why, he'd talk the paint off a door. Goes on and on so's you can scarcely get a word in edgewise, which it can be very annoying at times." He nodded vigorously. "Got him a red vest, just like this one." The man unbuttoned his coat and swelled his chest to display a red vest with a green paisley pattern. "George didn't get his at the company store, where I got mine. His girlfriend give it to him for his birthday. Which she lives in Chinclaclamoose. That's where George comes from. Chinclaclamoose is a Injun name. George said it means 'no one tarries here.'" The man slapped the tops of his thighs and guffawed. "That hits me in the funny bone, so it does. 'No one tarries here.' Could be it's not be much of a place. Plagued with swarms of gnats, maybe. Or unfriendly people. I never been there, but with a name like that, I ain't sure I need to go." The man guffawed again.

"Where is George now?"

"Left a couple hours ago. I told him, George, I said, you oughtn't to travel. You see that red sky this morning? Means there's a storm coming. My leg says so, too." He hiked up his pantleg and exposed a hairy shin with a large pink knot. "Got kicked by a horse a few years back. Ever since then, I have felt pains in this leg whenever a storm is on the way. I call my leg my weathervane. Durn thing aches right now, so it does. Pretty useful, wouldn't you say, bein' able to predict the weather with your leg?" He let his pantleg fall. "I'm glad that hoof didn't hit a couple feet higher up and betwixt my legs, which is where a horse kicked Edwin when he was a little sprout. Ruined his balls. He never did grow up proper, still got him a high voice, and he can't beget. Ain't that so, Edwin?"

The owlish man kicked the ground.

"Where is George England now?" Gideon felt frustrated at having to fight through this thicket of jabber.

"Mum's the word," the owl squeaked again. "Mr. Thompson finds out you told, Edgar, you'll get raped over the coals."

"Now Edwin," the low-browed man said. "This here is the county sheriff. You can tell by the badge he has on. Though if you ask me, he looks a bit wet behind the ears to be a sheriff. Anyway, fellow says we are bound by the law to answer his questions."

"George went off on iron company business," the owl piped up.

"What kind of business?"

He shook his head. "Ain't permitted to say."

Gideon looked at the sturdy man, who stood shifting from one foot to the other. "Edwin?"

"I'm Edgar," the man said. He pointed an elbow at his companion. "That's Edwin. George is supposed to go find somebody."

"Who?"

"A tramp," the owl said. He looked up triumphantly at the sturdy man. "An old tramp with a white beard and a buck tail hat."

Gideon felt like a fist had slammed into his stomach. "Where can this old tramp be found?"

"I heard Mr. Thompson telling George, 'Go to the logging camp at the head of Egypt Hollow,'" the owl said.

Gideon turned Maude and touched her with his calves. She shot ahead. Then he stopped and walked her back. "Where's Egypt Hollow?"

★★★

Maude cantered. Gideon felt sick to his stomach. If only he'd known about this stable before he went to the ironworks this morning. Now George England had been gone for a couple of hours. And all because of what I said to the ironmaster, Gideon thought.

Rain began to fall, heavy drops in stuttering bunches. The clouds' bellies smudged the ridgetops. Gideon pulled on his slicker. Maude ambled through the rain on the road down Panther Valley. They passed gleaned fields and brushlands. The way led through a wood of twisted locust trees, their trunks black and thorn-studded and blotched with yellow lichens. Gideon looked for a tall lightning-struck pine that marked the turnoff to Egypt Hollow. A half hour later he found the pine, a pale vertical wound where the bark had been blasted away by lightning spiraling up the tree's trunk.

The branch road led steeply upward. The rain swept across the hollow in sheets. Foam collected at the bases of trees. The wind shook the treetops. Gideon tilted his head forward, sluicing water off his hat brim. His hands, gloved in sopping leather, were numb.

The dun came trotting toward him on the muddy road. Its rider never hesitated. He put the dun into a gallop and raced past. With no time to draw his pistol or pull the rifle from its scabbard, Gideon leaned toward the rider and lashed out with his arm. The inside of his forearm struck the man in the head. George England yelped and his hat flew off. He lost a stirrup and lurched sideways. He clasped his arms around the dun's neck and scrambled back into the saddle and booted the dun in the ribs.

Gideon watched him gallop away down the hollow. Should he chase after him? Or ride on to the camp?

He had to know.

The slab-sided lumber camp loomed black in the rain. He jumped off Maude. The cabin's door was half-open. The feeling seized him again, pins and needles racing across his shoulders and back and up his neck. It stopped him in his tracks. He bent over and fought to draw breath. He balled his hands into fists. He put his fists on the tops of his thighs and pushed downward and straightened and lifted his head. He gulped in air. He forced himself to go in through the door.

In the dim light he made out an overturned chair and a big dark spot on the puncheon floor. A dark smear led across the room and out through a back door. Outside on the ground, the smear showed red. He followed it to a patch of brush.

The tramp lay on his back. His face was white. His mouth and beard and the front of his shirt were soaked with blood. Hack marks covered his hands. His throat had been cut so deeply that the severed windpipe hung out the side of his neck.

Gideon fell to his knees. His shoulders knotted hard as wood. Pain throbbed where his shoulder had been clubbed. A feeling of evil overwhelmed him. Again he saw his *memmi*, her face, the cuts on her hands, the stab wounds on her breasts. He turned aside and vomited. He looked at the tramp again. He heard a high keening coming out of his mouth, a cry that was both a wail of anguish and a roar of rage.

★★★

He sat on Maude, walked her down Egypt Hollow. The rain fell. He arrived at the main road. In the fading light he could barely see the dun's tracks.

He turned and followed the tracks west down the Panther Valley in the direction of Chinclaclamoose.

*Life is the hour that God has given*
*To escape hell and fly to heaven*

# Thirty

⟨⟩

H E RODE DOWN THE SQUELCHING MAIN STREET OF THE TOWN. THE
night before, he had terrorized the residents of a cabin along
the road by banging on their door in the middle of the night and
demanding they let him in. He had caught a few fitful hours of sleep
curled up in a blanket next to the hearth. He had left the cabin before
dawn, with directions on how to get to the town with the strange-
sounding Indian name. He had made up his mind to go on to Chinclaclamoose in case George England indeed lived there, in case he
had decided to go home. There was only one way to get to the town,
along a poor road up a steep hollow that notched through the Allegheny Front before debouching onto an expansive plateau. The road
led straight to Chinclaclamoose.

It didn't matter how far he had to ride, Gideon told himself. It
didn't matter how elusive or dangerous George England was. He
would capture the man. He would catch the murderer, or he would
die trying.

He wondered again who had attacked him in Hammertown.
Had it been George England, and had he done it at Adonijah
Thompson's behest? If his assailant had used a gun, Gideon figured,
he might already be dead. Or if he'd used a knife—Gideon shuddered as he pictured the old tramp, then imagined a blade slicing
through his own neck or plunging into his back or breast.

He had failed to keep the old tramp alive. It was no one's fault
but his own. After finding the body, he had dragged it back inside the
lumber camp. A hasty search of the tramp's clothing and the inside of

the cabin turned up nothing—no papers or possessions that might point to his identity. Just some food, the poor fellow's knapsack and walking stick, and that fancy hat hanging on a peg by the door. Now, with the tramp dead, it seemed to Gideon there would be no way of finding out if Nat Thompson had come back to Colerain County. Unless George England knew who it was he had killed; knew and was willing to tell.

The rain dripped off the roofs of the buildings lining the street. It overflowed rain barrels and ran down the few windows of the mostly unpainted and dilapidated stores on either hand. Gideon passed two huge brindled hogs wallowing in the mud. They pointed their ears in his and Maude's direction but did not bother to open their eyes or lift their heads.

A man picked his way catlike across the morass of the street. Gideon asked him if anyone upheld law and order in Chinclaclamoose. The man directed him to James McGee, constable, who owned the dry goods store.

The whitewashed false front of McGee's store gave it a stature and an appeal beyond those of its neighbors. Even though it was Sunday, the door was unlocked. No customers inside. A small, trim-looking man with a white shirt and black sleeve garters was perched on a ladder restocking shelves.

"I wonder if you can help me," Gideon said.

The man looked down at him. "Maybe so."

"Would you please get down off that ladder?" Gideon said. "I don't like being looked down on when I talk."

"Well, all right, then." The man climbed nimbly down.

"I am Gideon Stoltz. The sheriff of Colerain County."

McGee smiled. "I've heard about you." He stuck out his hand.

"I am chasing a fugitive," Gideon said. "I believe he killed two men."

McGee ushered Gideon in to a room that doubled as a storage area and an office. He got out two chairs.

McGee appeared to be in his mid-thirties. He had dark eyes, dark hair pomaded heavily and parted in the center of his head, and a moustache whose tips curved downward below the corners of his mouth before curving up again to end in pointed tips. Gideon thought he looked more like a cardsharp than a shopkeeper and even less like a constable.

"Tell me about your fugitive," McGee said.

"He is a young man. Maybe nineteen or twenty. He's been using the name George England, though that may be an alias. I met him once on the road in Panther Valley, and he told me that he hailed from this place. From Chinclaclamoose. And I saw him again yesterday, near a cabin where a murdered man lay. I tried to stop him, but he got away."

"You say he killed two men?"

"The first one was a clerk, a young man about the same age. In Adamant, outside of a saloon. He smashed in the man's skull and then emptied his pockets." Gideon paused, unsure how much to reveal about the second murder. "He also killed an old man, a tramp. Yesterday. He stabbed him to death in a cabin near the ironworks at Panther."

"And you think he rode on to Chinclaclamoose," McGee said. "This is not a very big town. I know everyone who lives here."

"That's what I'm hoping." He described George England as closely as he could—he'd gotten a better look at the man during their brief encounter in Egypt Hollow, but he could describe him with no more particularity than having a lean build, light-colored hair, and fair skin. "He has a good horse. A dun. Long body. A strong horse, and a fast one."

McGee nodded, and sat back in his chair.

Gideon felt sleepy. His throat hurt, and his cheeks and forehead burned. He closed his eyes and saw the corpse of the old man pitched into the brush behind the logging camp. The old tramp who could have supplied answers to the questions that rioted in Gideon's brain.

"George England," McGee said. "Don't know the name. But you say the horse was a dun? That's an uncommon color, sure enough. Will you excuse me for a minute?" He went into another room. Gideon came out of a doze as McGee returned holding a tray with a teapot and two mugs. Gideon accepted a mug. The tea, scalding, warmed his mouth and gullet and chest.

"I believe I know who you're after." McGee drank from his own mug, then patted his moustache with a napkin. "There's a young buck lives here in town. I'd bet my bottom dollar he's behind a rash of thefts we've had over the past couple of years, though I haven't been able to catch him at it.

"George Baker is his name. Goes by his initials—G. I. B. 'Gib' Baker. He's the right age and fits your description. He more or less lives with his mother. The father ran off years ago; the father is from bloody old England, talks with a Johnny Bull accent. The son doesn't. He's as American as you or me. I haven't seen young Gib for a while. He has a good dun horse."

Gideon put his mug down. "What are we waiting for?"

While McGee closed up the store, Gideon drew the charges in his pistols and loaded and primed afresh. He told McGee it was of the utmost importance that the suspect be taken alive. "I think someone paid him to kill the old man," he said. "I need him as a witness."

Gideon, McGee, and McGee's brother-in-law, a heavy, splay-footed man who must have stood six and a half feet tall, slogged through the mud to Baker's house. The house stood by itself on a bare lot that encroached on the surrounding forest. The big deputy went around back. McGee and Gideon knocked on the front door, then went inside with their pistols drawn. They received a steady stream of invective from a gap-toothed woman as they moved quickly from room to room. A cat ran off and hid beneath a bed, then vacated that spot when Gideon crouched and peered under it. Cellar to attic, McGee and Gideon searched and did not find Gib Baker as the gap-toothed woman followed them from room to room showering them with abuse.

"There's one other place," McGee said as they went back outside.

The second house was on a back alley. They rushed in without knocking. In a downstairs room Baker and a girl were in bed. Baker woke up as Gideon grabbed him by one arm and pressed his pistol against the man's neck. Baker gave a loud yell and tried to pull loose. McGee hit him with a blackjack across the back of the head. He fell down half in the bed and half on the floor, his bare white buttocks in the air. The girl screamed. A voice from upstairs yelled at her to shut up.

Gideon felt weak and out of breath. Sweat striped his sides beneath his long johns. His hands shook as he let the hammer down to half cock and put the pistol back in his belt.

They got clothes on Baker and manacled his hands behind his back. The constable and the tall deputy frog-marched the groggy man through the mud to the dry goods store as residents of Chinclaclamoose came out in the pouring rain to watch, holding catch-as-catch-can items above their heads—a wooden platter, a folded newspaper, a frying pan.

McGee put irons on Baker's legs and shut him in a closet. He said he would keep a watch on the prisoner and get a boy to take care of Gideon's horse. Gideon thanked McGee and shook his hand. He supposed he should feel good about capturing Baker, but instead he felt low and wretched. He went back out in the rain. It was late in the day. The light in the sky was almost gone. He trudged down the street toward the tavern that McGee had pointed out. The hogs still lay in the mud, except now, instead of just two, there were four of them, all equally immense, all covered with mud and immobile. Gideon wondered if he was seeing double.

The tavern was low and rambling and sided with rain-darkened rough-cut lumber. In the main room a man got up out of a chair, blinking and scratching himself under one arm.

"I want a beefsteak," Gideon said. "And some fried potatoes. A bottle of good whiskey if any is to be had in this place. And when I'm done with the meal, I want a bath. Make the water as hot as you can." He looked around. Though he saw no sign of anyone else lodging in the tavern, he added, "And I want a bed all to myself."

*Jesus whispers consolation*
*And supports your fainting soul*

# Thirty-One

———❦———

"I WAS GOING TO TELL YOU NOT TO TURN YOUR BACK ON THIS RATTLE-snake, but then you couldn't drive this rig," McGee said. "I think we have him secured good and proper."

Gib Baker wore the wrist and leg manacles that Gideon had brought. The restraints were chained to an iron eye-bolt sunk into the borrowed wagon's bed. The prisoner wore a new hat, slightly too large for his head, and a rain slicker wrapped around his shoulders, both of which Gideon had purchased from McGee's Dry Goods. In a storage area under the wagon seat, wrapped in oilcloth, was a written statement from Baker's female companion and a sack filled with gold coins—along with a gold pocket watch with the initials YK engraved on the underside of the lid.

It felt strange to Gideon to be sitting there while a killer crouched three feet behind him. Farther back, Maude shuffled restively at the end of a rope tied to the back of the wagon.

Baker sat hunched over. He did not look comfortable or happy. McGee smiled at him. "I figured this one might stretch a rope some-day," he said. "Looks like that'll be your job, sheriff.

"Hey, Gib," he said to Baker. "Be a good boy for Sheriff Stoltz. Do whatever he tells you, and always talk polite."

"Go fuck yourself."

"I might come and watch you hang," McGee said.

"They got nothin' on me."

"Two murders," McGee said. "Don't worry, they'll only hang you once."

★★★

Gideon coughed, and pain rasped in his throat. His shoulder still hurt from where the club had hit him. He sat on the hard seat and let the horses pick their way along the road. It would be a two-day drive back to Adamant. Baker wasn't talking, and Gideon had no wish to speak with him anyway. Baker's half-lidded eyes sent a chill through him. He thought of the old man, Nat Thompson—it had to be Nat Thompson, who else could it be?—looking into those eyes, the last human things he would see, eyes that held no mercy, and the knife driving through his upraised hands, hacking them, knocking them aside, plunging into his heart, the hot blood spraying out, and how the terror must have cascaded through Nat Thompson's being when he knew his death had come.

*Don't let even a single thought of your* memmi *come into your head*, he told himself. *Or you might take the whip out of the socket and turn around and flay the son of a bitch to death.*

He drove east across the high plateau with its few impoverished farms and long stretches of low scrub oak and laurel and dense stands of chestnut and rock oak. The leaves were gone from the hardwood trees. The wagon's axles groaned as the rig slewed through the mud. Around midday the rain ceased, a gold slit carved itself in the clouds, and a shaft of sunlight fell upon the wagon. Harness fittings gleamed. Steam rose from the horses' backs. Gideon looked over his shoulder. Baker stared at him. His rain cape dazzled.

The clouds healed themselves and the rain commenced again.

Gideon chained the wheels before taking the wagon down the road where it descended into Panther Valley from the escarpment of the Allegheny Plateau. The road was narrow, banked with stone on the downhill side. Pull-outs had been dug into the slope on the high side of the road every few hundred yards, in case two wagons met or a wagon and a man on horseback. But no one else was traveling in this weather. The wagon skidded and bumped down the grade. The horses snorted and threw up their heads, holding back the wagon's weight. Gideon talked to them. "Easy, easy." A runaway now would kill them all. The horses' ears pointed back, telling him that they listened, that they trusted the man who was driving them down this slick, rutted road with a steep drop-off on one side. Above, dark hemlocks towered up a hundred feet, their tops lost in cloud. Below, a stream clattered unseen through a jungle of rhododendron.

Just before dark Gideon found the tavern McGee had told him about. The small log building stood on a lonesome stretch of road. Gideon knew he must have ridden by the place yesterday, but try as he might, he could not remember it; perhaps he'd passed it in the dark.

The tavern's occupants were all female. A white-haired woman cooked supper, a lanky girl with bobbed hair tended the fire, and a middle-aged woman with a claw hand served Gideon at the table. Baker ate sitting on the floor, his wrists and ankles shackled.

The claw-handed woman studied the prisoner. "What crime has he done?"

"He is a suspect in several crimes," Gideon said. "I am taking him to jail in Adamant."

The woman circled around Baker, her hands on her hips. "I know you, you little shite," she said. "You bought a meal here last month. Then afterwards you stoled our ax out of the woodshed." She looked up, an indignant expression on her face. "Sheriff, I want to press charges."

Baker laughed so hard he spat food on the floor.

After the meal Gideon shoved Baker out to a corn crib behind the cabin. He made him sit down and then ran a short chain around one of the wall logs and between Baker's manacled hands and padlocked the chain's ends together. He arranged a blanket over Baker's shoulders with the raincoat on top.

"Sweet dreams," he said.

Inside the cabin, the girl laid a dulcimer on her lap. She always looked down, or would present only one side of her face to

Gideon—had done so all evening. He wondered if she was shy, or fearful of the strange armed man who had come to her dwelling, or if someone had used her badly in the past. The girl strummed the dulcimer's strings with the quill end of a black-and-white turkey feather and sang about a girl named Barbara Allen and a boy named Willie Grove. *Though death be printed on his face, and o'er his heart be stealing, yet little better shall he be, for bonny Barb'ry Allen.* The dulcimer left a buzzing drone hanging in the air. The fire lit the girl's profiled face while putting her downcast eyes in shadow. She sang another song, and another, as Gideon and the two older women sat listening.

In the night Gideon dreamed that the girl laughed and kissed him on the mouth. She probed boldly with her tongue while her hands rummaged through his pockets. She was searching for something, the key to the lock on Baker's chains. He jerked awake. The grass-filled tick beneath him rustled as he sat up. His face burned and his breath wheezed. The pain in his throat made him swallow, which led to wrenching coughs. He pulled on boots and slicker and went outside. It was still raining. He began to cough again, the hacking stopping him, making him bend over. When he managed to quit coughing he pulled open the door to the corn crib. Baker sat there looking at him.

Gideon checked the lock and chain. They were secure. "You keeping dry?" he rasped.

"What's the matter, sheriff?" Baker said. "Are you taken ill?"

Gideon breathed heavily through his mouth. "I must have caught a cold."

"That's a pity," Baker said. "I hate it when anyone feels poorly. Y'know, I been thinking. About the wicked crimes I have done. My heart is burdened, and I feel the need to confess."

In the dark, Gideon could barely make out the whites of Baker's eyes and his teeth. "I admit it," Baker said, starting to laugh. "It was me done that awful crime. I stoled that ax from them whores."

★★★

Around noon the next day Gideon turned the wagon onto the narrow track up Egypt Hollow. At the logging camp he let himself down off the seat. He fumbled his way into the cabin. He wrapped the old tramp's body in a tarpaulin. He secured the tarpaulin with rope. Again he searched the cabin and found nothing of importance beyond the buck tail hat and the pack and staff. He had to rest for a while before boosting and shoving the corpse up onto the wagon bed. Baker pulled back against his chains, shrinking as far away from the misshapen bundle as he could get.

Gideon stood in the cabin's doorway, trying to get his wind back. Outside, the rain fell. He stared at the wagon, at Baker crouching there, at the old tramp's shrouded body. He tried to shake off his misery with the thought that at least he had caught Baker, taken him alive. But not before Baker had murdered the old tramp. A window onto the past had been shut. What if Baker refused to say who had paid him to kill?

He put the tramp's staff on the floorboards at his feet and stowed his pack and hat beneath the wagon's seat. He took up the reins and clucked to the horses. Carefully he drove down Egypt Hollow. Every few minutes a bout of coughing seized him. Each time it felt like his chest was being ripped apart. He felt hot all over, as if he were standing next to a huge bonfire, and then chills overcame him and he shivered and his teeth chattered. He pulled his coat tight. He sat hunched over. His vision swam. A hymn came to him, a shape-note hymn called "Claremont," and he sang it to himself over and over again: *Trembling, hoping, ling'ring, flying. Oh, the pain, the bliss of dying.* Was he dying? This was no cold, it was much worse. The poetry became embedded in his brain, droned on and on so that he did not think about it anymore but heard it echoing as he tried to keep his head up and feebly checked the horses with the reins and worked to hold the rig on the muddy branch road.

He turned onto the road down Panther Valley.

Later he turned again, onto the road to Adamant.

The road followed the creek through the gap in the hills. It led beneath the stark bare branches of sycamore trees. He saw the town far away. The courthouse, the academy on the hill. The graveyard on the other hill.

*Oh, the pain, the bliss of dying.*

He realized the wagon had stopped. Alonzo stood looking up at him.

"Good God almighty!" Alonzo said.

"Lock him up. Take the body to Doc Beecham. Some things under the seat . . ."

"You're going to the doc yourself," Alonzo said.

"No. I'm going home. True will take care of me."

*Not Jordan's stream, nor death's cold flood*
*Should fright us from the shore*

# Thirty-Two

⸺◦◦◦⸺

HE STUMBLED THROUGH MUDDY EMPTY STREETS. DARKNESS falling fast. His knees wobbled. He saw everything through a haze. True's mother met him at the door, her face drawn and her eyes red.

She gripped him by the shoulders. "She's sick," she said, "awful sick. The influenza." She looked at him more closely, laid the back of her hand against his forehead. "You're going straight to bed."

He staggered inside. "Where is she?" His father-in-law took his arm and led him into the bedroom. True's head lay against the pillow. Her face was pale. A moan escaped her lips. She opened her eyes, saw him, and tried to raise herself up, only to fall back on the bed. The word came out as a sob: "David."

The cradle sat in the corner. David's face was shrunken and collapsed. He didn't move, didn't smile, didn't reach up with his little hand toward his father. Slowly it dawned on Gideon. His heart breaking, he touched his hot fingers to his son's cheek. Cold.

"He passed early this afternoon," True's mother said.

And I wasn't here, Gideon thought. They wanted to take him elsewhere, separate him from his wife and child, but he fought out of their hands and got in bed with True. He wrapped his arms around her. He buried his face in her breast and wept.

★★★

He came awake as coughing wracked him. Opening his eyes, he seemed to view the world through thick green glass. He was alone. He didn't know where he was. He closed his eyes and felt a great wave come crashing down, tearing him away, dragging him down into cold silent depths.

He fought against it, seeming to rise from a dark and heavy realm and surface again into murky light. He realized he was not in his own bed or even in his own house. He cried out for True, tried to rise, felt the great irresistible wave drag him down again. Then he was running slowly and clumsily through the rain in a wood of twisted trees with black trunks studded with thorns and blotched with yellow lichens. In a clearing he came upon a cabin. He kicked the door open and went inside. His mother was there, seated in a chair, and he looked at her, and they were both sad, terribly sad, for she understood that her grandson David was dead. She took his hand in hers. Her eyes filled with tears. No words passed between them, no words could express their pain.

★★★

His mother-in-law spooned broth into his mouth.

"True . . . ?" he managed to croak.

"Alive. We thought we'd lost her. We thought we'd lost both of you."

His mother-in-law put her hand on his chest and gently pressed him back down on the bed. He slept. He slept for what seemed like ages. Then someone was shaking him by the foot. It was Davey Burns. His father-in-law did not say anything; he helped Gideon get out of bed and into his shirt and trousers. His big rough hands eased boots onto Gideon's feet.

As he let himself be dressed, Gideon held out his hand and stared at it, front and then back, and concluded that it was real, it was his hand, the fingers moved like his fingers had always moved, the skin stretched and wrinkled in the usual places, the scar winked white across one knuckle where, as a boy, he had cut himself whittling a little horse out of a chunk of basswood.

Davey Burns put his brawny arm around Gideon and held up his son-in-law while guiding him outside and across the street to Gideon's own house.

True sat in a chair in the kitchen. Gideon fell to his knees and put his arms around her hips, felt her hands settle on his head, her fingers grip his hair.

David lay on a broad pine board in the unfinished room that was supposed to be a parlor someday. He wore a gray linen dress. His eyes, collapsed, stared blankly beneath half-lowered lids. Gideon detected the smell of corrupt flesh, not quite masked by the lavender simmering in a kettle over the fire.

The house filled with people. They clustered around David and True and Gideon. They laid their hands on True's back, on Gideon's back. True's grandmother was there, and the people fell silent as she took a platter of something white and brown and held it up for all to see, then lowered it and placed it on the board next to David. The white was salt and the brown was earth. Gram Burns made True and Gideon both get up and touch David's body. Gideon felt his heart break all over again.

"I thought it was another baby sickness," True said. He could barely hear her voice, so quietly did she speak.

He kissed the back of her hand and held it against his cheek. He remembered True's dream of bloody white teeth. She hadn't reminded him, hadn't said "I told you so." He didn't want to talk about it. Maybe she didn't, either.

A coincidence?

And was it also a coincidence that she had dreamed about the judge and Rachel McEwan arguing with each other—and two candles burning low and guttering out at the same time? Two incidents that Hiram Biddle had described thirty years ago in a diary that True had never read?

Someone prayed in a voice that rose and fell. Then other voices took up song. They started off ragged, strengthening and becoming purer as more people joined in. *And am I born to die? To lay this body down!* It was "Idumea," the shape-note hymn Gideon knew so well. He tried to sing, but his voice cracked and his throat seared and he fell silent. He heard True's parents singing, and the jaybirds and their wives: *Waked by the trumpet sound, I from my grave shall rise; and see the Judge with glory crowned, and see the flaming skies!*

He realized that True wasn't singing. He looked up. Her eyes were dry. She stared straight ahead. Her face looked frozen. It wore an expression of deep pain, and something else. He thought it was bitterness.

The light in the room grew dim. His vision swam, and the water, cold and green, rose up and swallowed him again.

*Are there anybody here like jailers a-tremblin'?*
*Call to my Jesus and he'll draw nigh*

# Thirty-Three

THE STATE'S ATTORNEY CAME OUT FROM BEHIND HIS DESK AND HELD out his hand. As far as Gideon could remember, it was the first time the Cold Fish had ever offered to shake hands with him.

"Good work, sheriff," Alvin Fish said, pumping Gideon's hand. "Doing your duty, even with you being so ill, to the point of almost succumbing. And please, let me offer my condolences for the death of your child. This influenza epidemic has hit the county hard."

Fish sat back down and placed his spectacles on his nose. Their lenses turned his eyes into peppercorns. He indicated another chair. "Do sit down. I can see you are not yet returned to a robust state of health. A little friendly advice: You may wish to have yourself bled. It is an excellent restorative measure when the body has been weakened by disease." He cleared his throat, tapped his fingers against Gideon's report lying on his desk. "Thanks to the thoroughness of your investigation, I am reasonably certain that we will be able to convict George Baker for the murder of Yost Kepler."

Gideon nodded.

"It is largely a circumstantial case," Fish said. "But I believe the evidence will convince a jury. Yes, I predict that man will hang."

"About the hanging. I . . . I don't know how to do that."

"We'll figure it out, I'm sure. There have been hangings in Colerain County in the past." He paused. "But let's not get the cart before the horse. First we need to secure a conviction."

"About the killing of the old tramp . . ."

"Don't let it bother you."

"Baker also murdered that old man."

Fish joined his hands, carefully placing his fingertips together. He stared at them for a long while, then looked up. "Your report states that you met George Baker on the road in Egypt Hollow, approximately half a mile from the scene of that very recent killing."

"It was a brutal murder. He hacked that old man to pieces. Cut his throat so deep he almost took his head off. The coroner's report spells it out."

"Indeed. But let me be frank. There is little point in our focusing on that crime at this point in time. We can be thankful that, owing to your diligence and hard work, a depraved killer is now behind bars and the public is in no further danger. As I said, we will prosecute and convict George Baker for murdering that poor Dutch lad."

"And for killing the old tramp."

Fish contemplated his steepled fingers again. "No need for that," he said.

"The evidence for that case is strong, too."

"Let me evaluate the strength or weakness of any body of evidence." Fish separated his fingers and took off his spectacles. He pointed them at Gideon. "Should Baker be convicted of murder in the first degree for killing Yost Kepler, there is no need to try him for the second murder."

"What? Are you joking?"

Fish's eyes narrowed. "No, Sheriff Stoltz, I am not 'choking,' as you put it. Keep in mind that every trial costs the county a substantial sum of money. Particularly a trial for capital murder."

Gideon's throat tightened and he started coughing. Fish backed his chair as far away as he could get.

"Mr. Fish," Gideon said weakly. "That old tramp, he may have been Nathaniel Thompson, the ironmaster's brother."

"I read that in your report. Pure speculation. The ironmaster's brother has been dead for thirty years."

"The two men at the stable, they . . ."

"They allege that Baker stayed at the stable before going off on some sort of 'iron company business.'"

"It wasn't 'iron company business,'" Gideon said. "Adonijah Thompson sent George Baker to kill that old man."

"Soft-brains, both of those stable hands," said Fish, his voice heavy with scorn. "Completely unreliable as witnesses."

"Think about what took place in 1805," Gideon said. "The trial of the preacher, Thomas McEwan, his confession, his conviction and hanging—those things may all have happened because of a horrible mistake, or more likely an evil trick."

Fish scoffed. "The records for those events are gone, burned up. The trial was before my time. I did not come to Colerain County until eight years later. But I can say with complete certainty that all we know at this point—all we *need* to know—is that in 1805 the Reverend Thomas McEwan confessed to killing and burying Nat Thompson and was subsequently hanged for his crime."

"Other suspicious things have happened. Like Judge Biddle committing suicide the day after the tramp came to his house."

"Yes. The judge is dead. A most unfortunate occurrence. That is one less witness to talk to, about the trial or anything else that may have happened back then."

"The judge's journal . . ."

"It's around here somewhere. I took the liberty of having it brought over from the jail. It is simply a somewhat biased personal account of an old trial. Mildly interesting from an historical perspective, but not relevant. Certainly not anything I would be comfortable presenting as evidence in a court of law."

"I'll get Baker to talk."

"No one would believe him."

"I will question the ironmaster."

"You'll do no such thing. As the commonwealth's attorney, I order you to cease any investigation into the matter."

Gideon got up from his chair. Fish looked at him for a moment, then put his spectacles back on and began shuffling papers on his desk. He glanced up. Gideon was still standing there.

"I don't like this," Gideon said.

"I don't care whether you like it or not."

"I do not like the stench of this."

Fish's face hardened. "You are impertinent. Let me remind you that I decide which cases are strong enough to prosecute, and which cases are a waste of time and the county's resources. You are merely a sheriff." He relaxed his frown. "Don't worry, you'll get your conviction. You'll get to hang George Baker for killing your Dutch compatriot. Now, if you will excuse me, I have work to do."

Gideon considered slapping the spectacles off of Fish's head. Instead, he made himself turn and walk out of the office.

★★★

He dragged a chair down the aisle and set it facing Baker's cell. Baker lay on his cot, hands behind his head, staring at the ceiling.

"He don't say much." Alonzo leaned against the door jamb. "I thought he'd be a blatherskite, leastwise that's what the serving wench at the House of Lords said. But it appears he's a man of few words."

Gideon watched Baker's chest rise and fall. He wondered how God or nature could form a man like that, capable of taking life so brutally, so casually. Baker did not look any different than someone you might meet on the street or in church. A plain face, but not a bad-looking one, with clean features and clear gray-blue eyes. What lay behind those eyes Gideon could not comprehend.

His throat closed, and he let his own eyes shut. The grief was palpable and intense. These days it came on him often and without warning.

They had buried David in the cemetery at Panther, near True's cousin Emma, the girl whose skirts had caught fire during the making of apple butter. His son's little body had been wrapped in cloth and placed in a small pine box that one of the jaybirds had made. In the grave David's feet pointed east, so that on that final awful morn he would waken and behold the dawn, and rise up joyous, and ascend with the faithful to dwell in that place where pain and death were no more.

Gideon asked himself how a body claimed by worms, tiny bones fallen to dust, could ever be put back together. How a dead child could rise again, new made. He wanted to believe that which he had always been taught: In God, all things are possible. He tried to keep his mind away from the abyss.

The funeral service for David Burns Stoltz had taken place in the small Presbyterian cemetery on a fine late-autumn day. White puffy clouds proceeded in stately fashion across a brilliant blue sky. In his weakness, Gideon had needed a chair. He felt detached from the words that flowed so assuredly from the preacher's mouth. True stood behind Gideon, her hands on his shoulders. He looked out at the broad valley in which the ironworks sat. Parts of the valley were bathed in sun, other portions were cloud-shadowed. The terrain showed its intricate form, its folds and gaps, its benches and flats. On one side Muncy Mountain stood with its gently rounded flanks and notched water gaps, and on the other side of the valley the little narrow hollows rose toward the long pale line of the Allegheny Front.

He glanced upward again. The clouds were serene and solid-appearing, like sheep grazing placidly across the sky. By nightfall they would have dwindled and died away. People are like clouds, he thought. They seem substantial and important and long-lasting. Yet they are here for the briefest day, then gone.

Doctor Beecham had said that he, True, and David had been among the first in Adamant to come down with the influenza, or, as some called it, *la grippe*. The malady had started earlier in Panther, and it had stricken True's father, Davey Burns, who subsequently recovered and now stood here among the mourners at his namesake's burying. The doctor said that, oddly enough, those hit hardest by the illness tended to be healthy adolescents and young adults; older folk seemed capable of shrugging it off. Infants and children were of course very susceptible. In Adamant, between forty and fifty souls had sickened so far, and almost half of them had died. The doctor believed it was pneumonia, developing in the wake of the influenza, that carried the victims off.

A surprising number of people had come to David's burying. Burnses in their multitudes, also various near and distant relatives. He saw the pretty freckle-faced Virginia Ross, True's cousin who worked in the big house. Some people from church. And the headmaster. Horatio Foote had come up and clasped Gideon's arms as he bent low his whiskered face, his pale blue eyes appearing somehow stern and full of sympathy at the same time. Foote hadn't said a word, just kept hold of Gideon's arms for a long moment and then gave them a squeeze before letting go. Gideon felt touched that the headmaster would leave his students and come all the way from Adamant for the burial of a child he had never met, a child whose father the headmaster barely knew.

One face had been conspicuously absent. Although a member and a regular attendee of the Panther Presbyterian Church, whose minister conducted the funeral for the Stoltz baby, and although the aggrieved grandparents and the child's uncles and aunts worked for him, Adonijah Thompson was not at the burying. Gideon thought it would have been strange indeed had the ironmaster appeared. Word had swept through Panther and Adamant that the Dutch Sheriff had caught the man suspected of murdering Yost Kepler—and brought back with him the body of another, more recent victim of the same killer, an old man with a white beard, a poor tramp who some said might be Nathaniel Thompson, the ironmaster's brother.

But how could that be? Nat Thompson had been dead and in his grave for thirty long years. Nat Thompson, killed by the hotheaded preacher Thomas McEwan, struck down with a maul and secretly buried at night in the garden of the parsonage—within sight of the graveyard where the sheriff's baby boy was laid to rest.

Gideon surfaced from his musings and was momentarily surprised to find himself seated in a chair in the jail, looking through a cell's bars at George Baker. Baker lay on his cot and stared up at the ceiling. Gib Baker, Gideon reflected, must once have been an innocent child like his own little David. What had gone so terribly wrong? What miseries had this man endured such that he could take a life—two lives—so carelessly?

He closed his eyes again. After his talk with Fish, he had come to the conclusion that Adonijah Thompson, with his great power and standing in the community, and the force of his personality—and probably his money—had pressured the state's attorney into deciding not to investigate the old tramp's killing. Unfortunately, Gideon could not even begin to figure out how such a thing could be proven. And about one matter, the Cold Fish had been undeniably correct: Gideon Stoltz was just a sheriff. He hadn't even been elected, he'd been appointed to fill in for the real sheriff after Israel Payton had died.

If only he had checked the ironmaster's stable that morning over a week ago, and caught Baker there, and thus saved the old tramp's life. If only he'd been able to find Nat Thompson alive and deliver him to Fish, present him as a witness to the strange and troubling events of 1805. If only he hadn't needed to ride after Baker, first to Egypt Hollow and then to Chinclaclamoose. If only he'd been at home to help True when David became ill.

So often did his thoughts go wandering along such useless trails, faint paths leading to barren, desert places.

He wanted to return to order, clarity, peace. He wanted to get back to living, to being a husband and a father again. Yes, a father. He had told True, "Together we will make another baby."

He heard a tittering and opened his eyes. Henry Peebles, the assailant housed in the cell next to Baker's, was laughing. Gib Baker swung his legs over the side of his cot and looked at Gideon with an expression that mingled astonishment and disgust.

Gideon realized he had spoken those words out loud: "Together we will make another baby." He started to chuckle himself. Then he began to laugh. It hurt his lungs, but he couldn't stop. He sat back in the chair, roaring with laughter, his eyes filled with tears.

*A point of time, a moment's space*
*Removes me to that heav'nly place,*
*Or shuts me up in hell*

# Thirty-Four

❧

THE NEXT DAY, MOVING GINGERLY, HE AGAIN PLACED A CHAIR IN the corridor outside Baker's cell. The prisoner paced about for a few moments, looking off to one side, then the other, then above Gideon's head, and then lay back down on his cot with his face turned toward the wall.

Alonzo brought Gideon a mug of coffee. He had one for the prisoner, too, and called out to him, but Baker did not respond. Alonzo put the mug on the floor beside the bars and went away.

Gideon took a sip. He screwed up his face. Alonzo made very weak coffee, hardly worth drinking.

"That old tramp," he said in Baker's direction. "The one you stabbed to death in the logging camp. The other day they put him in the ground, up on Burying Hill. If you could look through that wall over there, and up the slope, you would see his grave.

"I went and paid my respects. No one else bothered to go. Nobody read him a service. They just wrapped him in a shroud and lowered him down and shoveled the dirt back in.

"The grave is unmarked for now, just a scar in the ground. But somebody really ought to put up a stone for that old man. Maybe I'll do it. I will have them chisel into the gravestone 'Nathaniel Thompson, 1778 to 1835, died in Egypt Hollow.'" He did not know Nat Thompson's birth year; he knew very little about the man, other than the few things Gram Burns had told him and what Hiram Biddle had written down thirty years ago. "I don't know if it would make sense to have anything like 'A Christian gentleman of the finest character,'" Gideon said. "I suppose it could say 'Called home by the Lord.'"

He took a sip of coffee, swirled the mug, and looked at the muddy particles whirling within. "Ah. I have it now. 'Here Nathaniel Thompson lies, for murder his blood for vengeance cries.'"

Baker sprang up from the cot, startling Gideon so that he spilled his coffee. Baker gripped the bars of the cell. He said in a choking voice, "I don't have to listen to your shit."

"You do have to listen," Gideon said. "I guess you could plug up your ears with your fingers. But that would grow pretty tiresome after a while, wouldn't it? So you may as well listen to the Dutch Sheriff while he *bob'ls* on."

Baker glared at Gideon. He turned, took a few steps, turned again, describing a small tight square with his pacing.

"The judge here in Colerain County died not long ago," Gideon said. "The president judge of the circuit neighboring us to the east will come here for the next quarter session. The state has decided to charge you with willful murder—murder in the first degree for purposely and unlawfully assaulting and inflicting grievous wounds on Yost Kepler, on the evening of October the twenty-sixth of this year, with those wounds resulted in his dying on the morning of October the twenty-eighth.

"The county will provide you with an attorney. He will try to confuse things and mislead the jury like lawyers always do. But the men on the jury will not be fooled. They will find you guilty, and the judge will sentence you to be hanged by the neck until you are dead. The sentence will be carried out within the confines of the jail—that means in the yard out back." Gideon indicated the wall at the end of the corridor with its single high window. "It won't be a public spectacle, the way executions used to be. It will just be you, me, a few deputies, the state's attorney, and twelve citizens as witnesses. A minister, if you want one. Also a doctor. After you stop kicking at the end of the rope, the doctor will check your pulse and pronounce you dead. It takes about ten minutes, or so I'm told. After you are dead, the doctor will take your body and cut it up—dissect it. Doctors like doing that. Especially the one we have here in Adamant.

"Understand, I will get no pleasure out of hanging you. However, it is my duty as sheriff to see that your sentence is carried out."

"I didn't kill that boy," Baker said.

"Witnesses will place you with Yost Kepler, sharing drinks in the House of Lords on the evening that Kepler was beaten. And kicked. Stomped to death, in an alley outside the saloon." Gideon pointed at Baker's stockinged feet. "My deputy took away your boots when he put you in the cell."

"Yeah. My fucking feet have been cold ever since."

"Yes, well. Your boots—the heel on the right boot has a big nick out of one corner. The coroner—the one who will cut you up when you are dead—he will testify that the bruises on Yost Kepler's body match the size and shape of your boot's heel. I also found the same kind of marks in the alley where you dumped the body."

"Nobody saw me do anything to him."

"Nobody needs to have seen you do anything. It's funny, but I'm told that this kind of evidence usually does a better job of convincing a jury than eyewitness testimony. The jurymen get a chance to put two and two together, draw their own conclusions. They will learn about you buying Kepler drinks in the House of Lords, getting him drunk. His body found nearby, hidden under trash. Your boot heel with the nicked corner, the bruises all over his body, your tracks in the alley. Oh, I almost forgot. Yost Kepler's watch, with his initials engraved on the lid, which we found with all that money in your girl's room in Chinclaclamoose. The jury will take about ten minutes to find you guilty of murder in the first degree.

"That's just the first trial," Gideon continued. "After you are convicted, you will be put on trial again, for murdering the old man." Gideon reflected that he was getting good at lying. "Did you know the old man was the ironmaster's brother? Maybe you were just told that he was someone who needed getting rid of. You were a tool—a dumb tool, like a hammer or a maul. You were paid to kill the old tramp. Whoever paid you didn't care any more for you than a beat-up old hammer he might use once and then throw away in the grass. Your girl put her mark on a statement setting forth things that you told her on the night after you killed the old man and fled back to Chinclaclamoose. She's scared half to death. And horrified at what you did. She will appear in court as a witness for the commonwealth, and she will repeat under oath what you said about being paid two hundred dollars in gold eagles to 'do a job for a big important man.' The ironmaster paid you to kill that old tramp, didn't he?"

Baker sat down on his cot.

"We found the gold and the watch in a sack in a wardrobe there in the girl's room. She told me you promised to take her with you and go west. If you had ridden off right away, I doubt you would have been caught. Stupid of you, to spend the night in bed with her, and most of the next day. Well, I hope you had your fun. Where were you planning to go, anyway? Ohio? Illinois? The Missouri Territory? What were you going to do with that blood money? Piss it away drinking and gambling?"

"Quit running your mouth, you Dutch blockhead. You got *nothing* on me. I never met that Dutch boy. I didn't kill him or any old man, either. I was just going home when you tried to stop me. I didn't know you were the law. I seen you blocking the road with your horse, maybe set to rob me. That's why I ran. Did you see me kill that old man? Did you find a knife on me?"

"How did you know he was killed with a knife?"

"Your big-mouth deputy told me."

"Yes, that's how the old man was murdered. He had thirteen stab wounds on his hands and arms, which he used to try to protect himself when you went after him. Once you got him down, you stabbed him four times in the lungs and three times through the muscle of the heart. The coroner says that any of those seven wounds would have been enough to kill him. Then you slit his throat. Even so, it took him a while to die, didn't it? That explains why there was so much blood on the shirt and trousers of yours that we picked up off the floor in your girl's room. No, I don't think we need to find a knife."

Baker lay down on the cot. His chest heaved.

"You are in a tight spot," Gideon said. And he figured he was, too. He had nothing to offer Baker for admitting his guilt and stating who had paid him to kill the old tramp. He had been ordered by a corrupt prosecutor to cease investigating the case. He didn't see any way that he could get Baker to incriminate the ironmaster.

★★★

True put clabber on the table that evening. It was a food she professed to love and one that repelled Gideon. Its lumpy curdled texture reminded him of puke. Its sour taste puckered his mouth. Back home, spoiled milk like this would be fed to the hogs. He spooned molasses onto it and tried to choke it down.

True sat across from him, eating silently, her eyes downcast. The whole house was silent. It felt empty, with just the two of them in it.

He pushed his bowl aside. "I miss him so much," he said. "True, honey . . ."

She swiped her hand across between them. "I don't want to talk about it." She shook her head. "I loved him too much."

"No, no. I just want to remember him. In a good way."

"All I can remember is the way he died." She dropped her spoon and held her head in her hands. He reached across and put his hands on hers.

"I did everything I could think of," she said. "I dosed him with mint tea, I poulticed him again and again. Nothing helped."

"You did all you could." *And I was not there with him, as a father should be.*

"I should have gone for the doctor."

"That doctor couldn't do a thing. A lot of people died from this. True, we're not alone."

"I wish my gram had been here. She would have found some way to save him."

"Maybe," Gideon said, "but I don't think so."

"I put my trust in God," True said. "He took my baby. He took David away from me."

"He was a good, sweet little boy." Gideon wanted to say something hopeful. He couldn't find the words. "I miss him so bad."

"I knew something would happen. That dream told me. I knew it, and I didn't pay attention." A tear ran down her cheek. "I listened to what you said. That dreams aren't omens, that they don't mean anything." She opened her hands and wove her fingers into his. "I'm sorry," she said. "It's not your fault."

He leaned across and kissed her. "It's not your fault, either. You did everything you could. You were a wonderful mother to that little boy. You didn't love him too much. You loved him just enough." He stood, still holding her hand, and urged her up out of her chair. He led her to their bed.

She sat down on it and stared at the floor. He kissed her again. He helped her undress. She began to weep. He caressed her, got her to lie down on the bed. He tried to be as gentle as he could. He thought that what they did could not be called making love. It was more like trying to assuage grief.

Later, he got out of bed. He went outside and got the red setter— he still had a hard time thinking of the dog as "Old Dick"—and let him in to the kitchen. He built up the fire and sat before the flames. The dog lay on the floor next to his chair. Gideon ran his hand along the dog's side, the ribs bump-bumping beneath his fingers.

Since he had ridden to Chinclaclamoose, more rain had fallen. At times the rain would change to snow, which melted when the temperature rose and the rain recommenced. The hills looked sodden, as if they'd been dredged up from the bottom of the sea. Muddy pools stood in the harvested fields. Ducks swam in the pools, having left the streams and creeks, which ran fast and high against their banks.

He had no desire to take the judge's gun and dog and go hunting for grouse in the thickets or for ducks on the ponds.

He would never take David hunting. Or hoist him up on his shoulders to watch a parade. Or teach him to saw a board or skip a stone across water or ride a horse. How many months would have to pass before his mind no longer went to his son a hundred times a day? What would it feel like to sit in front of the fire some evening and realize that all that day he had not thought of David even once?

Gideon believed he had thought of his *memmi* every single day in the years since he had found her murdered. Not good thoughts, either. Mostly the awful scene of her body on the floor, bloody and dead. Or his imaginings of her killing.

He went quietly in to the bedroom and reached under the bed where True slept. He slid out the heavy leather-covered case. In the kitchen he set the case on the table. He unbuckled the straps and lifted the lid. The smell of oil tickled his nose. Mixed with it was a hint of cigar smoke.

An image of a lean, strong-jawed face came to his mind: the judge enjoying an after-dinner cigar as he cleaned and put away his beloved shotgun.

Gideon assembled the Manton. He threw it to his shoulder and looked out over the graceful twinned barrels on whose oiled dama-scene surface the firelight danced.

Seeing the gun, the red setter had gotten to his feet. He stretched and yawned, gave a little stuttering whine. He came and stood next to Gideon. He looked up, wagging his tail.

"You think we're going hunting, don't you?" Canine optimism brought a smile to Gideon's face. "In the dark? I don't think so, *hund*. But we will. Someday soon, we will."

*The coffin, earth and winding sheet*
*Will soon your active limbs enclose*

# Thirty-Five

⟨⟨⟨⟩⟩⟩

THE MOON, SINKING BEHIND THE HILLS, CAST UP A PALE GLOW. A breeze pushed thin silvery clouds across the sky. As Gideon trudged up Academy Hill, the moon's glow faded and the stars became pure and ice-bright. He stopped and drew air into his lungs. The cold air started him coughing. The fit passed, and he stood and looked up at the heavens. When he was little, his *dawdy* had held him in his arms as together they looked up at *die schtaerne*. He remembered the raspy feel of his father's cheek against his. Scents of dirt and hay on his coat. His quiet voice as he pointed out *der Drache, der Rabe,* the big sprawling constellation called *der Grosser Baer,* the Great Bear, just below *der Naddschtann,* the North Star—his father said that of all the animals, the Great Bear was the only one whose coat was thick enough to let it venture into the frozen realm of the north.

It surprised him, finding that memory again after all these years. It told him his father hadn't always been so angry and mean. He felt a pang at the love lost between them—and a deep sadness at the thought that his father, too, must have suffered terribly from the sudden, harrowing violation and killing of his wife.

His eyes searched among the constellations, found the comet hanging there silent and aloof.

Climbing, he had to stop several more times to catch his breath. The doctor had said it might be weeks or even months before he got his wind back. Dr. Beecham did not think the pneumonia had scarred Gideon's lungs. *But be careful,* he had said. *You have had a great shock. Give yourself time to heal.*

Gideon figured that time was something he did not now have much of.

It was Wednesday, the seventeenth of November. This evening, the church would ring with shape-note harmony. He'd asked True if she wanted to attend, but her answer had been "Not yet." And so Gideon had sent a boy to the academy with a letter asking whether he might come there this evening and meet with the headmaster. Gideon had received a hastily scribbled reply from Foote inviting him to come.

He found Foote outside, bundled in a buffalo robe.

"The comet has reached perihelion," the headmaster said. "It is now as close to Earth as it will get. Soon it will sweep past our planet and return to the marches of the solar system. It will not return for three quarters of a century. Unless you live to a very ripe age, Sheriff Stoltz, you will never see Halley's Comet again."

Gideon looked at the comet with its gauzy tail trailing back from the bright, solid-looking head. "It seems that scientists can explain comets, more or less," he said, "but not some other things about the stars. It has always wondered me, why the night sky is so black. I've read that the universe goes on and on, that it is filled with uncountable numbers of stars as bright as our sun. If there are so many stars, why do we see black spaces between them?"

"I, too, have scratched my poor old pate about that," Foote said. "My conclusion is this: We see, with our feeble eyes and our poor telescopes, into but a very small portion of the universe, some minuscule percentage of the whole. We don't see the stars that lie at an unfathomable distance from the earth.

"Here's another question to tickle your brain," the headmaster continued. "Are some of the stars we view already dead? Are they so remote that the light now reaching us was given off in the deep past, and the stars that we see are, in reality, no more than burnt-out husks?" He laid a hand on Gideon's arm. "You should not linger in this chill listening to the cosmological theories of a scatter-brained academician. Let's go inside. I'll make us something hot to drink."

In the headmaster's quarters, as Foote prepared tea, Gideon heard a chorus of shrill chirps apparently coming from the fire. Crossing the room, he found on the hearth several small boxes made of thin sheets of basswood folded ingeniously and capped with woven rush lids. From inside each box chirped a cricket.

"*Gryllus assimilis*," Foote said. "Common field crickets. I keep 'em caged so that Merlin and Morgan—my turtle and snake—cannot eat them. Alas, the poor fellows do not have much longer to sing. Or, more accurately, to stridulate. They produce that sound by scraping their wing covers together, although I'm sure you know that already.

"Here." He handed Gideon a steaming mug. "You will also recall that I have a more stalwart libation, if such is your fancy."

"I wanted to thank you for coming to my son's burying."

"Not at all, not at all. I can't imagine the grief that you and your wife must be feeling."

"Mr. Foote," Gideon asked, "do you believe in an all-seeing God?"

Foote's brow knit. "Well, I might believe in a distracted God, an absent-minded one in some far corner of the universe. Or maybe a cross-grained old reprobate who doesn't give a hoot for us here on Earth and would rather complain about his hernia or his ingrown toenail. But in fact I believe in none of those deities, or any other. A reverend minister, Mr. Donald Braefield—why, he is the very man who conducted the burial service for your child; he holds the pastorate at Panther—Donald calls me a 'Nothingarian.' He's a good Christian who loves me in spite of my unbelief. He's also an avid collector of odonates, the dragonflies and damselflies. Donald wields a swift net. Well. Gone off the rails again, haven't I?" Foote gave his grating laugh and leaned forward in his chair. "Sheriff Stoltz, all godly thoughts aside: Were you able to identify the man who was stabbed to death?"

Gideon shook his head. "I believe he was Nat Thompson. I am *sure* he was Nat Thompson. But there's no evidence to prove it. No letters on his person, no monogrammed clothing, nothing like that."

"Have you learned anything from your prisoner?"

"He maintains that he is innocent of all crimes."

"Do you interrogate him?"

"I talk with him. I talk *at* him, mostly." Gideon sipped his tea. "Maybe he will open up to me at some point. But I can't offer him anything in exchange. He's been charged with murder in the first degree for killing Yost Kepler—a willful, premeditated murder committed in the perpetration of a robbery."

"The evidence in that case, is it strong?"

"It seems to me to be strong, even though it is circumstantial."

"Do you think he'll be convicted?"

"Mr. Fish says Baker will be convicted for killing Yost Kepler. That he will hang for it." Gideon squirmed in the chair. "He also told me he will not put Baker on trial for killing the old man."

Foote's eyebrows shot up.

"He won't even let me investigate."

"But . . ."

"I think the ironmaster got to him," Gideon said.

"Bought him off."

"Or scared him." Gideon described the evidence linking Baker to the old tramp: meeting him on the road near the logging camp where the tramp had been stabbed to death, Baker's flight, his blood-stained clothing, the gold eagles in the sack, the sworn statement by the young woman Baker was with in Chinclaclamoose claiming he had told her he'd been paid to do a job for "a big important man."

"Is there anything to directly connect Adonijah Thompson with this assassin?"

"Two men at the ironmaster's stable told me Baker stayed there. Simpletons, I suppose you'd call them. They heard the ironmaster tell

Baker to go find an old tramp in the logging camp at the head of Egypt Hollow. A camp that is owned by the ironworks."

Foote gave a low whistle. "And Fish won't let you investigate."

"When I got back from Chinclaclamoose, I went down with the influenza and was out of my mind for a while. My deputy knew that the old man had appeared at the judge's house on October 18. So he brought the judge's housekeeper to the jail to view the corpse. Mrs. Leathers went there practically kicking and screaming, not wanting to lay eyes on another dead body. But she looked at the old man, and she said yes, it might be the tramp who had shown up at the judge's house that evening."

Foote drummed his fingers on the arm of his chair. "'Might be.' That's not exactly a positive identification. Nothing that would cause a grand jury to indict anyone."

"No," Gideon said. "And anyway, Fish would never agree to convening a grand jury for this."

Foote and Gideon had finished their tea. It was not difficult for the headmaster to persuade Gideon to have some of the stronger stuff.

As he sipped the whiskey, Gideon described the old tramp for Foote: his stature and build, similar to that of the headmaster; the length and cut of his beard; his wooden staff; and his clothing and hat, the latter adorned with a white buck tail. All of those personal items were under lock and key at the jail.

"How well do you know the ironmaster?" Gideon asked Foote.

"I don't believe I've ever met the man."

"You'd remember it if you had. My wife told me the ironmaster says the law stops where his ironworks begins. I met him there in Panther one morning when I was hoping to arrest the man I knew then as George England. When I faced the ironmaster, I was afraid. But my wife tells me that Adonijah Thompson is not without fear himself. She says he's terrified of spirits. Of ghosts."

Foote snorted. "You could say that about most of the people around here."

Gideon swallowed the rest of his drink. An idea had come to him. A wild idea. A dangerous plan. But it just might work.

"Your friend, the Reverend Braefield," he said. "The one who likes to catch dragonflies. Does he believe in the Ten Commandments?"

"I assume so. He's a preacher, ain't he?"

On the hearth the crickets chirped, their notes slower, fewer. They're dying, Gideon thought. As we all are.

*Who is this that comes from far,*
*With his garments dipped in blood?*

# Thirty-Six

~⚬~

"'THE HEART IS DECEITFUL ABOVE ALL THINGS, AND DESPERATELY wicked: Who can know it?' Word of the Lord, as told by the prophet Jeremiah, chapter seventeen, verse nine."

The Reverend Braefield had a booming voice for such a slender man. His eyes were large and set wide apart in his head. Gideon thought they made Braefield look a bit like a dragonfly himself.

The preacher's eyes, flitting about the sanctuary, seemed to momentarily find and bore into those of each and every congregant at the Panther Presbyterian Church.

"The English dramatist John Webster writes that 'Other sins only speak; murder shrieks out.'" The minister paused. "I am certain that all of us are reeling at the news of two murders in this county within the last month." Again his gaze raked over the congregation. "Can you not hear the shrieks of those poor wronged souls? And can you not hear another shrieking, older and yet persistent, coming from the walls of this church, from the garden next to the parsonage—from the house where I, your pastor, make my home?"

The minister clasped his hands behind his back and paced from one side of the pulpit to the other.

"Murder is a grievous sin, whose severity and depravity are shown by God's placing the commandment 'Thou shalt not kill' at the head of the second table of Mosaic law. Committing murder burdens the mind with a heavy guilt, a guilt that grows harder to bear with each passing day—each month—each year."

Gideon had filed in with the last of the worshipers and taken a seat in back. By leaning forward, he could watch Adonijah Thompson, three rows in front of him and across the aisle. The ironmaster had placed his top hat on the pew next to him. No one sat close, out of either respect or fear. The ironmaster wore a fine frock coat whose dark gray color matched his hair, combed back and flowing down over his collar. Seen from the side, Thompson's face appeared stern and unmoving.

"The Bible says that each of us suffers from the sickness of a deceitful, wicked heart," the Reverend Braefield said. "Into this condition we are born, and throughout our lives the evil in our souls causes us to do many things we know to be wrong. We bear false witness. We cheat and steal. We grow wrathful and fierce. We may even strike out violently against our fellow man and kill.

"All of us are sinners. *You* are a sinner; *I* am a sinner. Make no mistake about it, a man of the cloth, a so-called man of God, can be as base and abject a sinner as any other. Such a one was the Reverend Thomas McEwan, who once preached from this very pulpit and who urged his fellow men and women to be pure in heart and soul and Godly in thought and conduct—when he himself was not.

"Sinner that he was, McEwan fell upon a person, a man in his employ, and smote him with a maul. The attack took place outside the parsonage. I am sure the older members of the church recall McEwan's act of violence, and some here would have witnessed the events that followed it—events that took place thirty years ago. Is that such a long time? No. Thirty years is but a fleeting blink before the all-seeing eye of the Lord."

Gideon saw the crease running from the ironmaster's nose to the corner of his mouth deepen and darken.

"In the courthouse in Adamant," the preacher said, "in November of 1805, the Reverend McEwan was convicted of murdering Nathaniel Thompson with a blow to the head, and then secretly burying his body in the parsonage garden. Justice—man's justice—was swiftly dispensed, and McEwan was hanged. It is said that he struggled at the rope's end for nigh onto a quarter of an hour, before his body, which had been powerful in life, gave up the ghost."

A murmur passed through the congregation.

"The Lord Jesus Christ, our Savior, recognized our sad and perilous condition when he said: 'From within, out of the hearts of men, proceed evil thoughts, adulteries, fornications, murders, thefts, covetousness, wickedness, deceit, lasciviousness, and evil eye, blasphemy, pride, and foolishness: All these things come from within, and defile the man.'

"But Thomas McEwan," the preacher continued, "went to his death a forgiven soul. For as surely as the Bible tells us that all men are sinners, it also reveals the path to divine forgiveness and final salvation, saying: 'For with the heart man believeth unto righteousness: and with the mouth confession is made unto salvation.'"

The preacher's voice strengthened. "God promises that *all* who repent their sins, who call upon the Lord for forgiveness, shall receive it.

"Before his life was forfeit, as he stood on a cart beneath the gallows tree, a rope around his neck, McEwan confessed his sins—of evil thought, obstinacy and pride, cruelty and violence. He confessed to the murder of Nathaniel Thompson, although in this we must entertain the possibility that he was deceived—not by the guiles of the Common Enemy, the Prince of the Power of the Air, but by one who lives among us still."

The minister paused. The congregation sat in silence.

"We sometimes think we can hear souls shrieking around us. Souls which have become debased; souls belonging to our brothers and sisters whose lives were cruelly and unfairly cut short. We hear people speak of ghosts and phantoms, spirits and revenants. Some of you here believe you have seen the spirit of a man called Calhoun, who labored in the ironworks until he met with a deadly accident and was immolated in the furnace.

"Why do we believe in ghosts? Why do they appear before our eyes, their cries assail our ears? Is there a shifting, barely glimpsed world that parallels the one in which we dwell? Or is it our own guilt that creates these spectral beings, our own deep and abiding guilt that calls them forth and presents them to our senses?"

At that moment the side door to the church opened. A figure stood in the little-used entry, lit from behind by the low autumn sun: a man stooped and bent, leaning on a staff, wearing a broad-brimmed hat from which a long white buck tail dangled.

A collective gasp came from the churchgoers. As Adonijah Thompson turned his head to look at the visitant, his face became open to Gideon's scrutiny. The ironmaster's eyes began to blink rapidly. The skin over his cheekbones paled.

The stooped man eased the door shut. His clothes were ragged and stained. His head was held low. The extravagantly decorated hat shaded and obscured his face; beneath its brim a white beard could be glimpsed. Gripping his staff, the man hobbled to the nearest pew, a front row bench where no one else sat, and lowered himself onto it.

"The source of murder," the preacher went on, "as of all human perfidy, is that Original Sin, which the hearts of men are full of, the ever-flowing spring that sends forth its perverse and wicked stream."

Slowly the ironmaster rose. He stared at the man seated alone at the front of the church. Adonijah Thompson's hands trembled. His shoulders shook. He cast quick glances about him, at this man, that woman, then back at the old man in the buck tail hat. The ironmaster picked up his own hat and clutched it to his chest. His mouth worked convulsively. He began stumbling along the pew, the people shrinking back or half-rising to let him pass. "No," he groaned. He stopped to stare again at the ragged man sitting hunched over in the front row. "*No!*"

The ironmaster turned and staggered up the aisle toward the door at the rear of the sanctuary.

Gideon edged down his own pew, reached the aisle, and turned to follow the gray-clad back. He felt the eyes of the congregation on him: people he had never seen before, people he vaguely recognized, and people he knew, among them True's parents and brothers and sisters-in-law. Their eyes were wide and filled with fear.

*Death, like an overflowing stream*
*Sweeps us away; our life's a dream . . .*

# Thirty-Seven

—⚬⚬⚬—

MAUDE SOON CAUGHT UP WITH THE GRAY-CLAD MAN STRIDING down the blue road. Gideon slowed her to a walk. Thompson was breathing heavily. He looked up, blinked. "What are you doing here?"

When Gideon did not reply, the ironmaster turned his face back to the road. He stared straight ahead. He kept walking. "Get off my place," he said.

"I will keep you company. In case you want to confess anything to me."

They continued on. Anyone seeing them might have concluded that they were two friends out for a Sabbath-day constitutional, one walking and the other horseback.

They passed the furnace. Smoke rose from the stack. The deep-throated roaring of the blast reached their ears. A man's voice could be heard from inside the building, calling out for stone and coal.

The ironmaster muttered to himself. Spittle clung to the corners of his mouth. He looked up at Gideon, then stopped abruptly. "Why should I confess anything to you? Clear off my ironworks now, you double-Dutch bastard."

"Mr. Thompson, you know that I am the sheriff of Colerain County. I go where I need to go to see that justice is served."

"Go roll your hoop, boy." The ironmaster strode onward.

Gideon clucked to Maude, who resumed her steady pace.

They came to the big house. The ironmaster bounded up the steps and went inside. As he sat waiting, Gideon gave Maude the

263

reins. She began shearing off grass next to the road. Her head moved from side to side, her lips exploring the tussocks, gathering the withered tan blades into her mouth. She blew through her nose, a sound of contentment. Gideon looked up. Clouds were creeping in from the west, turning the sky to milk.

The ironmaster came out of the house. He had taken off his coat, revealing a white shirt with bloused sleeves. He wore knee-high black boots, brilliantly polished, with silver-roweled spurs. He was hatless, his hair queued up behind his head. He ran down the steps. Maude raised her head. The ironmaster strode up to Gideon. He drew a pistol from his belt, cocked the hammer, and aimed the gun at Gideon's breast. Gideon felt heat wash upward through his body. His pulse pounded in his head. The pistol in his boot and the rifle in its scabbard seemed miles away. *Fool.* He felt a stab of grief at how he had failed True yet again. He had not taken her warnings seriously enough. He would die at the hands of this man. It would destroy her.

The pistol's octagonal muzzle framed a round black hole. Gideon stared into the ironmaster's eyes. They were fierce and unyielding. Then slowly they became dull and inward-looking. Adonijah Thompson's chest heaved. "Dear God," he said. He turned the pistol and placed its muzzle against his temple. He pulled the trigger. The hammer fell. If there was powder in the pan, it failed to ignite. The ironmaster slowly lowered his hand and dropped the pistol in the grass. He turned and staggered off.

Gideon took a deep breath. He sat up straight and gathered in the reins. He felt the reassuring link between himself and Maude, the charge of empathy going through the reins from his hands to her mouth and coming back to him again. He held the reins lightly but firmly, as if holding two small birds, one in each hand, not wishing to harm them and not willing to let them fly free. He felt Maude playing with the bit, biting it softly and then releasing it. He clucked to her, and she began to walk. His hips moved in synchrony with her limbs. It felt like he was walking through her.

Together they followed the gray man who went quickly and disjointedly down a road through a grove of tall pine trees until he came to the stable.

When the ironmaster emerged through the open double door, he sat bareback on the stallion Vagabond. Glistening swirls marked the horse's black coat. The stallion's nostrils flared, and his neck arched. He flicked his ears toward Maude. She gave a whicker and cut a little flirt to one side, and the stallion whinnied in a guttural way and stepped toward her. The ironmaster, using the reins and the pressure of his legs, turned the stallion and made him hew to a straight line down the road, headed away from the ironworks.

Maude ambled forward to walk alongside the black.

Gideon said, "You paid George Baker two hundred dollars to kill your brother Nathaniel. You told him he could find Nat in the logging camp at the head of Egypt Hollow, where you had stashed him away. Baker went there and stabbed your brother to death. Baker is now my prisoner. He is prepared to testify that you paid him to kill Nat."

The ironmaster stared ahead between the stallion's ears.

"Your brother is not the first person you have killed," Gideon said. "Many years ago, you shot an Indian boy to death not far from this spot, while he made a sound like a turkey, trying to lure you in to an ambush."

The ironmaster looked at Gideon, his eyes wide.

"Then in the autumn of 1805 you killed some other man, whose corpse was later dug up in the garden of the parsonage by Sheriff Bathgate, and misidentified as your brother Nat, while Judge Biddle and the Reverend McEwan stood watching."

"I didn't kill that man." The ironmaster took both reins in one hand. He combed the fingers of his other hand through the stallion's mane: a strong hand, age-spotted, the tendons sharp beneath the skin. "One of my workers. A woodcutter. He died of some disease, probably the diphtheria, in a bark shanty down the valley. Hadn't worked for me much above two weeks. He came from away, no next of kin that anyone knew of, no one to miss him." The ironmaster looked down the road. "He was the same size and build as Nat, had the same color hair. I dug him up out of the shallow grave they'd laid him in and carried him to Panther in an ore wagon. I had sent Nat to go work for McEwan in the first place. Told him to provoke the old preacher. It wasn't hard, let me tell you."

He smiled his tight upside-down smile. "That overbearing bastard got what he deserved. What he so richly deserved." The ironmaster spat. "He spoke with such piety about God and Jesus and 'loving thy fellow man.' An arrogant bully. Proud as a louse."

"At the trial," Gideon said, "a witness, a teamster named Samuel Lingle, swore he saw a man in a dark robe and a white cap, at night under the full moon, digging in the garden at the parsonage."

"Lingle worked for me. I had him walk by that night and then tell the sheriff what he'd seen. I myself had seen the reverend out one morning early, standing in his garden, wearing his robe and cap. That night I stole into his house as he slept. I put on his robe and cap. I went back out and buried the dead man—I'd dressed him in Nat's clothes, put Nat's ring on his finger. I made sure he had wounds on his head."

"Your brother left this place . . ."

"The day Nat came home and told me the reverend had struck him with a maul, I almost cried out with joy. I spirited Nat away, made sure no one saw him. I gave him enough money that he could have set himself up handsomely. He agreed to never come back. We shook hands and said goodbye—forever."

"How could you do such a thing? Your deception caused Thomas McEwan to be wrongly hanged. You cheated Hiram Biddle and Rachel McEwan out of a life together. In the end, your treachery drove the judge to take his own life."

"You should have seen how McEwan talked himself into believing he'd gone sleepwalking and buried my brother. Oh, he was guilty. He might as well have killed Nat when he hit him with that maul.

And the honorable Hiram Biddle, the high-and-mighty judge, proved no more perceptive than the self-righteous Bible thumper."

"It's true the preacher could have been brought up on charges for assaulting your brother," Gideon said. "But what you did was much worse."

"He got his comeuppance. All that rigmarole about confession and salvation. No. He burns in hell."

"As you will."

The ironmaster's mouth twitched.

"This has preyed on you for thirty years," Gideon said. "Just as it preyed on Judge Biddle." He reached into his boot and drew out the pistol. He cocked back the hammer and pointed the gun at the ironmaster. "I arrest you for murder. Not for what you did thirty years ago, but for hiring George Baker to kill your brother."

The ironmaster stopped his horse. "Tell me. In the church. Who was that?"

Gideon kept silent. Would Adonijah Thompson now submit? Had he swallowed the lie Gideon told, about Gib Baker incriminating him? Did he think the state's attorney would now have no choice but to prosecute him? Did he believe his brother's ghost had really come back?

Or was it now dawning on him that Gideon had played a trick almost as devious as the one the ironmaster himself had played thirty years past?

Gideon stared into Adonijah Thompson's eyes. A weary look overcame the ironmaster's gaunt, sharp-featured face. It reminded Gideon of the look on Hiram Biddle's face, as the judge had stood in the brush, holding in his hand a dead grouse, on that last day when they went hunting together.

"You'll not shut me up in jail," the ironmaster said. "You'll not put me on trial or hang me." He straightened. "Go ahead. Shoot me dead."

Gideon had wondered from the beginning if he would be

capable of that. He thought about what this man might have done to True. He thought of all the people that Adonijah Thompson had harmed. How he had probably sent George Baker to Hammertown, to watch for the Dutch Sheriff and kill him if he could.

They sat looking at each other.

"So. You will not release me." The ironmaster looked at Maude. "That's a nice mare. You ride her well. But I don't think she can catch this black."

"She has a big heart, and she doesn't give up," Gideon said. "We will follow you as far as we must."

"Then follow me to hell." The ironmaster spurred the stallion, and the black horse lunged forward.

Gideon didn't have to ask Maude to follow.

The ironmaster never looked back as he galloped down the road. After a ways, he turned the stallion off into the brush. Vagabond jumped over rocks and fallen limbs and crashed through brambles. Gideon slowed Maude. He put away the pistol. He let Maude pick her way over and around the worst of the obstacles. By now the ironmaster was out of sight. Gideon followed by sound, then by finding the trampled brush.

The stallion's hoofprints turned onto a path. The path left the brushlands and descended through forest to the bank of Panther Creek, then turned east.

The creek ran high and fast. The water surged and braided itself in white strands around rocks. The path came to a hill that the creek bent around to the left. The stallion's tracks led up the steep hill. On top of the hill Gideon found a clearing with a rock face at its edge. The creek went brawling along in its bed, sixty feet below. The ironmaster could have ridden off through the woods downhill and away from the creek. But a slew of tracks told Gideon that Adonijah Thompson had asked the stallion to do something, and the black had refused him.

Gideon rode all around the edge of the clearing to make sure. No tracks led off into the forest. The only thing the stallion could have done was go over the cliff and into the creek below.

He looked but didn't see anything, only Panther Creek raging past. He turned Maude away from the brink. He leaned back in the saddle as she muscled her way down the hill. At the bottom of the hill, the path led back to the water's edge.

Rapids in the creek roared. White water sideswiped boulders and spumed into the air and toppled onto rocks.

As they followed the path, the creek calmed and broadened. They came around a bend. The stallion stood in the shallows, his head low. Blood ran down his flanks from gashes made by the ironmaster's spurs. His sides heaved. He stood on three legs. One front leg was broken. The jagged bone stuck out through the hide.

*An empty tale, a morning flow'r,*
*Cut down and withered in an hour*

# Thirty-Eight

GIDEON SWALLOWED AGAINST THE LUMP IN HIS THROAT. "WHAT A noble, beautiful animal. I got down off of Maude and ended his suffering."

Horatio Foote rose from his chair and broke up the blackened logs in the fireplace with a poker. It was a raw, rainy night on the cusp between fall and winter. The headmaster placed a log on the embers. It caught fire quickly, flames crackling and leaping up its sides.

Gideon took a sip of the headmaster's whiskey. He pictured again the black stallion, so cruelly used. He thought of the lives destroyed by what Adonijah Thompson had done thirty years ago, and the crimes he had recently committed.

He thought of his mother, dead now a dozen years, the good memories of her hidden away in his mind. Could he find them again? He thought of David, tried to picture the bright and cheery baby and saw only the still, vacant face. He thought of True, and his heart filled. What could he do to ease her pain?

He could love her. Maybe it would be enough.

"When I got back to Panther," he said, "my deputy had arrived. We went down the creek with some men. We found the ironmaster's body in an oxbow a mile downstream from his horse."

Gideon watched the flames lick up from the fire and vanish into the chimney's maw.

Many questions now had answers. Gideon had even figured out how his brother-in-law Jesse Burns had been linked to the murdered Yost Kepler. This morning, in a store in Adamant, Gideon had encountered a Dutch man newly arrived in Colerain County. The man told Gideon that he had bought a farm in Sinking Valley, where many *Pennsylfawnisch Deitsch* were settling. The man had a beard lining his jaw and wore plain clothes, one suspender crossing his breast, and a broad-brimmed black hat. To Gideon's questions he replied in halting English, in an accent thicker than *nudelsupp*, "This man, Chesse Burns, a farm for me he found." It turned out that Jesse got a commission whenever he located property for some Dutchman to buy. Gideon wondered what would happen when word got out that Jesse Burns was bringing in the damn Dutch. He certainly wouldn't be the one to tattle on his brother-in-law, but no doubt the truth would out.

He looked over at his host. "And you, Mr. Foote? What did you do after the ironmaster left the church and I followed him?"

"As planned, I removed myself from the sanctuary. I limped out through the same door I came in. I never raised my head or spoke to anyone, and no one followed me. The Reverend Braefield said the congregation sat frozen in place. He continued with his sermon, taking another half hour. By the time church let out, I was long gone." The headmaster stroked his white beard. "Tell me, how did the state's attorney react to the ironmaster's death?"

"He was very displeased. Both with me and over what he is calling the ironmaster's 'unfortunate accident.' Mr. Fish doesn't believe what people are saying—that a ghost showed up at the church in Panther. I told him I was there that day to thank the Reverend Braefield for conducting the funeral for my son. I said that for some reason, Mr. Thompson got up and left during the service. He didn't look well, so I thought I should follow him."

"Many people believe Nat Thompson really did come back," Foote said.

"Yes. They say the ironmaster paid the boy from Chinclaclamoose to murder his brother in the shanty up Egypt Hollow, and it was

Nat's restless spirit that came to the church to haunt him. They now believe that Thomas McEwan did not kill the ironmaster's brother in 1805, and that he was hanged for a crime he did not commit. There's even a rumor that a trickle of blood ran down the preacher's gravestone when Nat Thompson was knifed to death."

Foote harumphed. "Superstition. I suppose people will never rid themselves of it."

"They're under a great deal of strain. They worry about what will become of the ironworks, whether they'll lose their jobs."

"And . . . ?"

"The ironmaster left a will. He had it drawn up only a few days before his death. Maybe he knew something was about to happen. He has given the ironworks to a great-nephew of his, a recent graduate of some scientific institute in Troy, New York. He's on his way to Panther now."

"Well, that's good news," Foote said. "I must say I was surprised not to see you at the burying today. Myself, I couldn't stay away. Curiosity; it will kill me some day, I expect."

"I've been to more than enough funerals lately."

"A brief ceremony, with but few in attendance."

"Don't you find it odd, that the ironmaster did not choose to be buried at Panther?"

"That would be too common for Adonijah Thompson," Foote said. "He has long owned a grand lot on Burying Hill with a commanding view of the town. I've heard that a large monument will be erected there. Granite, carved in the shape of an anvil, and brought here, at great expense, all the way from Vermont. Granite is an exceedingly hard stone. No doubt it will outlast every other marker in the boneyard."

Gideon was only half-listening. He rose and told the headmaster that he must be going. He didn't want to leave True alone for too long. Besides, she'd smell the whiskey on his breath.

He realized he had not heard rain on the roof for some time. He crossed to a window. As he approached, he saw his face mirrored in the glass.

He drew nearer. His image dimmed and darkened and then vanished. He cupped his hands, pressed them to the glass, and looked out.

While they had been talking, the rain had turned to snow. Adamant lay white in its valley. Through the falling flakes Gideon could make out Burying Hill. The twin to Academy Hill, it loomed up pale and ghostly. The snow fell steadily there, on the graves of the preacher, the ironmaster, and the judge.

# Acknowledgments

For many novels, I suspect, there's a story behind the story. The one behind *A Stranger Here Below* began years ago when my wife bought a beautiful little book at a used book sale: *From the Danish Peninsula* by Steen Steensen Blicher. A minister in northern Denmark, Blicher lived from 1782 to 1848. The book, published in 1957 by the Tourist Association of Jutland, included a tale "The Parson at Veilby." That narrative inspired the interior story of *A Stranger Here Below*: the plot within the plot, related in the journal of Judge Hiram Biddle.

I thank my wife, the writer Nancy Marie Brown, for her steadfast encouragement and support, and for her astute editorial advice while I wrote and revised. Deep thanks and appreciation go to Natalia Aponte, my agent, who suggested a new and better beginning to the novel, and who worked long and hard to find a publisher. At Skyhorse, I thank my editor, Lilly Golden, whose excellent edits and suggestions have made this a better story.

Thanks, too, go to Harlan Berger, Denise Brown, Richard Fortmann, Alfred Gallifent, Carl Graybill, Betty Grindrod, Joe Healy, Randy Hudson, Cynthia Nixon-Hudson, Doug McNeal, Doug Madenford, Jackie Melander, Bill Jordan, Peter Jurs, Elaine Jurs, Garet Nelson, Mark Podvia, Sheila Post, Suzanne Rhodes, Stephen Roxburgh, Leonard Rubinstein, Alice Ryan, Ralph Seeley, Earl Shreckengast, Pamela Smith, Sandy Steltz, Jeff Swabb, Linda Wooster, and the staff at Cobleigh Public Library in Lyndonville, Vermont. I especially thank Paul Fagley, cultural educator at Greenwood Furnace State Park in Huntington County, Pennsylvania. Paul is a fount of knowledge about charcoal-making, ironmaking, and life in central Pennsylvania during the 1800s; he very generously read the manuscript and pointed out ways in which it could be improved.

Claire Van Vliet created the beautiful map depicting Adamant and Colerain County.

Both Colerain County and the town of Adamant are fictional places modeled loosely on the part of central Pennsylvania where I grew up.

I relied on many sources for historical and cultural information. These books were especially helpful:

*Albion's Seed: Four British Folkways in America*, David Hackett Fischer, Oxford University Press, 1989.

*Death in Early America: The History and Folklore of Customs and Superstitions of Early Medicine, Funerals, Burials, and Mourning*, Margaret M. Coffin, Thomas Nelson, 1976.

*Foreigners in Their Own Land: Pennsylvania Germans in the New Republic*, Steven M. Nolt, Pennsylvania State University Press, 2002.

*Making Iron on the Bald Eagle: Roland Curtin's Ironworks and Workers' Community*, Gerald C. Eggert, Pennsylvania State University Press, 2000.

Shape-note song lyrics that appear in different parts of this book, the short verses introducing each chapter, and the title *A Stranger Here Below* are all drawn from shape-note hymns published in tunebooks and widely sung in rural America in the early 1800s.

www.charlesfergus.com

Take a Peek at the Next Novel in
the Gideon Stoltz Mystery Series

# Advance Praise for *Nighthawk's Wing*

"What a fantastic book! Strong, well-drawn characters, rich attention to natural detail, and a haunting narrative make this a series to get excited about."—Paul Doiron, author of the Mike Bowditch Mystery Series

"This beautifully written mystery combines harsh realities with moments of sheer wonder. A murder mystery that has at its heart a praise hymn to America's rural past."—Patricia Bracewell, author of the Emma of Normandy trilogy

"Spellbinding historical fiction. Fergus is a wonderful writer who will entrance you with his sense of time and place."—Kate Flora, author of *Death Comes Knocking*

"An intricate mystery alive with well-paced narrative and brutal realism."—Castle Freeman, author of *The Devil in the Valley*

"I absolutely loved *Nighthawk's Wing*—I read it straight through in one day, and it's haunted me ever since."—Kristen Lindquist, author of *Tourists in the Known World*

"High-tension, high-stakes law enforcement and crime solving in a fascinating culture of immigration, frontier, and survival in early America."—Beth Kanell, author of *The Long Shadow*

"An atmospheric page-turner . . . I was borne away by *Nighthawk's Wing*, and you will be too."—Edith Maxwell, author of the Agatha Award-winning Quaker Midwife Mysteries

"A darkly engrossing tale in which a young sheriff struggles to understand and unravel not only the workings of the complex and dangerous souls he encounters, but his own tortured soul as well."—Jeffrey Lent, author of *In the Fall*

"A fresh and original take on the historical mystery, *Nighthawk's Wing* fills the stage with characters whose concerns will resonate uncannily with those of 21st-century readers."—Tim Weed, author of *A Field Guide to Murder and Fly Fishing*

*God of my life look gently down,*
*Behold the pains I feel*

# Chapter 1

◦◦◦

H E FLINCHED AND SHOT A GLANCE OVER HIS SHOULDER.
Nothing there but the empty street, hot and dusty and
flooded with light.

Gideon Stoltz faced forward again. He was a tall, broad-shouldered
man who normally stood up straight, but now his head hung and his
shoulders slumped.

He squinted at the sky.

There it was again—the thing that had *shpooked* him. The strange
blurry object hung in the upper right corner of his vision. Like an
errant cloud, or a dirty cobweb. It had been there, he reckoned, since
he had fallen off Maude and hurt his head.

He didn't remember falling off his mare. He didn't—couldn't—
remember much of anything from that time.

He wiped the sweat from his face with his shirt sleeve. His head
*schmatzed* him something fierce, and pain also throbbed in his neck.

He checked and made sure no one had been watching when he
startled and looked behind himself. He didn't want to appear daft, or
scared of his own shadow. He was the sheriff of Colerain County. A
sheriff was supposed to be sensible. Brave.

The Dutch Sheriff, they called him. Said he was too young.

Well, he was undeniably *Pennsylfawnisch Deitsch*, Pennsylvania
Dutch, unlike most of the other folk hereabouts. Maybe he *was* too
young to have the responsibilities of a sheriff—although for the life
of him he couldn't recall exactly what those responsibilities might be.
Anyway, he wasn't *that* young. He was . . .

He frowned. Why couldn't he remember how old he was? It was

1

now 1836; August of 1836. He had been born on April 1, 1813. He tried to subtract: thirty-six take away thirteen. He let out an impatient huff of breath. Finally it came to him.

He was twenty-three years old.

Twenty-three and addlepated from a fall off his horse.

Was he daft? Maybe only a *verrickt* man would go out in the sun on a blistering day like this. But he needed to walk around town. Sheriff Payton, his predecessor, had said it was part of the job: to patrol the town and county, to travel about and be seen, keep an eye peeled for strangers and potential lawbreakers, nip any trouble in the bud.

The sun stood high in the sky. He blinked against its glare. He tried to get a look at the gray cobwebby thing, but it leaped sideways, his eyes chasing after it until the object darted off his field of view.

He looked forward again, and there it was, hovering on the upper right edge of his vision. Like it was watching him. Judging him.

He set off down the street, his boots sinking in the dust.

He passed brick and stone and log and wood-sided buildings, stores and shops and dwellings on both sides of the street, some of them separated by empty lots grown up with pokeweed and briars.

Clanging from a smithy beat against his ears, followed by the screech of red-hot iron quenched in a slack tub.

He smelled rotting garbage and cooking meat and wood smoke and burning charcoal.

He trudged three more blocks until a dizzy spell hit him. He found a patch of shade cast by a small barn and steadied himself with a hand pressed against its wall. His stomach felt queasy. Pain rippled through his shoulders, his neck, his head.

After his fall, True said he should go see the doctor. He had nixed that idea right away. Doc Beecham would bleed him or burn him or dose him with some vile potion that would make him gag and puke. No, he wanted True to nurse him. She was his wife; she ought to take care of him. Which she'd done—half-heartedly, it seemed, maybe even grudgingly. He set his jaw. He didn't like this unease that lay between them. He wished she would get over her grief and return to being a real wife to him. He needed her. Needed them to be together again.

He pushed off from the barn. The heat rose up around him. He went through an alley, intending to head back to the jail. Rounding the next corner, he ran into a wall of stench.

In the street lay a dead horse. Nearby a wagon listed to one side, its tongue in the dust.

He pinched his nose shut. What the devil happened here? Then he remembered. Yesterday, Old Man Greevey's horse bolted and crashed his wagon into the watering trough. The horse broke a leg. Greevey pitched into the street, breaking his own leg. Gideon's deputy, Alonzo Bell, shot the horse. They carried Greevey to the doctor, the old man moaning that they might as well shoot him, too.

Greevey's son said he'd get rid of the horse. Clearly he hadn't done it yet.

Gideon asked himself why he hadn't remembered the horse as soon as he smelled the stench. Or before he went out for his walk. Or maybe he *had* remembered it and had gone out from the jail to check on whether the horse had been removed, and then forgotten why he'd ventured out in the first place.

Why couldn't he remember such things?

Why couldn't he write a clear sentence, or sign his name with facility, or add up a column of numbers?

Why couldn't he remember anything about his own accident, getting thrown off Maude or otherwise falling off her, striking his head on the ground, and (so he'd been told) lying insensible on the road?

He worried about the gap in his memory. He didn't know how far back it went.

He edged around the dead horse until he was upwind of it. The horse lay on its side, belly bloated, legs jutting out save for the left front, whose hoof and part of the cannon bone hung down below the knee, the bone's jagged end sticking out through the hide. Flies swarmed over the carcass. Greenish fluid leaked from the horse's anus. A Christ-awful stench. Soon they'd be bombarded with complaints to get the thing off the street before contagion spread.

Greevey's son said he'd get rid of the horse. Clearly he hadn't done it yet.

Gideon realized it was the second time in less than a minute that his mind had registered the exact same thought.

He skirted the broken wheel with its splintered spokes and shattered felloes and twisted iron rim. He stopped at the stone watering trough. Water trickled into the trough through wooden pipes from a spring in one of the brushy hills that hemmed in Adamant. In the past, those hills had been forested; now they were studded with stumps, here and there a single tree standing like a confused and bereft survivor of what had once been a great tribe.

He took off his hat and set it on the wagon's seat. He bent over the trough, cupped water in his hands, and splashed it into his face. He ran his hands through his short sandy hair and wiped the back of his neck. He picked up his hat and put it back on his head.

Setting off down the street, he stared at round marks in the dust made by horses' hooves, straight lines unspooled by wagon wheels, irregular scuffings of human and animal feet.

He passed two hogs lying in the patchy shade of a box elder, their sides slowly rising and falling. He stopped for a cart piled with hay, pulled along by a swaybacked horse, the driver standing in the bed holding the reins in one hand and a sun-shielding umbrella in the other hand.

After the cart he found himself confronted by a dozen gray geese. They waddled along, panting, driven by a hatchet-faced woman carrying a stick. The geese seemed to have angry expressions on their faces, but then all geese looked that way. Beneath her sweat-stained bonnet the woman looked angry, too.

The geese gave Gideon a wide berth. He figured they were butcher-bound.

He passed the courthouse, three stories tall and easily the most elegant structure in Adamant. A portico held up by white columns shaded the courthouse's polished walnut doors. Twelve-over-twelve windows interrupted the gray limestone walls. Dazzle from the building's copper roof struck his face like a slap.

Climbing the hill to the jail, he felt sweat running down his sides beneath his shirt. He took his time ascending.

Inside, the jail was cool and dim. Alonzo sat behind the desk. He looked up from the newspaper lying open on the desktop.

"What are you reading?" Gideon asked his deputy.

"An account of the massacre at the Alamo."

Gideon drew a blank.

"The Alamo," Alonzo repeated. "In the Republic of Texas." He returned his attention to the paper.

"The battle happened back in March," he said. "Don't know why it took our so-called *news*paper five whole months to print a story about it. Listen to this: 'The event, so lamentable, and yet so glorious to Texas, is of such deep interest and excites so much our feelings that we shall never cease to celebrate it.' Wait, it gets better. 'Who would not rather be one of the Alamo heroes, than the living merciless victors?' Well, that's up for debate, since all of them heroes got bayoneted or shot." Alonzo stuck his face closer to the paper. "'The Mexican force being six thousand strong, having bombarded the Alamo for two days without doing any execution, a tremendous effort was made to take it by force, which they succeeded in doing after a most sang . . . sang . . . *sangui-nary* engagement lasting nearly an hour.'" Alonzo looked up again and folded the paper shut. "Them Texians got wiped out. The Mexicans heaped their corpses in a pile and burned 'em."

Gideon vaguely recognized the words "Texians" and "Mexicans," but little else of what his deputy had read made any sense. "Corpses," however, jogged his memory.

He sat down on the couch. There was something he needed to tell Alonzo. Something about a corpse. Or was it a carcass? He gazed at his deputy, trying to recall. Alonzo was twenty years Gideon's senior. A bachelor, he lived in a boardinghouse but slept at the jail when they had a prisoner. Right now Gideon couldn't remember whether any prisoners were housed in the cells or not.

What was it that he needed to tell Alonzo? Gideon stared. Coarse black hairs bristled from his deputy's nostrils. Alonzo was bald as an egg, built dumpy, competent at most every task. Like cleaning a firearm, or tracking down someone to give them a summons, or putting a broken-legged horse out of its misery.

"There is a dead horse on . . ." Gideon paused.

"On Decatur," Alonzo said. "Bill Greevey said he'd borrow a team and drag it off. That horse still there?"

Gideon nodded.

"I'll get after him," Alonzo said.

Gideon blinked. "Can you tell me about my accident?"

"Again?" Alonzo scratched his pate, causing small flakes of dried skin to drift down onto the desk. "All right. 'Proximately 'bout two weeks ago a peddler found you laying in the middle of the road to Sinking Valley. Just before dawn. Said he didn't notice you till his horse stopped short of stepping on you. A Jew man, he was; must've been a Good Samaritan, because he got you up on his cart, which it weren't much more than a yellow-painted cupboard on wheels, tied your horse in back, and brought you here." Alonzo jutted his chin toward Gideon. "The Israelite even fetched your hat."

Gideon reached up and touched his hat's brim. He took his hat off and set it on the couch.

"We laid you down right where you're at. You had a big knot on your head and blood all over your face." Alonzo's bushy eyebrows bobbed. "You don't remember that?"

Gideon shook his head. No memory of a peddler or a cart, yellow or any other color. However, he did seem to recall lying on the couch. Aching all over, pain sheeting through his skull. When he opened his eyes, he saw double: two Alonzos hovered over him, not a pleasant sight.

After a while, a woman came in through the door. She was handsome and shapely, and even in his misery he found her agreeable to look at, though there were two of her as well. He stared up at the woman until the figures coalesced and he realized he was looking at his wife. Something was wrong with her. Her dark hair, usually clean and pinned back, hung drab and lank. Her cheekbones were sharp, as if she'd lost flesh. At about that time, he faded out again. Then he remembered sitting in a chair in the kitchen of their house while True cleaned the blood off his face. She wouldn't let him crawl into bed. She kept him sitting in the chair the rest of that day, a damp rag over his eyes. Now and then she removed the rag and made him drink tea that left a bitter taste in his mouth.

Suddenly he wanted to see her in the worst way. He picked up his hat and got up slowly, in stages, from the couch.

"I'm off home," he said.

As he stepped out of the jail, he saw a boy coming up the street on a mule. The animal's long upper lip stated that it grudged being ridden. No saddle. The boy sat on a girthed sheepskin with the fleece side down. He held a loop of rope tied to the bit rings on both sides of the mule's broad, disgruntled mouth. The boy was small, and his legs stuck out sideways from the mule's sweat-slick barrel—uncomfortable enough, Gideon thought, even for one so young.

The boy's bare feet were mottled with grime. He wore a broad-brimmed straw hat and a pale homespun shirt above breeches held up by a single leather suspender crossing his chest.

The boy hallooed the closed door of the jail, clearly not realizing that the man standing in front of him, his hat pulled low to block the sun, was the sheriff of Colerain County himself.

"Why don't you get down off that mule," Gideon said, tipping back his hat, "and tell me what it is that you want."

The boy looked at him.

"I haff for the sheriff a message," the boy said.

Instantly Gideon recognized the *Pennsylfawnisch Deitsch* speech pattern accompanied by an accent even thicker than his own.

"I am the sheriff," Gideon said.

The boy's face opened with recognition. "You came to our farm this spring. The Trautmann farm. In Sinking Valley." The last word came out as "walley."

Gideon groped down in his memory and vaguely recollected going to a farm in Sinking Valley, a place where many Dutch families had bought land. He'd gone there to sort something out, a dispute between neighbors.

"... dead body," the boy was saying.

It woke Gideon up.

"In the *sinkloch*," the boy said.

The word meant "sinkhole." One of those strange depressions that pocked the land in areas underlain by limestone rock.

"A dead body?" Gideon asked.

The boy nodded.

"Whose body is it?"

The boy looked down at the mule's broad back and shrugged.

"A man or a woman?"

The boy raised his eyes. "A woman," he said. "*Meeglich*."

A woman. Probably?

"And you rode here to tell me."

"Father sent me. Jonas Trautmann." The boy pronounced his father's first name in the *Deitsch* manner: *Yonas*. "You talked with my *dawdy* this spring about the *bissel feld* down by the stream, the one the Rankins own, but they can't get to it because the bank is too steep there. We planted on it corn. You said to pay them for what we harvested."

This gushing of information was too much for Gideon to take in. "Why don't you get down off that mule and have a drink of water and tell me more about this dead body."

The boy shook his head. "I don't know more. They wouldn't let me look. *Dawdy* told me to ride to town and tell you and come straight back."

Gideon studied the boy's face. The Trautmann farm. In Sinking Valley. Likely he would remember how to get there. If not, Alonzo would know.

A dead body in a sinkhole. Probably a woman. Maybe an accident. Maybe something else.

He said to the boy, "Tell your father I will be there tomorrow."

The boy nodded. He pulled on one rein, bending the mule's thick neck. He tapped the mule with his calves. A john mule, Gideon noticed. The mule didn't move; clearly he did not want to go any farther on this hot day. The boy lifted his heels and kicked. The mule kept his big hooves planted in the dust. His eyes hardened, and he laid his ears back. The mule seemed to Gideon to be contemplating the unjustness and perversity of the human race, and weighing whether or not to buck this flea off his back. Then a resigned look slackened his features. The mule sighed, turned ponderously, and started off down the street, walking at first, then, as if exacting a sort of vengeance, commencing to trot, the boy trying to grip with his thighs while jouncing along on the mule's back.

*That boy will be very sore tomorrow*, Gideon thought.

He went back inside the jail and told Alonzo what the boy had said. He instructed his deputy to have a team and wagon ready first thing in the morning, and to come pick him up at his house. In case he forgot about it.

# Gideon Stoltz's America

⸺⸺⸺

Today, in central Pennsylvania, abandoned iron furnaces still dot the landscape, truncated stone pyramids that once gouted smoke and yielded great quantities of pig iron. The heyday of the charcoal-fired iron industry was in the early 1800s, and central Pennsylvania, with its abundant wood, ore, and limestone resources, was a key ironmaking region.

In 1835, Sheriff Gideon Stoltz patrolled the town of Adamant, Pennsylvania, at a time when our young nation was flexing its muscles and finding its identity—*Waking Giant* is what the historian David S. Reynolds called his seminal book about early 19th-century America.

Andrew Jackson, also known as "Old Hickory" and "The Hero," was President. He carried around a pistol ball lodged near his heart, the souvenir of a duel he had fought as a younger man. A populist, Jackson sought to carry out what he believed to be "the people's will" during his presidency. He displaced more than 45,000 Native Americans from the South, forcing them west into the "Indian Territory" (now Oklahoma), leading to hot speculation by whites on their expropriated lands.

In the South, planters grew cotton, rice, and sugarcane, relying on the labor of African slaves. (The slave-owning Jackson ran a plantation, The Hermitage, near Nashville, Tennessee.) Settlers advanced westward: Michigan, Iowa, and Texas were on the frontier.

A period of religious zeal known as the Second Great Awakening was underway, with folks attending revival services across the land. Circuit preachers depicted heaven as a paradise to which all true believers could ascend. They also described the terrors of hell to frighten sinners into giving their souls to Christ. Western New York was called the Burned Over District because of all the fire and brimstone spouted there.

Schisms and sects abounded. You had Millerites and Mormons, Swedenborgians and Shakers, Quakers and Rappites and Zoarites and Finneyites and Universalists and Pietists and Transcendentalists and Adventists and Dunkards and Unitarians, not to mention Congregationalists, Episcopalians, Lutherans, Methodists, Baptists (at least seven sects), and Presbyterians (no fewer than eight sorts). Worshipers who embraced these various sects all thought they followed the one true religion.

The country was a ferment of new ideas. Controversy raged over foreign immigration, prison reform, free education, birth control, the rise of capitalism, a growing inequality of wealth, the first labor unions, increasing urbanization, who should have the right to vote, whether alcohol should be prohibited, and that overarching and hugely incendiary issue, slavery.

In addition to the wagoners and peddlers and drovers who moved about on the poor roads with their freight and wares, their flocks and herds, average Americans in the Northeast (including the residents of my fictional town, Adamant) could encounter polygamous prophets, traveling mesmerists and phrenologists and teachers of shape-note singing, radical abolitionists delivering scathing lectures (and sometimes getting tarred and feathered for their trouble), escaping slaves and pursuing slavecatchers. Also oddities and freaks: In 1836, P.T. Barnum began a three-year tour showing off Joice Heth, a blind, partially paralyzed black woman whom he declared to be 161 years old and George Washington's nanny.

Scientific discoveries proliferated. New machines cleaned cotton and wove it into cloth; steam power sent boats chugging up rivers and railroad engines huffing down their tracks. The bicycle, the mechanical reaper, the steel plow, percussion-ignition and repeating firearms (Gideon Stoltz's gun-nut deputy Alonzo Bell would have filled his ear about such modern weapons), the tele-graph, the sewing machine, and the daguerreotype photograph all arrived on the scene.

Yet the early 1800s was also a primitive era in many ways. In lightly settled regions, roads were little more than traces cut through the woods with tree trunks chopped off just below wagon-axle height. When the weather was dry, the roads were fairly passable, but when it rained, huge ruts could develop, making travel even more difficult or downright impossible. People got around on horseback, in wagons, in carriages (though not in backwoods areas where the roads were rudimentary), in stage coaches, and on foot, known as traveling by "shanks' mare." Folks engaged in fisticuffs (organized and not), no-holds-barred wrestling matches, dog and cock fights, horse races, and turkey shoots. They drank like fish. Each year the average American gulped down more than 7 gallons of absolute alcohol, about three times today's per capita consumption.

Doctors were often illiterate and had no idea of how illnesses arose (the germ theory of disease would not gain acceptance until the century's end) or how to cure it. A family might lose all of its children to the bloody flux (dysentery) inside of three days. Influenza, yellow fever, tuberculosis, cholera, smallpox, and typhus scythed the population. Some people said that disease was "God's flail," his way of punishing sinners.

Bigotry and discrimination reigned. Many whites thought that African Americans and Asians were inferior and even subhuman. In many places, immigrants were deeply resented, particularly the Irish, who began entering the country in large numbers around 1820 (almost two million would arrive between 1820 and 1860). Germans poured in by the millions, along with other Europeans.

Many writers have set novels during the American Revolution and the Civil War. Yet the tumultuous period between those events, some scholars suggest, may have been the richest in American history and the time when the foundations of the modern United States were laid.

For those interested in reading more historical novels set in the era, I'd recommend *Mr. Emerson's Wife*, by Amy Belding Brown (set in Massachusetts); *Lost Nation*, by Jeffrey Lent (New Hampshire); *Ahab's Wife*, by Sena Jeter Naslund (Nantucket Island and Kentucky); *The Known World*, by Edward P. Jones (Virginia); *The Last Runaway*, by Tracy Chevalier (Ohio); *The Good Lord Bird*, by James McBride (Kansas); and *The Whiskey Rebels*, by David Liss (Pennsylvania).

# A Note from the Author

―∞∞―

A good mystery presents rich and complex characters. It evokes a strong sense of place. It conveys the beauty and the power of language. If set in the past, it teaches us about history—painlessly, as we keep turning pages, caught up in a story, wanting to know what happens next.

Most mysteries include murder, and they revolve around characters who must confront horrific crimes. Murder is, after all, a real human phenomenon. Murder happens to people, sometimes even to people we know.

In September 1995, my mother, Ruth Foote Fergus, a widow in her seventies, surprised a burglar in her home in State College, Pennsylvania. He stabbed her to death. I found her body the next day.

When I decided to write a novel that included murder, I wanted to depict, as honestly as I could, the reality of what happens when a human being takes another person's life. In my opinion, murder is not something to write about lightly. I don't often read the kind of mysteries known as "cozies," in which killings may be downplayed or even treated with humor. And it bothers me, in a mainstream mystery, when an author creates and knocks off characters with no thought or acknowledgment given to how those deaths affect family members, friends, communities, even the people who must investigate those murders.

My main character, Gideon Stoltz, is a young sheriff of Pennsylvania Dutch extraction, making him something of an outsider in fictional 1830s Adamant and Colerain County, Pennsylvania, occupied mainly by clannish Scotch-Irish residents. I wrote several drafts of the novel and was not fully satisfied with Gideon as a character. Then someone I'd asked to read the story, and who knew my personal history, suggested that I draw on my own past and give Gideon the experience of having lost his mother to murder.

At first, I resisted. Creating for Gideon that kind of backstory would mean that I would have to revisit, and in some ways relive, losing my mother to a particularly cruel and violent death. Then I thought about how important truth and honesty are to the writing of fiction.

I hope you've enjoyed *A Stranger Here Below*—and that you stay with Gideon Stoltz as he works to solve more murders while trying to overcome his own griefs and travails.

# About the Author

CHARLES FERGUS is the author of twenty books. A native of Pennsylvania, Fergus now lives on an old farm in Vermont's remote Northeast Kingdom with his wife, the writer Nancy Marie Brown, and four Icelandic horses. A member of a hospice chorus, he sings in small groups bringing a cappella music to people in their last days and final hours. He is also part of an American roots trio called Yestermorn, which sings Appalachian, folk and shape-note songs, including many from the early 1800s—the kind of powerful, spiritual music that would have set Sheriff Gideon Stoltz's wounded soul soaring again.

www.charlesfergus.com